I0592758

Richard Machin

Joining In

LegallyBoundBooks
Redmond : WA

Library of Congress Control Number: 2018911438
ISBN (print): 978-0-692-18123-2

LegallyBoundBooks
www.LegallyBoundBooks.com

To us. To all of us.

And of course to them, too.

"Glory be to God for dappled things –
For skies of couple-colour as a brinded cow;
For rose-moles all in stipple upon trout that swim;
Fresh-firecoal chestnut-falls; finches' wings;
Landscape plotted and pieced – fold, fallow, and plough;
And all trades, their gear and tackle and trim."

— Hopkins, G.M., 1877

"I don't know. It's all some sort of natural throwback I'm told.
Just color and whatnot. God knows. I'm not involved in any of
that and neither is Herr Stammbaum."

— Boss, Geoff's, 2018

Joining In

1: The end

THE EVENTS LEADING to Newman leaving for good with a pair of binoculars, a memory stick, and an RV full of fish were remarkable and not the typical end to a successful career at Ziegler Genetics Corporation.

The binoculars were a gift from his team, who were keen to provide him with something useful for his new life at the lake. The fish of course were a key part of his next project, but at his departure their very existence was unknown to anyone apart from Newman.

The memory stick he stole, as it contained everything that had been forgotten about the fish.

As far as Newman's boss Steve was concerned, and apart from the last few days, the project had been a success. The budget had been increased for the second three-year period, justified by fish that proved strikingly attractive and grew at a furious rate. Over two inches a month was previously unheard of, and weighing ten pounds in under a couple of years. That, and the coloring. They had a deep metallic iridescence that took your breath away as they jumped and darted vigorously around the holding tanks.

Steve wasn't so much surprised as he was dumbfounded by the way things were going. Against his better judgment he was almost ready to relax about the commitments made and the correspondingly massive expenditure involved. Secretly, he had all along been convinced that at some point the whole thing would unravel leaving him, Newman, and the rest of the division high and dry.

His fears were realized when the project was abruptly canceled, fish ordered destroyed, and all records erased.

The end came on a Friday afternoon when, as Newman was undergoing his weekly one-on-one in Steve's office, a short phone call, a knock on the door, and the entry of two suited individuals all happened in quick succession.

"Donoghue, Legal," said the first. "Stevenson," said the second.

"Here's the situation," said Stevenson, sitting down, opening his briefcase and addressing no-one in particular. Donoghue seemed fixed on Steve, his eyebrows raised in apparent anticipation of Steve's response.

"You're done with the fish project. We need signatures from everyone involved indicating that all materials have been destroyed, any patents abandoned, down tools, reassign staff, *non fumus boni iuris*, *nemo auditur propriam turpitudinem allegans*, and so on, and so forth," said Stevenson.

"What the—" Steve's exclamation was interrupted by Donoghue.

"Johnson. Heard of him? Works in your division."

"Well no but—"

"Ate the fish, you see. Ended up with orange teeth and a staggering settlement agreement."

"Ate the bloody fish? What was he thinking?"

"Not thinking clearly, apparently. He was, after all, intoxicated almost to the point of comatose after attending an event sponsored by the company. And organized by you.

'Friday Food Fracas' I think you call it."

"Yes, well, morale you know . . . ate the fish? Orange teeth? You heard of any of this, Newman?"

Until now Newman had been feeling relieved to be left out of it.

"I am familiar with Johnson," he said, taking time to choose words that would indicate distance. "Well-liked by his colleagues, I gather. Highly thought of by immediate management. I think he came up with the idea for . . ." Newman noticed Stevenson turn a challenging gaze directly toward him. "well, better not discuss that now. Eating the lab specimens is clearly off bounds, goes without saying. Can we be sure of all this?"

"Oh, his colleagues confirm his demonstration of trout-tickling," said Donoghue. "Given his condition, surprisingly dexterous in whipping the fish out of the tank and slapping it on your Friday Fracas barbecue."

"A new twist on fishing off the company pier, eh?" said Steve. Donoghue shifted his expression to one of alarm. "I mean — oh god. Anyone else eat it?"

"Not that we know about. And we would know about it, you see, because whatever you allegedly did to engineer that consumer-friendly orange color is claimed to bind it irreversibly to tooth enamel, producing a very evidently fluorescent orange smile. Only a massive *ex gratia* disbursement proved enough to cover the restorative dentistry required to correct the matter."

Newman knew Steve would be waiting for him to come up with something. Some "wildcard shit" that Newman often pulled, according to Steve and appropriately enough, "out of his ass". Newman was well aware of the number of times he had been so called upon to save the day when budget, schedule, or headcount was threatened, and on this occasion he caught Steve's exasperated glance. But Newman wasn't thinking about Johnson and his teeth, Donoghue and Stevenson, or even Steve any more (whose look appeared increasingly desperate).

"Can I speak off-the-record?" he asked.

"Go ahead," said Donoghue.

"I can imagine where this might have happened. This project attracted a few, ah, idiosyncratic geniuses that may have been tempted to go off-base a little in the genetic alteration department. I heard talk of splicing-in a little redfish along with the color gene from salmon. So the orange binds with tooth enamel — I'm sure no-one was expecting that." Newman seemed to drift into thought for a moment. "I wonder if there's a trait in Great White Shark that might compensate somehow. Hmm. Could sell that idea to Drugs."

"Joint project with drugs?" said Steve. "Food that whitens your teeth, eh? Ahead of you Newman. Oh my god, I like that — and think of the budget!"

"Let me stop you right there," said Donoghue, rising ever so slightly from his chair before sitting back down again. "We come to bury your project, not to justify further funding. Really. Mr Stevenson — perhaps you could wait outside for a moment while I discuss a solution? *Credibile est negata* and so on."

Stevenson snapped his briefcase shut and got up before unlocking his gaze from Newman and leaving the room briskly, no doubt happy to avoid further responsibility for what was likely about to be proposed.

"Mr Newman; let's speak, as you requested, *in*

confidentia." Steve repositioned himself in his chair and leaned forward a little. After a momentary smile, Donoghue continued.

"In short — can you take care of this? It seems there was a transgression of professional practice in the documentation and in the execution of this project, which threatens to put Ziegler under the regulatory microscope in a general sense. It seems unlicensed steps may have been taken, in a manner of speaking. Unprofessional, even. Splicing experiments that resulted in clearly unanticipated or should we say, erm, unforeseeable results. Fear will be that orange teeth are just the tip of what might turn out to be a criminal iceberg. My colleague Mensing in Drugs is particularly apprehensive of being cast in the same light, *in pari materia* if I may. And we can't appear as though our right hand doesn't know what our left hand is doing, you see. The CEO, Herr Stammbaum himself, just claimed publicly that we are above all an information company, so as a consequence it falls to us to avoid appearing ignorant of what the hell is going on in our own back yard. In short, we need this whole sorry episode erased, shredded, rendered entirely the stuff of myth and fiction."

Donoghue paused and looked at Newman for a moment with a slightly furrowed brow, as if wondering if Newman had fully understood, or if he could have put things any more clearly.

"As Director of Comestibles, Mr. Newman, can you do that?"

Steve saw an opportunity to contribute. "My best man," he said, looking at Donoghue, with a tilt of the head toward Newman. "Nobody better at starting, running, and dare I say canning a fish project. I mean if anyone can land in shit and come up smelling of roses…"

"Quite, quite," said Donoghue. He turned an inquiring look toward Newman.

Normally Newman would be immediately drawn to unraveling a transgenic blunder such as this; it had all the technical, comic and even alcoholic potential that, at this stage in his career, was the most enjoyable part of the job. But now, all at once, in a flash of inspiration he saw a much grander opportunity.

"Speaking of shit and roses, fish and cans, I think in this situation we need to clear out all the mess first, putting one person in charge of the remainder who can then leave and take the residual smell away with him. I mean our IT wizards can do a forensic cleanup of all the data, we are already familiar with disposing of experimental waste, we have the cash and the legal expertise to deal with the staff. That just leaves the reason for the whole business."

"Hmm. Carry on."

"The project has a considerable following in the trade press and of course among investors. We committed massively to it and were predicting huge success only last month. So once it's dead, we need someone to bury it. Then the poor sap with all the remaining answers must disappear and take them with him."

"I see," said Steve, although it didn't look like he did.

"Very creative," said Donoghue, who clearly did see. It sounded like he had already anticipated the conclusion of the plan, and he continued Newman's thought for him. "We would need to devote — errm — appropriate resources to that process of closure, *maritimae res postularent*. I imagine whoever took that role would merit generous compensation for his selfless efforts to protect the future endeavors of the corporation."

"I agree," said Newman, sitting back in his chair. "The usual handshake, golden double helix and 'best wishes for your future endeavors' would be nowhere near apropos."

After a moment's silence, Steve stood up, more than a little exasperated.

"Can we cut to the chase here? In terms I can follow?"

"I'll do it for early retirement and a boatload of cash, and I'll sign whatever you want," said Newman.

"Done," said Donoghue.

2: The beginning

IN TRUTH, ZIEGLER Genetics had never really suited Newman. Or, rather, his career had never followed a conventional corporate path. He was a big ideas guy, he loved investigating problems but was less interested in crafting solutions, and he got swept away by his own obsessions. What he lacked in productivity, he overcompensated for in enthusiasm. He was completely uninterested in company politics, in working his way up the corporate hierarchy, or in strategizing and positioning himself for success. As a result Newman's career had developed an unexamined life of its own, bearing him onward and up through the corporation while he — eventually to become Director, Comestibles Research and Productization — was occupied looking for something more interesting to do.

More interesting to Newman had been hanging around with real geneticists, chewing over interesting problems and coming up with ideas for promising research projects. And his colleagues were only too happy to co-opt Newman as a resource, indulge his compulsions, and exploit his willingness to take their work and run with it — to management, to marketing, but most importantly to potential sources of funding.

Half a lifetime ago Newman, fresh from the University of Washington with a joint major in biology and business studies, had arrived at Ziegler for his meeting with

Steve. Steve had drawn the short straw and was on point for interviews that day.

Steve's team did food research, known internally as Food, and competed for funding with Drugs, which was currently the investors' favorite. But Food was moving into the spotlight, and great things were expected of Steve's projects. As a result there were a lot of interviews to do; the potential for genetic "interventions" in food production was about to explode, and Ziegler had identified huge profit from the future fallout.

Steve was a pragmatic manager, and contrary to the expectations of most of his interviewees that day was not looking for a genius. He was looking for a new hire that would be enthusiastic, unambitious, and would above all else reassure his higher-flying reports by gravitating toward the middle region of the team's performance curve.

Newman's entry into his office gave Steve an immediate impression that this day might not be a complete loss.

"Come in, come in. Sit down. Joint major, eh? What the hell?"

"Sorry about that," said Newman, recognizing an English accent from Steve.

"The business studies thing was supposed to help me figure out how to make a living doing biology."

"Well genetics is as much business as it is biology round here anyway. That and a bucketful of politics, of course. Shit."

Steve squinted slightly as he looked out of the window for a moment.

"Damn' politicians."

After a moment's reverie he seemed to snap back to the present.

"Anyway, what's with the English thing, Mr. Newman? Where d'you get your accent?"

"Came over here to study. Dad liked the place, told me I should come. See no reason to go back now. How about yours?"

"Ha! Worked for the Ziegler sub in Slough. Yes, Slough. I suppose you can take the man out of Slough and so on. Thank God, eh! Well I started some research looking into GM fish. Project showed so much promise corporate moved it, and me, over here to U.S. H.Q. Wife took the opportunity to jump ship and marry a dentist from Bracknell. So." Steve slapped the desk. "Everything worked out for the best."

He beamed at Newman for a moment.

"What were we talking about? Oh yes. You. And politics. How are you with politics?"

Newman wondered for a moment if Steve had heard about his arrest for protesting a nuclear reprocessing plant when he was in high school. It wasn't so much his actions that had got him, as opposed to his comrades, arrested so much as his relative lack of athletic ability when it came to escaping the police. But it did nearly cost him his student visa.

"Not the most interesting part of business studies," he replied, carefully. "But I understand how important politics can be in any organization. I learned that much."

Steve casually checked the 'team player' box on his interview form.

"Well what did Shakespeare say — something about politicians circumventing god, eh! Some say our geneticists do a bit of that, too. Matter of fact my team plans to improve His food." Steve grinned and waited for his joke to register. No immediate response, so he added "So what do you feel you'd bring to the table? Ha ha."

Newman was relieved the interview was steering clear of hard questions and, above all else, anything involving the whiteboard, where he'd never felt comfortable.

"I bring my bachelor's in Biology, 3.9 actually," (he was still unclear on how he had managed that) "and a specialism in aquaculture, which I assume helped me get an interview with you." Newman heard himself getting a little overconfident, but it was too late to back off. "But mostly, and apart from what's on my application, I'm quick on the technical uptake and I get along with non-technical people too. So I'm generally useful. And of course, I'm familiar with food. I mean to say . . . " (Generally useful? Familiar with food? He heard himself talk and wondered what he was thinking.)

"Well one thing we don't need is a useless, hungry person, no matter how damn' smart he is!" Steve said, in less an interruption than a merciful intervention. "Of course, everyone round here is qualified. Your aquaculture and biology would be trumped by a boatload of damn PhDs in genetics. But you're right; we do food research, and we're involved with fish, so you might just fit."

Newman felt like he'd been compassionately slapped.

"And you're probably better at dealing with stuff than my PhDs!" Steve added, then with a wide grin: "Most of them are assholes."

Newman was unsure what exactly was meant by dealing with stuff, but he already had experience avoiding stuff that he couldn't successfully deal with, and he was feeling generally confident about all possible outcomes from the interview when Steve stood up, and Newman took the cue that the interview was over. He shook Steve's hand and turned for the door. Steve said, "See you Monday after lunch. Now we have a British quorum we might buy a company teapot; you can be in charge of that, Newman! And not to put too much on your plate, but you can also help run my fish research program."

"Well. Thank you!"

"Don't thank me til you've been round here for long enough to get a better idea what I dropped you into. Ziegler's a big pond, with a lot of bloody odd-looking fish I can tell you that much for starters. Most of 'em in Drugs."

As Newman left he heard Steve shout after him: "You'll have to call in at HR before you go; waste of time but there you are. Oh — and keep the whole PhD assholes thing between you and me, eh."

Steve was right about Newman, and he ended up doing well in Food. He seemed a natural choice for the research division of Ziegler Genetics, or at least for Steve's piece of the research division and the way Steve liked to run it. He understood the engineers and could direct their work without appearing threatening; or as Steve put it, he managed to keep those damned geek octopuses in the string bag. And he could work with management. They felt informed, that the projects were important and deserved the considerable resources Newman had persuaded them to invest. He danced the fine line between pure research and product deliverables, attracting funding for crucial investigations while avoiding commitment to any sort of hard deadlines.

Semi-annual project reviews were Newman's forte.

"Semi-annual is coming up." Steve's tone used to signal resignation, perhaps capitulation. Something unavoidable was about to happen that they had to make the best of, and he was reluctantly relying on his team to help him somehow get through it. But now, now he had Newman. Newman seemed a natural for semi-annuals, and today Steve's "Semi-annual is coming up" had an almost chipper feel to it.

"Let's give those bastards what they want and take what we need, eh Newman? Drugs can whistle for it — Food needs cash for the fish project."

Steve had come to regard Newman as "a safe pair of hands", and the increase in the number of projects he oversaw, and the funding that they attracted, was in no small part due to Newman's ability to quietly, without any fuss, get stuff done. It was almost as if Newman's successes in this regard were incidental — he didn't seem to put any effort into it. One minute he'd be in the break-room debating arcane experimental scenarios with an engineer or a data scientist, next he'd duck into the conference room to deliver a presentation that would be met with applause. Applause. When it had been Steve's responsibility to do the reviews, he felt lucky to emerge from one with his job. Newman, on the other hand, appeared completely free of nerves and almost oblivious to the excitement he generated among those "damn' wallet-hugging dinosaurs".

After this latest review, Steve shared the dinosaurs' elation.

"I don't know how you do it," he said. "But you must

keep bloody doing it. We're awash in cash and the new fish project is a go. Somehow or other you've given 'em cause to regard us as crucial to Ziegler's success without actually creating any dependencies for us. Damn' genius is what you are."

Steve's enthusiasm had been no doubt fueled by the celebratory lunch he'd enjoyed at the local pub, but after years of subjugation to Drugs he was in no mood to hold back.

"Damn the consequences, Newman — I'm recommending you for Director of the new division."

Steve's generosity was not entirely without self-interest. Newman had succeeded in attracting enough attention to Food Research that the creation of an entirely new division had become an inevitability. It would be called Comestibles Research and Productization, and it would need a Director to report to Steve, who would be Vice President of the Food division. Steve needed someone with Newman's albeit largely unconscious skills to protect him against the intervention of real-world responsibilities suggested by the term 'productization'.

"I'll tell you what; I don't like the sound of it Newman. Bound to happen sooner or later. They want us to start 'monetizing'. No longer enough for research to just keep up with the competition and generate patents. Well as Director, I expect you to turn them away from asking 'why' and back to 'how'. They're on track to make us responsible for some sort of payback and I don't like it."

By now Newman had been at Ziegler Genetics for a good many years. He had risen rapidly through the ranks of various forms of management — assistant, project, program, general, and now with this latest reorganization he was Director of a department that occupied an entire building, with a budgetary responsibility Steve would describe after a beer or two as making him "shit bricks".

All this was more due to Newman's presentation skills than it was to his technical smarts. He was an email wizard, he could perform alchemy with proposals and pivot tables. There was no vague idea he couldn't make solid and compelling with well-chosen phrases and graphical sleight of hand. It helped that he wasn't in himself any sort of an intimidating figure; over the years many of his more intellectually or physically overbearing colleagues, inspiring fear and suspicion in their corporate superiors, had fallen by the wayside or been consigned to some hopeless backwater. But Newman had sailed on, turning what-ifs into why-nots, preempting why should we with why wouldn't we, and offering up his opportunities for great progress with free transfer of ownership to anyone who could pip his or her peers to the post.

Newman looked up and nodded in that generic fashion that confirmed to Steve that he hadn't really been listening. Regardless, Steve was confident he had the right man for the job, and this latest fish thing Newman had proposed sounded like it would keep the suits happy, and his new Comestibles Research and Productization division staffed, busy, and above all else, fully funded.

When it came to the battle for resources with Drugs, Steve had referred to him as "Food's secret weapon", and it had been to Newman's advantage that he had to-date remained secret. Success through stealth; he liked to think of it as hiding in the limelight.

This fish thing, as Steve thought of it, turned out to be the biggest research investment Food had yet made. By now, management regarded Newman as a solid performer who could tell it like it is or, rather, in terms that they could understand. And what it is, they had evidently decided, was less important than how confident they felt that Steve's division had it under control and would likely make a success of it.

"It's complicated shit Newman, no mistake," said Steve one morning, staring at his Danish so intently that a casual observer might think he was talking about breakfast not fish. "It's a good job Drugs has its own crap to deal with so they don't look too closely at ours."

The fish project was just up Newman's street. It was more or less pure research, which he preferred, but as Steve pointed out this did make it more vulnerable to losing funds to a more revenue-oriented effort from Drugs. On the other hand, Newman had presented what was a long shot series of expensive hybridizing experiments as the first step toward a paradigm shift for open water, lake-farmed GMO fish production. He had hinted at massive opportunities to expand Ziegler's patent portfolio and the likely insatiable market for big, cheap, healthful, good looking fish for which Ziegler alone held the license to breed. He intended to unleash his best engineers — "transgenic rockstars" — on a project that, in time (he struck out the adjective 'considerable') could turn out to be the very foundation of the new Ziegler, and the establishment of Food as its signature division. Newman boiled it down at the close of his management pitch:

"We think we can leverage the unique, leading-edge skill-sets and technologies available to us at Ziegler to design a trout that grows quickly and tastes marvelous. The meat will be an attractive color — no more 'color added'. In fact the fish will look bright, clean and colorful in the water and on the slab — it will finally justify the term 'rainbow'. It will be easily farmed in freshwater lakes and will be naturally disease resistant so no need for antibiotics. Attractive, healthy, healthful, and inexpensive. Farmers will be falling over themselves to get hold of our fry, and consumers will be falling over themselves to get hold of their fish."

Fully anticipated responses questioned cost, liability, and competition. Newman pointed out that Ziegler had key procedures for combinations of genetic modifications sewn up with watertight patents; they were already ahead of the game. They would use isolated facilities to contain the experiments, and costs paled in comparison to likely benefits of their work — particularly in view of the potential for more widespread application in Comestibles. The term 'GMO', said Newman, will be taken off protesters' placards and will finally get the respect it deserves. Not just consumers, but the entire food production industry will be thankful and owe a debt of gratitude for the decision made today to invest in this project.

Newman had, at a stroke, appealed to management's defensive, avaricious, and philanthropic natures. Everyone found something to be happy about. He got the go-ahead for a renewable three-year investment schedule the amount of which was a surprise even to Steve.

"That's a shitload of money Newman. So the one thing I need ASAP are the reasons we failed just in case we do. I'm too gunshy to fly without a parachute so let's get our excuses in order along with our ducks."

"Don't worry," said Newman, ignoring the haphazard rhetoric. "You don't need ducks or excuses. One way or another, we'll make this project a success."

3: The move

NEWMAN'S OPTIMISM HAD been justified; fish had flourished, careers had been forged and Steve's doubts were unfounded. At least until the lawyers stepped in.

And winding up the fish project was just about Newman's best opportunity so far. He saw in that assignment a means to bring together so many loose threads; early retirement to a beautiful part of the country, a new project under his full control, a practical application for what he'd learned about genetics, and a chance to exercise his skills for making things happen. And this time all for the benefit of himself and the little community of staff and visitors at Glacial Lake.

Well, that's the way he liked to spin the story whenever he thought about it. Truth is, there was to be a little jiggery-pokery required in order to help everything fall into place.

He'd seen the potential of the lake years ago when he and a Ziegler geologist were on a scouting trip to find locations for farming hybridized fish at scale. Taking such projects into the wild requires caution bordering on paranoia, and experimenters are policed with masses of rules and regulations, and threatened by potential financial and corporal punishment in case of transgression. When things do go wrong the result can be anything from mild loss of credibility, through bankruptcy, all the way to incarceration.

It follows that Newman's mission was by no means straightforward but among all the places he'd visited, those eight or so square miles of largely landlocked water among the inland hills above Coldwater Bay were the most memorable. Owned by the National Parks Service, Glacial Lake had only ever been an outside candidate for Ziegler's study; there was never any real chance of deployment. Of course Parks would never agree to using such a national treasure for genetic experimentation. But Newman engineered a good few trips there ostensibly to learn about the geology and the biology of these natural environments, along with the issues that might arise around moving in experimental fish. In practical terms he was less interested in moving in fish and more interested in longer term plans for moving in Newman.

While thinking about the needs of the fish, Newman got to thinking about the broader needs of the lake. It could do with a boost. It had everything going for it, which was immediately clear to anyone who actually visited. But in an area of lakes aplenty it needed an edge to get people out there in the first place; it was already on the map but it lacked something to make it stand out, to get it talked about. The fish, he decided in a flash of inspiration, didn't need a lake so much as the lake needed his fish. The fish had the potential to bring the lake alive, to draw people the three miles off the main road to come see them and then stay for the boating, the hiking, the swimming and the glorious scenery.

The license to operate the resort was coming up for bid. The current licensees were aging out of the whole process and the Parks service was clearly looking for someone who could generate more revenue from the operation. And in recent years reviews from the few visitors that stumbled across the place had been trending downward, with talk of lackluster facilities, unhelpful staff, and too many better alternative locations nearby to spend their precious vacations. If the resort business thrived on return visits, then this one was clearly in its death throes. Although at that time Newman wasn't sure where he would get the money for the license or who he would get to help manage the place, here was a project he could sink his teeth into — one of those sows ears out of which he'd spent a career making silk purses. It was a challenge, and he was always up for a challenge.

Newman eventually became convinced of the merits of his plan, and borderline enthusiastic about its execution even without being in possession of all of the essential elements — notably cash, fish, and Parks lease. But when he went ahead and put the wheels in motion he was surprised by how quickly things began to move forward.

If the Devil is in the details, then the Devil visited with those very details required to complete his plan shortly after Newman was appointed to get rid of the fish project for good. The license to operate Glacial Lake was granted to him by the Parks service, more than enough cash required to pay for it would be provided by his settlement from Ziegler, and the disposal of the fish was completely, officially, and untraceably placed in Newman's hands.

"Right. Where do we start?" said Steve, who had already decided to start with an off-site planning session with Newman in the pub. "Never know who's listening," he'd said, "better take this off-base."

"Patents," said Newman. "We patent almost everything we officially did, put it all into the public domain, bring everything above board. Then we can draw that work to a close as a practical matter."

"A practical matter?"

"Oh we justify it with talk of assessed viability, limited near-term product potential, opportunity cost recalculation, redeployment of resources. That sort of thing."

"Oh, right, yes. I like that — wring a little more out of your 'research as a path to product' thing?"

"Yes, but whereas our unstated goal used to be an endless path, now we can publicly focus on the positives of canning the fish — we can apply those patents to other areas of work where we feel real-world applications offer broader opportunities to advance the cause, bring long-anticipated benefits to market faster, solve world hunger in shorter order and so on. Well, something like that."

"I like it. Warrants another pint at the very least." Steve attracted the attention of the bartender by waving his glass and holding up two fingers. "But what about the organization — what do we do with the people? I still don't know how much extra-curricular fishmongery we were involved in. Apart from this idiot Johnson and his redfish mouth business."

"We'll use carrots not sticks I think. Besides, throwing boffins under the bus never works, or looks good for that matter. Donoghue and Stevenson are adding legal gibberish to some paperwork I put together, praising contributions, pointing out the advances we made and the patents we've been granted and so on, and of course stressing the need for absolute secrecy around this crucial work to the point of dead silence. That's where the legal bit sews it up, King's shilling sort of thing — everyone involved takes the money as part of a binding agreement, beyond the non-disclosure they signed when they joined Ziegler, and the additional tenting agreement they signed when we brought them into the fish project. Standard legal threats and insinuations follow regarding the horrible consequences of a breach."

After appearing to mull this over for a moment, Steve pensively drained half his glass, then asked, "Sounds like they would be definitively stitched up then, once they sign. But what if they won't sign?"

"We round them up and throw them under the bus."

Steve slapped Newman on the back as he got up to collect his beers at the bar. On his return he handed Newman a pint and said, "I expect you feel a little guilty over the fact that you're probably a lot better off after this cockup than you would've been if the project had continued?"

"Oh yes, devastated," said Newman, meeting Steve's raised glass.

"Cheers!"

"Cheers!"

Back at Ziegler, the plan was going well. Steve had come up with a timeline for what he called "project Tuna" and, thanks to Newman, everything was on track. The entire team had been given positions on new and current projects, and their efforts toward a raft of new patent applications were rewarded with bonuses, salary increases and in some cases promotions. Some, especially a few in Drugs ("meddling ingrates" Steve called them) feigned puzzlement, questioned the overall success of the project and had difficulty identifying precisely where all that value was to be found.

But on the one hand the patent lawyers were experts at creating something out of nothing or — as they preferred to put it — identifying opportunities for surfacing intellectual property and enhancing Ziegler's competitive portfolio.

And on the other hand Newman was in charge, and on form.

He was called upon to deliver a post-mortem presentation to upper management. The room was packed; the presentation was broadcast globally across Ziegler's internal networks. "Should have sold tickets," Steve said, "this'll get better ratings than the damn' Oscars".

Newman as usual rose to the occasion. He spoke about new relationships forged with academic institutions, advancements in the state of the art, new techniques that can be applied across Food's animal and plant hybridization efforts, and the need to go boldly and without restraint into the dawn of this new age of previously unimagined genetic adventures.

"We must remain agile," said Newman, as images of darting schools of fish were projected behind him. "We have demonstrated our ability to be nimble, to intervene, push forward and, at the right moment, take our winnings off the table and apply the advantages we have gained to meeting new and lofty challenges elsewhere. Leveraging the indisputable talent that characterizes our organization is key;" (a broad sweep of the room here with his laser-pointer hand and a glance at the camera), "unifying our people in team collaboration, or setting individuals free to unleash their unique creativity. We will never stop searching for the best way to reach our goal for Ziegler and for you all: to be the best, smartest, and most profitable we can possibly be."

Newman was met with rousing applause. He had turned the fish project on its head, and what was initially thought to be a near total disaster was now a poster child for leading-edge project management. Many who had never really seen let alone worked with Newman before were moved by his passion. Even the few who were left with nagging doubts didn't dare speak negatively for fear of appearing disloyal, or worse, ignorant. Transformational research techniques, agile development practices, a whole new culture to take the company boldly into its next stage of growth; who wouldn't want to be a part of that, somehow? And throughout the entirety of the presentation, no-one noticed that Newman hadn't really mentioned the demise of those rainbow colored fish that began it all and that were expected to embody the brave new genetically modified world he had just described.

But the fish, though absent from his speech, were certainly top of Newman's mind as he shook hands, sipped wine, and nursed an artificial-looking slice of cake at the post-presentation social.

Newman was thinking of the fish because many of those very same had begun a new life in Glacial Lake shortly after he'd agreed to dispose of them.

He had been taking his RV up to his favorite spot each weekend for a while now; ever since the visit from Donoghue and Stevenson and his appointment to wind up the project. He always towed his cabin cruiser, ostensibly to enjoy a little peace and quiet on the lake during the off-season. The real reason he was taking weekly trips was known only to Newman. And Pete in Holding.

Pete spent his time in a warehouse full of water tanks arranged in ranks, each of which capable of holding huge numbers of fish at various stages of development. At that time Newman's project occupied the entire facility, and all the occupants had in common the Fish project's genetic interventions. But Pete didn't care about any of that; Pete's expertise was in simply keeping them alive. He nursed fragile eggs through their eye stage, at which point they became a little more robust, and on through fry and up to four or five inch fingerlings. The larger, table-ready fish enjoyed secure swimming-pool sized accommodations outside.

So it had been more than a mild surprise to Pete when, under Newman's orchestration, he received a visit from Legal who asked him to sign some paperwork in return for what amounted to a little over a couple of years' salary. Shortly after, Newman himself arrived to speak with a newly energized Pete about the disposal of the fish.

"There'll be a new project coming in shortly," said Newman, "so we'll need to clear these out. As you know, this is all hush-hush, confidential leading-edge stuff. Discretion is key."

"Discretion is my middle name," said Pete, whose middle name was Simon. "I will miss these little buggers for sure — never seen anything quite like 'em. Don't know how those whizzkids do it."

Newman leaned towards Pete and spoke quietly while looking him squarely in the face. "Well, the key thing here, Pete, is that they don't. Never did," he said, with a tap of his nose.

"Oh yes, right."

"Now as part of closing things down I will need to come in and do a little, oh, stocktaking in here. Need to move a few things around, a little offsite archiving for legal compliance sort of thing — no big deal. I can give you the go-ahead to flush the tanks when I'm done. Meantime don't worry if you see me in and out with the live transport trailer."

"Of course," said Pete. He didn't quite follow much before the "flush the tanks" bit, except "legal compliance" which, from what Mr. Donoghue had told him, sounded key to receiving his cash.

"This was an important project, Pete, I don't have to tell you I'm sure. Part of history and all that. We should be discretely proud, eh. I trust the company's compensation package adequately reflected the importance of the part you have played?"

"Oh definitely," said Pete. "Very generous. In fact I think it may be enough to kickstart me and the wife's B&B plans for her mother's old place by the ocean."

"New beginnings. Sounds good to me," said Newman.

Newman's boat could hold thousands of fingerlings in its water tanks, and thousands more in the live well. And the RV, modest in size though it was, was home to who knows how many fry, aerated and oxygenated in coolers for the trip out to Glacial Lake.

As he drove through the countryside the uniquely individual keys to his new project sloshed around behind him. Newman thought about how the fish project's success now depended, ironically enough, on maintaining the illusion that it had never happened. It was hard to see how anyone involved could possibly benefit from blowing the whistle. Certainly not the whistleblower, whose complicity was already proven by their signature on the settlement documents. And not Ziegler, who risked its continued ability to do business. Any disclosure would be met with vigorous outrage and denial from all others involved, backed by the legal alacrity of Donoghue, Stevenson, and a whole host more just like them from Ziegler Legal. All paper evidence had already been erased, and biological evidence in the form of surplus fish would shortly, when Newman was ready, be subject to Pete's protocol for not so much a figurative but, Newman thought in a reflective moment, a sadly literal flush down the toilet.

At this time of year there wasn't much activity at the lake. The resort was officially closed and the resident manager, Doris, had followed the last visitors out with a favorite among all her normative signage: "Closed. Keep Out." As Newman negotiated the chain across the entrance, it was clear the place was deserted except for a large, rust-colored truck that he thought had been either criminally dumped by a local or casually parked by the maintenance man. The maintenance man would be here year-round, of course — what was his name again?

"Robert!" shouted a short, wiry-looking figure darting out from between the cabins across the field.

"Hello! It's Newman actually. I'm the new—"

"Yes yes I'm Robert," said Robert, appearing next to Newman almost immediately. Robert was clearly a Scot by accent and by kilt. "I live here. My home from home, you understand. And I know who you are I can tell by the haircut. The only other haircut like that round here would be Fred

Jesperson's. Ha! And you're clearly not Fred."

"Fred?"

"That's right. Corporate style back and sides. Twin haircuts, you and Fred. Haircuts separated at birth you may say. Anyway I heard about the new licensee, was waiting for you to show up. Is Doris OK with all this then?" he said with a wink. Like all previous visitors Newman was familiar with Doris. "There's plenty of room for change around here, that's for sure, but easiest to do it either with Doris's blessing else on the QT if you're canny."

Newman was beginning to think Robert might have some sort of sixth sense. "I'm here to take stock, do a little boating, get my bearings."

"Aye, aye. Need a cabin? Plenty to chose from." Robert waved an expansive hand at the sad-looking line of individual accommodations above the lawn that looked to Newman as though they were last painted by Lewis or Clark.

"Not this time — brought my own accommodation. All set." As Newman spoke, Robert was already off and striding toward the lodge with an "Alright then, see you later!" and a backhand wave.

Newman climbed back into the RV and headed for the boat dock, and it was approaching dusk by the time he'd negotiated the ramp and had the boat along with its tankful of shiny souls off the trailer and into the water. From there it was a simple matter of loading up the coolers full of fry and taking off across the glassy lake with a boatload of new residents.

The light was fading and the temperature was perfect as Newman released the fry among the rocky shallows where cold clear water relentlessly pushed and welled its way into the lake. About half way around the North side, where rock walls rose almost vertically up from the depths, breaking the surface and climbing into the surrounding pine-topped hills, he washed the glittering masses out of the water tank. He spent time drifting silently, sipping a beer, listening for owls in the trees, watching the lights from the few occupied cabins on the distant shore, and mulling his plans.

A five or six thousand acre lake like this would support a half dozen adult fish per acre easily. By the time he took up permanent residence he would have made a couple more visits like this, and by his calculations introduced more than enough to compensate for all imaginable environmental and predatory misadventures they might meet on their journey to adulthood. These trout were capable of growing more than a couple of inches a month; Newman reckoned they would start making their appearances after the first year or so, after Newman had his chance to settle in, and after the Ziegler thing had pretty much blown over. Plenty of time to put the wheels in motion to get Glacial Lake on the map. He would invest in social media, hire people who knew about such things, put together events — fishing competitions, corporate retreats, summer concerts on the lake, maybe gourmet dining in the off-season — all themed with some sort of branded spectacle of a rainbow fish.

The dining idea brought Newman out of his reverie with a jolt. There was the whole teeth thing to deal with. There were longstanding local laws governing use of the lake and its inhabitants. Although the catch and release mandate was vigorously enforced by the rangers you couldn't be certain that some scofflaw like Johnson wouldn't fry up a fish just for the hell of it. Then what? Maybe this generation wouldn't carry the orange thing. Or maybe some bright spark of a reporter might put the fluorescent dentistry, the fish, and Newman's history at Ziegler together and at the very least drum up enough suspicion to put a wrench in the works. Better at least ensure his U.K. passport was current in case he needed to add physical distance to his separation from Ziegler.

But then, mustn't get too paranoid at this early stage.

It could quite simply end up being a bit of a triumph. The opportunity to turn Glacial Lake into a commercial success teeming with visitors was a challenge, and Newman had always enjoyed a challenge. It had a mix of technical, commercial, and rhetorical aspects to it that was his specialty. Allowing himself for a moment a little optimism, he started to relax and felt his heart rate slow. It was a challenge, and a project. It was an ideal retirement project, a doable challenge, and in an ideal location.

Well we'll have to see, he thought; see how it goes. See how popular it will be. See how the adult fish turn out in a few years or so. He yawned. There'll be plenty of opportunities to figure things out between now and then.

Newman took the boat back in, tied up at the dock, and plodded back to the RV for a sound night's sleep. He dreamed of fish, of sparkling clear water, and of busloads of tourists being released onto the lake. He could see the fish grow in size and splendor before his very eyes; the grounds became greener, tourists more numerous, the cabins newer, the staff more friendly. As time passed, his plans flourished along with his bank account. Everyone was happy. Things were working out.

4: The golden years

YES. THINGS DID, in fact, work out. Surprising really, given the many and varied scenarios he'd anticipated along the way where the entire adventure ended in personal, financial, or even legal disaster.

Newman drifted around his favorite spot on the lake. His boat rocked gently, water lapped against the idle paddles, and he lay back to listen to the children splashing and shouting on the shore. Now and again a fish flipped, breaking free for a moment to reflect a metallic rainbow against the blue sky in the afternoon sunshine before returning to the gloomy depths. A dog bark echoed across the water. There was the sound of clapping. Crows joined in for a brief, raucous response from the treetops. He heard the distant whine of a golf cart as housekeeping completed their rounds of the cabins. Visitors were leaving and arriving; Doris in the lodge would be signing them in and out with a mix of efficiency and disinterest that comes from years of experience. The restaurant was preparing for dinner, and in his waterside cabin ranger Dave reviewed his lecture on those marvelous and uniquely iridescent trout.

It had been a few years since he'd taken over the resort having none of the experience required to run it, but enough of the cash required to assume the National Parks license. After all, he hadn't had to run anything so much as make sure all was in place for it to run itself. Keep the buildings, the grounds, the lakefront and of course the staff in good shape to ensure a fair shot at success. He wasn't one for effusive optimism, but in his previous life and while still perched unsteadily atop the corporate ladder, he had painstakingly listed the pluses and minuses of his new venture and landed more or less on the plus side.

And of course there were the fish. The fish had been only the last project of many Newman had participated in at Ziegler. But they had been possibly the brightest of his ideas and those fish were the very genesis of his decision to leave for good, for his new and as far as he could foresee most likely successful enterprise.

Yes, he thought. Yes. Despite the ups and downs, his time at Glacier Lake Resort he judged to have been, on the whole, and so far at least, surprisingly successful.

He sat up, grabbed the oars, and rowed back to the dock with a contented sigh.

In the Glacial Lake lodge, Doris was indeed busy with a sizable melee of incoming and outgoing visitors. She had her own long-established method for managing the couple of dozen cabins, smattering of campsites, and the RV fields overlooking the lake.

"What's this?" she said. A bespectacled man looked hot, bothered, and was encumbered with at least two small children. He waved a set of keys in the air.

"I'd like to check out". Of course he would. Doris knew exactly what he wanted, but this was another of those procedures for which she had a tried, tested but above all personally preferred way of doing things.

It was changeover day and with changeover came the

weekly opportunity to confirm that, after all these years, everything still revolved around Doris. There was nothing she didn't know about running a resort, and long ago she had learned enough to recognize the satisfaction to be derived from policing the limits on the joy her visitors might derive from the natural splendor of the place.

Doris was the only manager anyone could remember there ever having been at the resort. Over time her personality had been stamped on every aspect, beginning with the unique system she'd developed for registering her visitors, and ending with the ritual of receiving the keys and — perhaps — returning the deposit. Visitors will remember her, she hoped, making dramatic appearances on occasions between their arrival and their departure; glaring at infractions of posted rules; gliding theatrically through the restaurant. They may recall her hesitating over the assistant's shoulder at the gift shop cash register, sometimes flashing a suspicious glance toward them before stepping back with a "hmph". Over the years she had developed what she felt to be a guiding personality as strong and impressive as the natural scenery. More than a fixture, she had become a presence that disturbs, among returning guests she was as memorable as the towering trees, the almost overbearing hills, and that gloriously deep, cold, sparkling lake.

In short, her purpose was to ensure people knew and remembered their place, and wherever that place is, it was not here. Not for long anyway. This was her place, and people were to be cautiously accommodated. She saw her task as not so much to ensure the smooth and happy melding of visitor and nature so much as to protect whatever it is they want from whoever these people are who want it.

"Check out? Oh. I see," she said slowly, quietly almost, as if surprised by the key-bearing man's response. "Would you wait for a moment while I check this family in?"

Not that he had any choice in the matter. Doris reached for her grease pencil and in a single motion dampened it with a flick of the tongue. She fixed both smile and gaze on the increasingly beleaguered-looking man for just a little too long, just long enough to make him even more uncomfortable. She noticed his spectacles were slightly fogged; that was good. The children were starting to tug him toward the door as she turned away and pointed her pencil at the incomers.

"You have a reservation?" she said, widening her eyes and tilting her head in order to convey doubt.

"Yes — Thorpe," said the woman, "please," she added. Doris liked to see visitors recognize the need to maintain politeness given that, after all, they were guests and they were asking for a favor.

A key part of her operation involved what she called "the System". She relied on the System to manage season after season of visitors, cabins, camp-sites, RV hookups, boat rentals, fishing licenses — everything that needed managing. Many, many temporary workers, here only for the summer season, had struggled to master the System only to be told that they had fallen short. "There's always something to know," Doris might say with a dramatic pause, raising her eyes and pointing a finger heavenward as if about to impart a pearl of hard-won wisdom, "that you don't."

The System was a collection of items starting with the grease pencils and including a huge wooden board with gridlines on it, sheafs of clear plastic overlays, and a rolodex-like affair. Finally she had a massively thick, many tabbed, and strikingly imposing book of the sort newsdealers once used to track newspaper deliveries for an entire town. The book looked like it weighed as much as a reasonably hefty dog, or an old-school television. It was only ever deployed as a final arbiter in case of any dispute about anything; she would turn to the book, shuffle pages for a while and then slam it shut, often with an accompanying smile and "I'm sorry". And that would be the end of it. The book was the supreme court of appeals in Doris's System.

In this case she didn't need the book; the Thorpes were in the System, confirmed with a curt "That's right."

Newman walked along the dock and crossed the lawn that reached down to the water. Despite being changeover day, it was good and busy with people swimming, boating, fishing, playing and many simply stretching out in the sun. It was mid morning and already the low-lying cloud had burned off the lake. It promised to be another day of clear warm air, bright light, and intense natural colors. He felt excited, even enthusiastic, as he walked through the gift shop and ice cream bar, stopping to decant a fresh cup of coffee and add a spot of cream. He paused to rearrange a few misplaced flip-flop sandals before entering the lodge where he opened the door for a sweaty-looking luggage-laden man and his children.

"Morning Doris," he called over his shoulder. As he turned he noticed a couple at the counter apparently debating which cabins were which, while Doris was busy leafing through her book. She's busy, he thought, and decided to head out toward the ranger station to see if Dave was in.

He liked to walk around the grounds. He felt like a secret shopper, observing and listening to staff and visitors, developing a feel for how things were going in order to provide feedback to Doris which, of course, she largely ignored. "It gives him something to do," he overheard her say perhaps to herself as he left after tentatively delivering a few suggestions.

Ranger Dave was in, and he was admiring a large stuffed and mounted trout that was intended for prime position in the lodge.

"Morning Newman!"

"Morning Dave — I'd have brought you a coffee but quite frankly I couldn't be bothered."

"That's alright Newman I'd rather drink the lake water than your coffee anyway."

"Wait a minute, Dave," Newman said, "is that one of the jewels in our crown? Certainly looks like it."

The trout, even in its current inanimate state, seemed to generate sunlight even in the shadow of Dave's ranger cabin. It was a sight to be seen, intensely mirrored color in glistening stripes that only recently, with thousands of its tribe, graced the clear waters of Glacial Lake. And thankfully, it was a sight seen by increasing numbers of visitors who were drawn to the well-publicized lake with its famous inhabitants.

"Biggest one so far since they showed up," said Dave.

The trout had been officially identified as unique to this particular location, their markings, patterns, and their characteristic dorsal fins heralding their celebrity and making them a must-see for vacationers, biologists, geologists, and season-long successive parties of schoolchildren.

"You speaking tonight?" Newman asked.

Dave was an enthusiastic ambassador, giving regular lakeshore lectures that he tailored for each particular evening's audience. But he always included the geography of the place, how ice bore down and gouged out a huge punchbowl from the earth, and how it pushed out all those scrapings before slowing to deposit them into a colossal plug behind which Glacial Lake came into being. He talked about the nearby coastal tribes of the Coldwater Nation and invited representative experts to speak of hunting, fishing, and the spirits from the shores that haunt the hills surrounding the lake. But the highlight was always his presentation of the uniquely magnificent trout, and during evening sessions he called for a dramatic period of silence at dusk while his audience scanned the surface of the lake. The fish seldom disappointed, leaping for clouds of emerging flies that hovered above the ripples, wowing onlookers with iridescent flashes of the reflected sunset.

"Speaking? No," said Dave. He always said the same, with a barely concealed smirk. But of course he was — it was changeover day, and he liked changeover day because people would be out strolling around in the evening, taking in their new surroundings, and he had the chance to stake his place among the attractions.

Newman gave his usual response. "Good. Tedious nonsense. See you later Dave."

He walked up the hill to the housekeeping cabin, where a procession of golf carts retrieved the spent and distributed the freshly cleaned essentials on which the cabin business depended. It was their busiest time, following people out so they can prepare as quickly as possible for people eager to get in. These, Newman thought, are the worst jobs at the resort and he was sorry anyone had to do them. But the temporary housekeepers — mainly students home for the holidays and a few retained for year-round visits — didn't mind so much, given that during the week there was plenty of time for water skiing, tanning, and otherwise partying. That, and generally avoiding Doris, made housekeeping a decent enough way to spend a summer.

As he completed his tour of the facilities he thought how, even on vacation, the tyranny of hierarchy was still evident. The cabins beside the lake with bathrooms and kitchens were top of the chain, next the rustic variants further up the hill offering only bed and bath, then the dormitory cabins among the trees sharing facilities with the campsites. Floating somewhere below cabin and above tent would be the RV community, set apart geographically and philosophically from the others, and comprising a broad diversity of characters to match the motley collection of vehicles enjoying the lake-view field that is devoted to them. These were the modern-day travelers — at least for a few weeks a year — and he was always impressed by how easily each creates a fleeting and often idiosyncratic snapshot of home out of their assigned full, or partial, hookup.

He was reminded of the way his former corporate colleagues would be assigned offices. Features such as windows, corner, guest chairs, projector were markers of rank and longevity, but could be supplemented with personal items (rugs, coffee machines, pictures, knickknackery of every sort) in an attempt to express personality or at least eschew uniformity.

He returned to the lodge and relaxed once more in a

particularly uncomfortable Adirondack in front of the lawn, overlooking the lake and the towering hills beyond. Three years ago he had a very different life, he thought, but let's face it he had enjoyed a very nice office, as offices go. He was close enough to the top rung of the corporate ladder to heed real ladder warnings about not overreaching, and was blessed with more than enough space, facilities, equipment, and influence. He held enough sway and had gained enough confidence by that time to walk the halls and shoot the breeze, to duck in and out of meetings as he wished, to garner funds and present results. There was no longer any question too revealing for him to ask, no argument he favored that he hadn't been prepared to make.

You know you've reached the top when there's no-one left who intimidates you. And now, now in his retirement, these must be the glory days for Newman and for the resort at Glacial Lake.

5: The enlightenment

IT WAS TRUE; there was indeed an entirely different atmosphere around the resort these days. It had something it always used to lack, something that even Newman hadn't anticipated: a solid sense of place, of identity. Newman, and of course his fish, gave it a sense of renewed purpose, a self-confidence and a unique character to rally around. Staff and return visitors alike felt the difference.

The change extended even as far as Doris, who after all the years she had spent there had a new attachment to the job, and was, she dared to think, for the first time in a very long while somewhat proud of her role as manager of the entire affair.

Her habit had been to avoid visitors as much as possible, at least during the day when they seemed most needy. She preferred to direct operations from the rear and to make appearances strictly on her terms. She would spend the hours prior to the evening and a glass or two of wine in a perpetual state of mild annoyance. But now she rose in the morning ready to meet and greet as she made her way down to drink coffee at a table on the lawn. She felt part of the attraction, and imagined herself as somehow both directing and starring in the movie of each and every visitor's Glacial Lake experience.

Much of this was down to two changes in her life: Newman's intervention and his subsequent changes at the resort, and a book entitled *Practical Buddhism: Opening the Unenlightened Mind*, given to her by a young woman she had scolded for using a singing bowl in a public space, namely the end of the dock ("Sorry dear, we haven't got a music license," she spat). She had started reading the book almost accidentally as an excuse for a sit down, a cigarette, and a glass of house red; this unplanned event in itself made it seem even more providential to her after she had almost unconsciously completed the entire book in one sitting. The book revealed the many years she had spent alienated from the place she lived and worked, an unexamined endurance in which she developed petty strategies to come to daily terms with the drudgery involved in accommodating vacationers. But now, now she felt enlightened in a spiritual and in a physical sense. She trod more lightly, she felt uplifted, she was supported by the place rather than depressed by it.

But she did still enjoy playing the part of the old Doris from time to time. After all, she couldn't escape doing what she'd become so very good at.

It was harder of course for her to realize, let alone acknowledge, the degree to which Newman had played a part in this transformation. Maybe it was just coincidence, she thought, that the whole place should seem to have gained a new sense of identity when Newman arrived; certainly the discovery of the fish gave the lake purpose, and brought many more visitors intent on catching a glimpse of them. Previously it was just another place to swim, boat, fish, or lay around in the sun. Now the place had a distinct character that set it apart and seemed to impart a reason for everything where previously there didn't seem to be one. She liked that.

She'd taken to developing a wardrobe that reflected

the new-found character of the resort. A little sparkle during the day, and, as now, a touch of color to add drama to an evening outfit. Of course she felt she needed to be wary of appearing overly dramatic; she felt, at her age, she needed to avoid anything garish, and she wasn't yet ready for the red hat society. She aimed for subtle but memorable, she wanted to reflect and be reflected in the richness and the beauty of her, yes her, resort. She felt she should embody her recent revelations as to the importance of the here and now. And she certainly wanted to be noticed.

She glided into the restaurant and saw Newman sitting in the corner. She waited for him to notice her.

"Doris! Please do join me if you have a moment."

"I will," said Doris, adjusting her almost luminous black, red, blue and yellow shawl as she took a seat. After a pause, she said "You're not like the last licensee."

"I'm here and she's not, I suppose, but apart from that?"

"I never saw her for one thing. I'm told I frightened her off early on, but that would have been such a long time ago I can't remember. When you signed up I was expecting some sort of a clean sweep, wondered whether I would stay on. The place was hardly thriving. But now it does seem like we're doing better. I'm not sure now whether it was you or the fish that came to save the day."

"I'm a big believer in enabling things to work out for the best," said Newman. "Put the environment in place to make things happen. Help everything thrive."

"Well it's working."

It was working a little too well in some respects, and the sort of people arriving at Glacial Lake these days had higher expectations. They had traveled further, they needed more, and they more readily showed both appreciation and frustration. As a result, managerial decisions had been made that led Doris to suspect that her System may be thought to have reached its limits. There seemed to be an inevitability about the intrusion of new processes and procedures to manage everything. Doris's tone became slightly more critical.

"But I dare say what's not working is the new booking system."

Newman had called in a disturbingly youthful collection of individuals and given them free reign to mess with the entire place, connecting it to the sky or something, 'hooking up', 'firewalling' and otherwise gradually but irreversibly replacing her System, her pencils, papers and book, with styluses, screens, and 'online databases'. She couldn't suppress her delight when the new machinery was 'offline' and she was given the opportunity to dramatically brush aside the checkin screen to drop her book in its place, and drop it from a height that caused a 'whump' leaving no-one in any doubt that her System had stepped back in to restore order.

"Seems to me," she said, "the tail is wagging the dog with that thing. It notifies me, it informs me, warns me, that thing — when it's working — tells me — me — it tells me what to do."

Doris was getting into her swing.

"And another thing — I challenge you to find anyone over seventeen years old who knows how to work it."

"Well I certainly don't know," said Newman in a transparent attempt to humor her. "But that's the point — we need all this technology these days I'm afraid. Parks almost demand it so they can keep tabs. But I am relying on you to provide a steady hand at the helm. I need you to play to your strengths as the bedrock of all that persists, is consistent, reliable and permanent round here. And you're right; people who understand that stuff are two a penny. But someone who can anchor the entire operation in experience and common-sense, who can step in and take the reigns when the technological horse bolts — a dog ... " Doris was enjoying the rhetoric of his pep-talk, but now her eyes widened slightly and Newman recognized his blunder, "oh let's see, a dog if I may borrow your allusion, Doris, a dog that is in full control of its own tail — now that's something rare, and something we're very fortunate to have round here."

Doris saw by Newman's expression he was uncertain whether he had managed to turn that whole thing round, and she chose to keep him on the hook a little longer.

"A dog you say? Well there is certainly a value to loyalty and continuity. Not much round here I haven't seen, avoided, prevented, or fixed. But while we're speaking directly, one thing I don't get is why you're here, what you plan for the place, and how long you're going to stick around."

Doris took a slow sip of wine and looked at Newman over the top of her glass, indicating that she was ready, waiting, and had plenty of time for a comprehensive response.

Newman said he'd had the idea of living there since his first visits when he was working for a big corporation. He'd wanted to leave corporate life, but he wasn't ready to retire, so what better way to leave his job and move without retiring than to become the licensee? The opportunity had come up, so he jumped.

"Besides making a living and satisfying the Parks department, I had no real plans. But I could see there was plenty of scope to improve the place. I intended to fix it up then market the crap out of it. The fish were a big help — who knew? The social media firm surprised me with the interest they were able to drum up with that."

"Social media. Contradiction in terms as far as I can see."

"I see your point but look at all these happy people that are coming these days — half of them are here because their friends recommended us, and a good portion of the other half are repeat bookings. It's a miracle."

"I wouldn't go so far as to call you a miracle worker, Newman." Doris put her glass down abruptly. "Where to from here?"

"I think things are going pretty well, aren't they? If I have plans, they would be based on not messing things up. Doing my best to keep things moving along as they are. I don't much see the need for any big changes, do you?"

Doris stood up.

"No big changes! Here's to that."

She drained her glass and swept towards the door, pausing to unleash a fixed smile at a wandering child, who quickly returned to his parents' table.

That particular afternoon Newman had somehow managed to nod off, uncomfortable though he was in his Adirondack in front of the lodge. He was brought to consciousness by an altercation in the gift shop.

A woman had bought one of the trout-shaped 'Happy Birthday' balloons and was clearly upset. Doris was already there, using her slightly hurt look as the woman claimed that charging for the balloon, then extra to inflate it, was "criminal". Once the woman became frustrated enough to raise her voice ("What use is a balloon with no air in it?") Doris seemed satisfied, and made a great show of pushing and swiping at the cash register, repeatedly polishing the woman's credit card and holding it up to the light. She eventually and with considerable demonstrated effort managed to reverse the charge for the helium that, the woman had shouted, makes a balloon a god damn balloon. Doris allowed plenty of time for the woman to reflect on the fuss she had made.

Newman got up and walked into the shop. As he passed Doris, who was now making a suitably theatrical exit, she said at a level slightly above a whisper, "Perhaps we should adopt a rule that our tourists must come with brains in them."

Newman made a note of another suggestion he should offer during his next one-on-one with Doris.

Things were otherwise going very well at Glacial Lake. As far as he could tell, forecasts for the density of adult fish proved to be if anything conservative. They were thriving, and Newman's concern about the whole orange thing had been alleviated by a conversation with Steve a short while ago.

Out of the blue, Steve had called to discuss a vacation at the lake.

"I have to visit, Newman," he said, "damn' place sounds more fun than Disneyland. Mind you I can't stand

Disneyland. Anyrate, I think I'll prefer the fish to the mouse."

Steve arrived. Newman met him in the Lodge and straightaway asked him what he had meant about the mouse. And the fish. Apparently Steve, with time on his hands, had looked at the history of Newman's lake and it had a reputation for being a pleasant enough place, but nothing in particular stood out. It was a place to stay, and a good base for hikers and campers visiting Coldwater Bay with its boating, beaches, and tribal interest a few miles away. But then Newman arrived, and the fish emerged to greet him. A previously ignored and presumably secretive though spectacular species of lake trout had put Newman and his resort in the news and on the map. Newman was a regular Walt Disney with his park full of colorful animated characters to bring in the crowds.

When Steve was done, Newman said he couldn't possibly imagine what he was getting at.

"I'll tell you straight Newman, my retirement is bloody boring and your story is the most entertaining thing that's happened post-Ziegler. Not sure how you did it, not sure when you did it, not sure I want to know, but I love it."

Newman and Steve reached a tacit agreement whereby they wouldn't talk much more about the fish, relative to the mouse or in any other regard. After a dinner in the Rainbow Restaurant spent picking over their shared past, conversation took on a more confidential tone.

"I had a pint with Geoff from engineering," Steve said. "It's kind of fun to go over all that stuff that never happened. Anyway, we were having a laugh about Johnson's teeth when Goff said it was kind of ironic, because that redfish gene is subject to reversion. Turns out it would've died out next generation anyway, if we'd bred 'em."

"You mean we could've paid off Johnson, weeded out the rogue geeks, and carried on regardless?" said Newman in what was less a question than an amused observation.

"Well maybe, maybe not. Geoff is convinced there was a lot of other shit going on that might've surfaced anyway if Johnson's teeth hadn't put the kybosh on the whole deal."

"Other shit?" Newman was suddenly more interested.

"He doesn't know for sure, but he thinks there was a small group of nerds in charge of the gene gun that went wild with that thing."

"What? How does he know?"

"Well, he says one of them likes to impress the ladies with his geekly exploits and regularly shot his mouth off in the pub, presumably trusting that most people wouldn't know what the hell he was on about. One of those ladies worked with Geoff and asked him if he thought it was bullshit. That, and Geoff reckons there were a bunch of other species in the transgenics tanks that weren't part of any official project."

Newman, although maintaining an outwardly neutral view of all this, was suffering a little inner conflict. That conflict lasted long after dinner with Steve. On the one hand he was relieved that orange was unlikely to be an issue in future — even for those lawless enough to eat them. On the other, he didn't like the sound of those cocky geeks playing with gene guns and unofficial genetic donor fish. He wondered if there might be any "other shit" that he should know about. So much so that the following morning as Steve was leaving, Newman passed him a memory stick and asked him a favor.

"Give this to Geoff, will you? Ask him if it helps figure out what they were up to with that little after hours project."

"Oh now this really does sound like fun," said Steve. "But is there anything on here that might compromise the plausible nature of any deniability? I mean, in particular, from my point of view?"

"It's just data, don't worry. Anonymous. Only someone who already knows where it came from would be able to make any sense of it."

"Well Geoff won't need any encouragement. This sort of detective work is right up his street. I'll let you know, Newman."

It was a warm summer. Newman was enjoying some relief from the air conditioning in the lodge, sitting in his office upstairs above reception, when there was a knock and the door cracked open. Doris peered inside.

"Visitor for you Newman. Fred Jesperson."

"Fred Jesperson? Who is that? I remember being told I share a hairstyle with him, that's all I know."

"Oh you'd be surprised. President of the Coldwaters."

Before Newman could say more, Doris flung open the door and ushered in two visitors, backing out behind them with a smile.

The first was a strikingly tall woman with a classic corporate back and sides haircut, dark business suit, and a pair of hiking boots. Following close behind was a shorter man of thirty or so, a more casual figure dressed in t-shirt and jeans. On his t-shirt was written "Ask for fireworks. See what you get."

"Fred," said the first. "Fred Jesperson, Coldwater. I know; father didn't realize it was supposed to be a man's name. Surname due to preponderance of local Swedes. If you feel more comfortable you can call me Running Water or something."

Newman was already feeling overstimulated and he'd barely sipped his morning coffee.

"Only pulling your leg, Mr Newman — but do try to keep up. This is my assistant Fargo. At least we call him Fargo."

Fargo stepped in. "Many Branches," and with a glance at Fred, added "but call me Fargo if you wish."

"Morning all, Fred, Fargo" said Newman, with a cheerfulness beyond what was required for polite introductions. "Newman — I've been the new licensee for a while now, I'm pleased at last to meet my neighbors."

"You've created quite something here Mr Newman," said Fred. "As a student of this resort for many years, or rather of what the National Parks service has chosen to do or not to do with it, I'm pleased to see the improvements you've made. And also those brought to you by the lake."

"Oh, you mean the fish?" asked Newman.

"The fish have been what you might call a blessing, for sure. Beautiful, aren't they?"

"Beautiful on the outside," muttered Fargo. Fred continued.

"I'm sure they've helped turn this place around. I see people flocking here now, and I even hear it said the fish have granted the lake some magical powers."

"We do have people coming here for retreats and the like," said Newman. "Spiritual stuff you know. Classes and such."

"Funny. That used to be our department, Mr Newman. Are you trying to put us out of business? Is he trying to put us out of business do you think, Fargo?"

"It is our duty rather than our business I think," said Fargo. "He is perhaps taking over our duty, leaving us with what? Our duty is to the spirits who stride among these hills, who inhabit this lake, who are one with its inhabitants. I'm not sure that duty is so easily discharged, not to mention transferred."

Fargo stopped and looked at Newman. Fred smiled and also regarded Newman. Newman felt a little uncomfortable as he tried to unravel what he'd just heard. He wondered where all this was going when Fred pushed a mop of hair back across her forehead and said:

"Well. That's as maybe — you must forgive my assistant for bringing to this occasion a little cultural gravity that may be, let's say, premature. He takes his calling very seriously, you see, whereas I'm more — aah — excited about things. About prospects, shall we say, for this beautiful place. And my visit today is to celebrate your success! Oh and to let you know about my little project on behalf of the Coldwater Nation."

Still uncomfortable, but pleased to get off the subject of fish, Newman said "Oh yes please do — what's that?"

"Well although Fargo and I are not entirely in accord on this, I am architecting a scheme to get our youngsters into colleges of higher learning. I feel until we open our own such institutions, we need to take advantage of those offered by outsiders." An audible urr-hmmph from Fargo. "I would like our students to take our culture out into the broader world, and bring important techniques from the outside back into the Nation."

"There's nothing for them to learn," muttered Fargo.

"You see where our disagreement lies, Mr Newman! Fargo fears that there is little out there for our young people to discover, and that in the very attempt to find it something will be lost. My view is that we will learn, and we will learn not what, but how. I have labored over the distinction. Outsiders know how to do many things, but do they know what they are doing? We will learn the how — we already know the value of the what." Fred turned to Fargo. "You never know — they may learn something from us in return."

"More lob-sided trades," murmured Fargo as he poured himself a coffee from the carafe on Newman's desk.

"Excuse us," said Fred, "we're a little sensitive at times. But despite Fargo's misgivings, I do have the backing of the council and I've started the process. My nephew Walker is in the vanguard — actually he's fishing your lake right now, he's up here on a break from his third year at Yale. I'm very proud of course."

"Of course!" said Newman. Law? He thought. Must be law.

"Genetics," said Fred. Geez, thought Newman. "A classic 'how to', don't you think? Leads naturally to and from the 'what'. The boy has talent, no doubt. But then again, you have dabbled in genetics in the past, Mr Newman. And you know, among no doubt many other things, what it takes to get into Yale — and to stay in Yale!"

Newman had wondered before, superficially and on

visits to the Coldwater tribal museum, what precisely it was that those folks knew. Now he felt a more immediate urge to figure that out.

"Oh I was more of a biologist, and even then I managed things rather than did things, if you know what I mean."

"Well you have certainly done something here Mr Newman and we are all very impressed! Enjoy this day, Mr. Newman." Fred abruptly turned and walked toward the door, which was still open, Fargo in tow. Newman heard the sound of subdued remonstration from Fargo as they exited the lodge; Doris rushed in and closed the door, as excited as Newman had ever seen her.

"OK cut to the chase Newman I heard everything!" After a pause, "What the hell did she say?"

Ignoring the contradiction for a moment Newman said, "She seems to like the place that's all — not sure about Fargo's thoughts but she seems very impressed with what we're doing. At least, that's what she said."

"I know that's what she said, but she's too smart, Newman. She is very smart — if you think running this place needs some know-how, that's nothing. It's well known round here Fred has big plans for the Nation, and she wouldn't waste time up here with her nephew congratulating you unless there was something else going on, you can bet on it."

Newman, of course, had his own concerns. He reassured Doris that Fred was just looking to meet and greet with locals involved in the overall development of the region, but inside he was reflecting on Fred's apparently carefully chosen words and thinking she was indeed smart enough to be one or more steps ahead of him.

"Don't worry Doris. There could be some opportunities to work together here; Fred wants a piece of the new action perhaps, and, well, we could find a way to benefit from the whole tribal angle."

"I hope you're right, Newman. I hate to have to play the Fargo to your Fred, but it makes me nervous. And by the way — never again say "tribal angle", OK?"

"Got it."

It took Newman a good few days before he stopped mulling over what was said at Fred's visit. Maybe she was after all just here to show Fargo that everything was fine, that their neighbor was doing good things, and that everyone would be better off for it. And the whole spiritual retreat thing that had sprung up around the fish was ripe for expansion; Fargo's comments about spirits in the lake and so on might present a whole new marketing angle. Some sort of symbiotic relationship with the Coldwaters might be just what the place needed next.

Then the phone rang; it was Steve.

"Newman — I've got Geoff here. He has some news about the analysis he's been doing on that data, so I thought I'd get you on the line to hear it. Here you go."

"Mr Newman?" The voice on the other end sounded nervous and, to Newman at least, unexpectedly young. "This is Geoff. I work in analytics. At Ziegler."

"Yes, hello Geoff. Many thanks for your help. I was pleased to learn that the orange thing was recessive after all that nonsense, eh. We can say goodbye to that whole thing with a clean slate."

"Oh yes," said Geoff, "haha. Excuse me. Well that was

good news, yes. I have some further information, based on that data you provided, and of course without biological investigation for confirmation and so on but I think I can be fairly conclusive. I mean after pretty comprehensive recursive analysis, that is."

Newman heard Steve in the background: "For god's sake Geoff get on with it will you? That's my long distance minutes."

"Oh excuse me. Yes. Well. Mr Newman?"

"Geoff do carry on."

"Yes, there's evidence of additional splices in the code for these subjects. I've chased up a few, of course it's not straightforward since the precise nature of the genes inserted requires further study you understand. But, in short, and without too much debate, we can get the gist of what's gone on."

"What's gone on?" said Newman.

"Interruptions here and there," said Geoff. "There are genes from a number of species including ... let's see ..."

Newman caught a background "Geez" from Steve. Geoff seemed to be shuffling papers.

"Well we have a rainbow trout for the canvas of course, with the recessive redfish, and I recognized the iridescent shark gene which of course will persist. But then there are a number of further ermm, further ah, interventions. The first I found was Burbot, pretty common to bypass the seasonal pattern and provide year-round growth. But then there's also a mahi mahi gene."

"Mahi bloody mahi?" Steve was clearly hearing this for the first time too. Newman was hoping the news stopped soon.

"Mahi mahi would be for accelerated growth, you understand. So there we have accelerated, year-round growth."

Newman couldn't contain himself. "Accelerated, year-round growth? What are we talking about here?"

"Well we can't know for sure of course purely from the data, what might or might not happen in practice. But mahi mahi puts on fifty pounds or so in a season."

"Christ," from Steve.

"Go on," from Newman.

"Oh and well, errm, I haven't finished analyzing all the data of course but there was one further modification I managed to wheedle out so far."

Newman heard Steve once again, distant now, perhaps even on the floor, "Don't tell me — you found Micky Mouse mixed in there?"

"Oh well — haha, yes. No, I mean — I found white sturgeon."

"Not familiar," said Newman. "Why would they do that?"

"Distinguishing characteristic of white sturgeon would be lifetime weight," said Geoff. "Lake sturgeon can be — oh, up to eighteen hundred pounds or so."

It sounded like Steve was now starting to laugh. Or choke. Newman asked, "Eighteen hu . . . Geoff. What does this mean?"

"Well we can't be sure of course. As you know, transgenics can be a bit of a shot in the dark, we would need to trial this in the field and see what the biology comes up with. But we know the iridescence took. And the orange. We weren't running long enough to see the rest of it."

Newman felt the need to pull all this together.

"So to get this straight, and accepting that you're not done with the data, if there were to be such composites out in the wild they could grow to be anything from merely spectacularly attractive table trout, to hideous eighteen hundred pound monsters. Is that about it?"

"Well yes," said Geoff. "Or somewhere in between. Mind you we would hope not to release any breeders. And of course given the trout and shark profile, if they were out in the wild they would be very successful predators. I mean they wouldn't be happy for long eating plankton, I'm sure."

Geoff seemed to be more relaxed after delivering his results, emitting a snort and clearly more amused by his last observation than either Newman or Steve. After a moment's thought, he added more seriously, "Make good fishing, I would think. Although once they reach three or four years old, better not fall out of your boat."

"Alright, many thanks Geoff I appreciate your work on this. Sounds like it's a good job we wound things up when we did. I'd appreciate it if you let me know if anything else crops up. If that's about it, then can you put Steve back on?"

Newman heard Steve in the background, shouting to Geoff about a pint sometime as the door closed. Then:

"Newman?"

"Steve. I suppose you realize . . . "

"Well let's see, I think I just shit my pants, so—"

"Exactly. And if this hits the fan there's no telling how far the spatter may spread."

"Well there's nothing specifically tying anything back to anyone is there. I mean how hard would it be reproduce all the stuff Geoff dug up, purely from the data?"

"Tough. Be hell trying to find all those data points by reverse engineering a fish. I'd say Ziegler is the only place capable of even attempting it let alone pulling it off, and in the event they'd drop that potato as soon as they were told how hot it might be. Oh and don't worry Steve — there's more than enough plausible deniability to go round at your end, if not quite so much where I'm sitting."

"Well alright, Newman. Have to see the funny side of it; here I am again, making bit of a gamble on you, not quite knowing what's going on but relying on you to carry it off. I thought we'd both retired."

"This is my retirement, Steve. And once these fish have run their course, given that per Geoff there should be few if any breeders, once they've worked their magic they'll be gone. Hey come up for some fishing sometime while they're still about. See if we can pull Moby Dick out of there."

"Too soon, Newman, too soon. But I'll be there, maybe not for the fishing. Though what did Geoff say? Successful predators? In case of accidents, I hope those damn fish of yours follow the Parks' catch and release rules too."

6: The findings

FRED HAD JUST had the most frustrating meeting of the tribal council. All they wanted to talk about was the popularity of the lake, and how many visitors it must get that they were missing out on down at the Bay. Granted, those sort of people wouldn't be interested in fireworks, or even gambling; on the other hand, maybe the reason they weren't making the trip to the Coldwater Casino Ballroom was simply because the average acts appearing there were well past qualifying for medicare.

"I knew things were heading in the wrong direction," said one representative, "when Fargo installed a defibrillator backstage. It's my job to look after the artistes, and where they used to want a sackful of doobies or a case of Jack Daniels, the last lot wanted talcum powder and *I Love Lucy* on demand."

Fred was well aware of the need to boost business. Everything was being taken over by outsiders; even traditional arts and crafts were cropping up in off-reservation gift shops, and she'd seen drums, dream catchers, and even a full sized totem pole bearing Made in China stickers.

She was in agreement with the council, something needed to be done and right now if she was to get her education initiative funded. She'd successfully sold her colleagues on the whole idea of sponsoring the finest students to attend the best universities they could get into, but now she had to find a way to pay for it.

She received a call from her nephew at Yale.

"Aunt Fred, I've been making some headway on a little project here, and I'd like to take a break, come up there and talk to you about it."

Walker's final year would require him to complete a research project, and he'd been trying to come up with some ideas. He'd been fascinated by the trout at Glacial Lake ever since he first landed one on his visit last summer. Aunt Fred it was who suggested he might take advantage of resources available to him in the Yale Genetics department after-hours to see if he could gain insight into the fish's unique characteristics. Now he had a project in mind, along with a suitably impressive title: *A Comparative Analysis of the Trout Genome with Special Reference to Quantitative Trait Locus in the Glacial Lake Phenotype*. So far the data he had accumulated on an admittedly illegally retained fish had provided him with surprising results, which he decided to share first with Fred rather than with his professors.

"I'm not sure how I can help, Walker," said Fred. "I can't really get past that title you came up with. But I'd be delighted for you to visit."

Fred had not, as was often the case, been entirely comprehensive regarding the truth when she spoke with Walker. Fred's approach was to be economical with information she felt others might not need at the present time. In this case she had her own ideas about the unusual circumstances surrounding the identification of a new species of trout, and while she was no geneticist, she was hoping that Walker's investigations might yield something useful to her overall plans for the nation.

When Walker arrived he seemed both excited and slightly conspiratorial. He wanted to speak about the fish.

"I was lucky," he said, once he was satisfied that he couldn't be overheard from their table in the Coldwatering Hole Cafe. "I ran some differentials against a partial trout mapping and came up with some unexpected anomalies. Signature transcription promoters for a start."

"Let's stop there for a moment," said Fred. "You've only been off reservation for a couple of years and already I can't understand what you're talking about. Maybe Fargo has a point after all. Anyway, assume I know nothing and you won't be far wrong. Now please continue."

"Sorry, yes. Well it's clear to me that these fish have been altered. It's too hard to figure out exactly what's been done, but it's pretty clear they used a common method to do it."

"Their genes have been messed with?"

"Yes. Some change, or possibly changes have been introduced rather than evolved. I can't say exactly what — it's like coming home to find your window open and wondering what's gone missing. But of course the colors."

"Oh yes, the colors — that's where they came from then. So is this some sort of smoking gun here Walker?"

"Well it's not clear when this happened. I can't tell for sure how many generations since this trait was established. One thing is that it doesn't match any registered modifications."

"Registered modifications?"

"Yes. With a GMO salmon, you can identify it and trace the modifications back by matching it to its patent filings. But not these fish. These are kind of genetically orphaned."

"So," said Fred, after pausing to take a deep breath, "All the curiosity, the excitement and the revenue around that rainbow hullabaloo we're seeing up at the lake is based on some sort of secret fabrication?"

"You could say that."

Fred thought fast.

"Walker, a couple of immediate ideas. This information may be very valuable to us. I mean, your project is already a success even before it's started. But we should think big here and regard this particular project as complete — you can't do this officially, with your professors. We need it kept under wraps at least for now. I want to speak with the Glacial Lake people, I feel there may be some opportunity for symbiosis here. Are you OK with all that?"

One thing Walker had learned early on was that information above all else was a valuable thing. You could tell that from the cost of a Yale education. Another thing was that Aunt Fred, whatever she appeared to be doing, was always on his side.

"Of course, Aunt Fred. It's strictly between us. And anyway, since working on this and thinking about that patented salmon I've come up with a bunch of other promising ideas around farming transgenics in the wild."

"Very good Walker, you've lost me again and that's the sign of a successful education. Well done! Now. Let's get lunch. Fish and Chips?"

"Thanks Aunt Fred."

Back at the Lake, Newman was still digesting the call with Geoff. Every so often he'd see a water skier fall into the water and he was compelled to keep watching to make sure she popped up again. He strained his eyes to scan the surface for odd-looking ripples. Whenever he asked a fly fisherman how's the fishing, he was reassured when he received only a modest report. But he feared it wouldn't be long before there was a new record-breaker pulled from the lake.

Part of Newman's problem was that he got few chances to leave the resort, so it was always with him; beautiful, relaxing, but now also a constant reminder that maybe he should be worried. He was starting to feel a little trapped, and despite having reassured Steve he wondered at times if he was currently in the middle of something he should be getting out of. There was no real telling whether the possibilities identified by Geoff would actually translate into living, breathing, and potentially homicidal fish. People might consider Newman's history and start to put two and two together. People who don't realize how little management usually knows about what's actually going on.

Maybe he was worried about nothing.

Or maybe he should put more effort into worrying just in case.

He had casually enlisted Dave at the ranger station to keep an eye out, ostensibly for fish impressive enough to replace the one above reception in the lodge. But that just made Newman all the more worried every time Dave hailed him or knocked on his door, even though usually it was just to apprise him of highlights from the latest lecture series, or to ask if he could enlist Robert to help crack down on illicit beer drinking at the picnic areas. (In truth the combination of almost a lifetime's investment in single malt whisky and total indifference toward National Parks rules rendered Robert the last person Dave should have considered for that task.)

So it was a welcome distraction when Steve showed up for a long weekend of fishing, reading, and relaxation. Steve brought a little of the outside world with him, a reminder of Newman's past life, and that there was still a universe of goings-on beyond the hills surrounding the lake. They met in the lodge, at the Rainbow Bar.

"Good to see you Newman! And glad everything seems to be going swimmingly here. Not that I'll be taking a dip anytime soon."

"Yes all is well. In fact so well that we'll have to start beating people off with a stick — we don't have enough places to put them or restaurant room to feed them despite building cabins and extending the lodge."

"Really? Well I'd have thought you'd be a little more cock-a-hoop then, Newman."

"Well yes, of course I am inside but years of remaining calm under corporate adversity, you know," said Newman, with the sort of nonchalance you might see in a cat about to be given a bath. Steve seemed to recognize Newman was itching for news.

"Ah well that comes in handy I'm sure, but I do have something more from Geoff. Good news is he's certain that whatever does or does not happen to emerge from that gene soup he was talking about, these damn fish won't turn out to be breeders. All females, eggs no good, end of story."

Newman was already imagining the lake back to how it was after a few stunningly successful years, and even starting to think about enhancements to his retirement plan, when Steve added:

"'Course every silver lining has to have a cloud, and

in this case Geoff did mention that there's no reason to assume these trout would live less than around thirty years, so along with the bulking up and so on, in that case we'd end up with fish that grow quickly and for a very long time, before they eventually kick the bucket as ferocious, frustrated, starving old monsters."

"Oh."

"Yes, and — here's something funny — he did say that given their predatory nature, after they've cleaned out the lake they will have a crack at each other. There is a scenario where you end up with a lake which is pretty much empty for a time apart from a few massive bastards waddling around the bottom stalking their roommates and surfacing only to drag in a boatload of sightseers."

"I see."

"Well, maybe not that funny."

Steve was clearly amused, and Newman was thinking his amusement may be the main reason for his visit. "Oh come on Newman. Doesn't sound likely to me. Hey maybe you should ignore the catch and release rule and have the tourists pay to yank 'em out of there for you while they still have the upper hand."

The levity passed right over Newman's head, who looked reflective as he said "Thought of that. Parks wouldn't go for it I'm sure."

Steve was close to extinguishing the flame of goodwill held for him by Newman, who was finding it hard not to lay blame. Blame for Steve's hiring him into Ziegler in the first place, for apparently enjoying the growing predicament, and — well — for being there. He was a little irritated and, although he knew it was unreasonable, he started to feel as though Steve and Geoff were eating bananas and tossing the skins about the place just to enjoy watching him slip up.

"There'll be a time when we look back with fond memories to these golden days, Newman, before the reckoning, so to speak. Before the emergence. Hahaha. Mind you," Steve settled into his imaginings at this point, and stared out of the window; "Feeding of the five thousand? One of those buggers could feed the entire town, eh?" He turned to Newman and added: "Or vice-versa, of course."

Steve ordered a gin and tonic with a decisive tone, as if he felt that although it was only midday his comic observations had fully justified it. Newman, about to ask Steve exactly how long he planned to stay, was interrupted by Doris who announced that he had visitors in the office.

Fred and her nephew Walker were standing at the window in Newman's office enjoying the lake view when Newman walked in, still thinking about what Steve had said about feeding villages. Before he had a chance to speak, Fred said:

"Penny for your thoughts Mr Newman!"

"Ah hello Fred. Good to see you. This must be your nephew?"

The "Yale Blue Genes" T-shirt was a big clue.

"Yes, Walker's taken some time off from his studies to visit us, but he spends most of his time up here at the lake."

"Well it's been suitably spectacular weather lately, for sure," said Newman.

Fred smiled. "Though a bit of a busman's holiday for Walker, you might say!"

"Really?" said Newman. "How so?" he asked, trying to sound like he assumed they were just making conversation.

"Oh he's fascinated by the fish. I'm sure you know how it is — anything unusual, these science guys want to unravel the puzzle."

Walker didn't add anything. Newman decided to test the water.

"Oh I do remember that. I used to work with a division-full of unravellers." Turning to Walker he said, "Fascinating variation we have here, isn't it? Really puts us on the map." And to Fred, Newman said, "Those fish have really brought a lot of business opportunities up here — you must see a lot more people down at the Bay, too?"

"Well, not as many as I'd like, actually. I'd like for us to be able to tap into that resource a little more."

Walker said, "Very unusual by all accounts, Mr Newman. I've researched landlocked species all over the world and it's hard to find any that haven't spread by birds, for example, to be found elsewhere. Your fish are, to my knowledge, geographically unique."

Newman maintained a smile, just until Walker went on to apologize for having removed a couple from the lake as part of his research. "I hope you don't mind — I know Parks has a catch and release rule but I was interested in trying to figure out where that shine comes from."

"Oh, I won't tell if you don't," said Newman, glancing back toward Fred. "The world of genetic mutation is full of both ugliness and beauty isn't it? We're lucky here that we can all benefit from the beauty, eh. Do you think there's enough here for your PhD, Walker?"

Fred intervened.

"First things first, don't you think Walker? We need to be sure where we are today before we think about where we're going in future. But you've served up a great opportunity."

Fred looked directly at Newman.

"And thank you for understanding the little transgression regarding the fish and the lake. Very nice of you."

"Well good, good," said Newman. He was still wondering why Fred was here again, thinking that she was withholding something but he wasn't sure what. After a pause, he added, "Was there anything in particular I could help with?"

"Oh no — not now — just here to introduce Walker since you're both in the same game. And I always enjoy a trip to your wonderful resort. Any excuse."

"And of course you're always very welcome," said Newman. He was disquieted. He felt that Fred had somehow got what she came for, but he wasn't entirely sure what that was. "Good to meet you Walker. And if you do decide to pursue research, then maybe I could put you in touch with a few contacts at Ziegler — at least, for so long as I still have any."

"Thank you Mr Newman — I'll definitely bear that in mind. As you know this sort of work always leaves you with more questions than you have answers so I'll need all the help I can get I'm sure."

"Well-said Walker," Fred added, "Enjoy the rest of this beautiful day Mr Newman - it's a great day for making plans, I like to say, but then again every day's a good day for plans, don't you think?"

"Oh of course," said Newman, who was none the wiser about her visit but pretty sure that, whatever they might be, he should be concerned about her plans. "Goodbye Fred, Walker."

They'd gone, and Newman sat down heavily in his chair to think as he fidgeted with the rainbow fish snow-globe on his desk. OK don't panic, let's just take stock here. He thought: what do we know. He knew Walker had found out something about the fish, and Fred seemed intent on letting Newman know that she knew, but so what? What possible good was all this to Fred anyway? It could have ended up in a PhD for her nephew. Did he want sponsoring or something? There was a lot more to it than that. He took the fish into the lab, but Geoff reckoned reverse engineering anything more than some obvious bits and pieces about the stripes or whatever was next to impossible. Mind you, whatever it is she thought she knew, she clearly didn't know the half of it. And thank god for that. Otherwise she'd be up there demanding he drain the lake or something before those monsters come after Fargo's precious hill spirits. No. Fred knew something, not much, but enough for her to test him out, and Newman was no poker player; he was more or less certain he'd given the game away a couple of times and let her know he was rattled. What was that she said? Transgression regarding the fish? Her Yale prodigy had shared a conclusion or two with her for sure.

Alright then, what was to be done? Only option: sit tight and wait for her next move. After all, the best-case scenario — which Newman couldn't, for sanity's sake, rule out — was that the fish enjoy a normal, spectacularly shiny lifespan and then die without reproducing. A rainbow flash in the pan, shortly to leave the resort bereft of its main attraction but still on the map, spruced up and by then with an established and faithful following of returning vacationers. That's it. Keep that in mind — Newman was calming down as he worked through this best of all possible cases.

On the other hand, there was extortion. What if that normally mild-mannered if inscrutable Fred figured everything out and threatened him with blackmail or something? Violence perhaps? Maybe that's what she hinted at with talk of mutual benefits and the like — did she want a payoff?

Newman felt something deep down in his internal musculature tighten as he imagined this less welcome turn of events.

After a visit to the bathroom he returned to the bar, where Steve was deeply ensconced and in intense conversation with Doris.

"Ah Newman, you're back. Doris was telling me about your neighbors down there at Coldwater Bay. Sounds like you've mended fences with them, eh? That would be up your street — he was ever the facilitator you know, Doris. The smoother-over of differences."

"I think we get on fine," said Newman. "Don't we?" He had his doubts, but he looked to Doris for confirmation.

"It looks like it, doesn't it?" said Doris. "Surprising, really, given the history."

Newman had never really delved into the history, and until now was largely unaware that there was any. "History?" he asked, as Steve leaned forward, raising both glass and eyebrow.

"Oh, well it goes back a long, long way of course. Way before Fred's time, before this whole area was taken over by Parks. Naturally, the Coldwater folks are still not happy."

"What do they want?"

"Always said it was clearly part of their land. They still talk about how before the lake was formed all that meltwater flowed down into the Bay. A direct connection with these hills they say. So the lake formed, spirits inhabit it, so on so forth, then eventually the government comes in and thinks it can take it away. They say, cutting off the head from the body of their land." Doris aimed an exaggerated smile at Newman. "So 'mending fences' sounds a little quaint, don't you think? Would certainly take some sort of political genius — are you that genius Newman?"

"I've seen him pull off a few stunts in my time," said Steve. "I think I've called you a genius once or twice haven't I Newman?"

"I realize you're pulling my leg, Doris. We didn't talk about anything like that. But yes, today's chat certainly left me feeling slightly queasy."

"Exactly," said Doris. "Did she say anything about making plans?"

"Well, yes she did actually. Said it was a good day for it, I think."

"She'll be back then. There's more to it. A couple of times she's left me with 'making plans', and before I've figured out what she means we end up organizing trips to her museum, selling her crafts in our gift shop, or having Dave invite tribal historians to give talks on 'Coldwater Lake'."

"I can't wait," said Steve, rattling the ice in his

otherwise empty glass.

"What time is it? Is it midday yet?"

"I'll have a gin and tonic too I think," said Newman. "Doris?"

7: The proposal

FRED GRACEFULLY OCCUPIED an Adirondack on the lawn overseeing the lake, sipping an iced tea. Newman sauntered over, a little over-casually, to join her.

Fred seemed not to notice Newman's approach, but as he was about to announce his presence she said, without turning to look at him, "Fargo says this lake is the heart of our inheritance, you know. When the government took it, we lost something central to who we are. Of course he's more of a historian than I, Mr Newman. But he says we've been struggling to find our center ever since, trying to recreate ourselves in an image acceptable to outsiders. Not paying attention to our selves and our loss." After a pause, she turned and asked "I don't know about that. What do you think?"

Newman eased himself into the classically resistant chair next to her and sat, uncomfortably, for a moment.

"You know I don't know what to think," he said. "Personally, I or my family never had anything so important taken away from us. But I can imagine it's something you never forget."

"Well as far as I can tell, it's never far from Fargo's mind. At council meetings he usually finds a reason to raise the issue of how the very name Coldwater ties us to the place higher up in the hills where the waters originate, not to the Bay where we live now, where those waters end up." She added, with a smile, "But then, that's Fargo for you. He likes to think he runs calm but very deep, like our lake."

Newman wondered if "our lake" signaled the direction today's conversation was heading, but he didn't have to wonder for very long.

"Actually I'm here to speak with you about the lake, Mr Newman. I'm not speaking on behalf of the council, you understand. I just have some thoughts I'd like to share — and to hear your ideas."

"OK great, go ahead I'm all ears," said Newman, his over-anxious levity and his discomfort in the Adirondack already having handed her the advantage.

Fred took off her sunglasses. Newman felt like she'd moved in and was treading on his toes.

"I don't know if you're a religious man Mr Newman, but those fish are no godsend, are they? It didn't take Walker long to tell me enough to be able to figure out that they're not exactly longterm citizens. Fish are essential to our culture and we take our fish very seriously round here, Mr Newman. But these fish are a joke." She took a sip of her tea.

"Just as well they're dressed like clowns."

Newman was still trying to decide how to respond when she continued.

"So anyway, while Walker was poking and prodding around in his lab, I have been checking your resume and I'm very impressed. I'd say if god couldn't make those fish, he might have asked someone with your qualifications to do it for him. Am I far off the mark?"

Newman's first reaction was to be impressed by Walker's detective skills. He decided to buy some time by following that tack.

"Goodness me, Walker must be top of his class! What a good student you have. Scholarship money well spent I'd say."

"Well there was one more piece of information he was able to provide."

Newman's stomach felt like it'd dropped under his chair. Walker's figured out the smorgasbord those geek Ziegler self-seeking shitheads had concocted, he thought. "Oh?" was all he said.

"There's some kind of technology being developed that enables these engineer folks to add a sort of genetic trademark. Walker says if he hadn't had access to the latest research equipment up at Yale he'd have missed it. Anyway it's like a sort of barcode he said, woven into the DNA somehow, used to confirm ownership of the particular genetic fiddling they've done. He found it, decoded it, and it turns out only Ziegler could be anywhere near being able to pull off this sort of thing. Oh — and apparently in this case it includes a sequence of characters that spell 'just say no to drugs'. Bizarre. Does any of this mean anything to you Mr Newman?"

Newman was thinking all those years he spent team building in Food by mischaracterizing Drugs had come home to roost in that simple message his underlings had left for him. But he was relieved to think that this might have been the sum total of what Walker knew. He thought as far as Fred's concerned, perhaps all we have here is a lakeful of illegally colored fish.

"I think we can agree on the general facts, Fred," he said, "but now what are your thoughts?"

"I'm thinking there's an opportunity here to help

each other out. I mean, we both have problems at the moment, don't we? I need to fund my education initiative, and I'd say you need to do something about these fish, don't you."

"Do something?"

"You don't think sometime down the road another Walker will come along, perhaps a little smarter or with a less visionary aunt, more sophisticated equipment, who will blow the lid off this whole shiny fish business?"

As far as Newman was thinking, this would have been the least problematic and most readily evaded scenario. Of all the future visitors he feared, human or aquatic, smarter Walkers weren't even on the list. Fred continued:

"Let's see. If I were you, what would have been my plan? Fleeing the horrors of corporate life in favor of retirement up here, maybe you were already familiar with the place; maybe you could see it was failing and spotted an opportunity to add some value? And why not. Five-fingered salute toward your former employer, take advantage of something maybe they didn't even know they had and give yourself a unique opportunity. Sounds good. And, if I were you, I would probably have thought the odds very much in my favor that no-one would ever be interested or capable enough to look into precisely how those fish came to be. Oh — and Walker said that these sorts of miracle fish rarely breed. So a self-limiting boost for you and your lake."

She paused.

"Are we pretty much thinking along the same lines?"

"You paint a pretty compelling picture, seems to me Fred. I could well imagine myself thinking the same thing, if only I had your imagination. So. What's to be done?"

"I was coming to that. I think the time may have come for the lake to leave the National Park, and reunite with the tribal land. What do you make of that?"

Newman didn't quite know what to make of it. He wasn't expecting that, for sure; once again Fred had taken him by surprise. He'd mulled over all the demands he expected Fred might make, and a grab for the entire lake was not among them.

"Of course, not just the lake," Fred added. "The entire resort. The complete operation." She seemed to be enjoying Newman's bemused look. "Starting with the fish, then the lake, the boats, the lodge, the hills, the trees, the cabins, your tame ranger, Doris. That little Scot, and naturally enough, yourself Newman."

"What on earth are you talking about?" said Newman. "You want the lake?"

"Oh, I've given this plenty of thought over the years. I've been waiting for an opportunity, but I must say even I was surprised when you and your precious scheme landed in my neighborhood."

"Wait — you want Doris? Robert? And me too? Just how does this all work, Fred?"

Newman was trying to appear slightly amused but not patronizing, inquisitive but not clueless, interested but not desperate, all at the same time. He realized his eyes may be a little too wide, and this damn Adirondack — never comfortable in the first place — put him in a poor position for any sort of authoritative negotiation. He did his best to sit up, bring his head above his knees at least.

"OK Newman. In a nutshell, imagine this. Parks are going to give up the resort and you are going to run it for us;

it will be hugely successful, and will generate the income I need for my plans at Coldwater Bay."

Fred held her arms wide, indicating that she'd given him the whole, big picture. Then she clasped her hands together.

"A bit of history for you. When the government assigned land to the nation, boundaries were drawn up according to where they decided we had primarily lived and worked. They decided we fished in the sea, and we ended up with chunks of the coast that fell short of including this lake. But those boundaries are technically subject to revision, as new facts about the Coldwater tribes may be uncovered. And now we have new facts."

This was a lot of information for Newman to digest. The best he could do, after struggling for a moment, was to ask: "What have my fish got to do with all this?"

"Well I do like you, Mr. Newman, and I have absolute respect and a fair bit of admiration for what you've pulled off — or I should say, achieved. But I wasn't sure how interested you would be in helping us, so your fish provide me with the — what should I say — leverage to have you use your considerable negotiating skills on our behalf when we speak with the Parks service."

She smiled as she recognized the first indications of comprehension on Newman's face. She could see he was ready for the final piece of information.

"You see, we need to tell them about the relics."

"The relics? What relics?"

"Walk with me, Newman."

In one fluid movement Fred got up and began to stride toward the beach. Newman struggled out of his chair and by the time he was done had to almost jog after her, loping awkwardly while his buttocks slowly released from their Adirondack-induced spasm.

When they reached the lake shore Fred said, "You see over there where the hills fold down into the lake — you can just about see the land flattening out towards the water's edge? Fargo's been over there, checking out reports of tribal fishing and cooking gear being found. He has some guys working around the lake, informally of course, looking for any other signs."

"Wait — he's found historical stuff in the lake? What sort of stuff?"

"Oh, he would know the details. Fargo is an expert on this sort of thing, and he's certain it's all very old, and very, very significant. The sort of things that may cause historians to rethink the way our ancestors worked this whole region."

"That's incredible," said Newman. "I mean, amazing. So what would Parks say?"

"They'll be surprised I'm sure. This may be enough to have boundaries redrawn. Fargo is convinced, but of course it's Parks and the government that really need to buy into it. And if it's not enough, then Fargo says he will look harder for further evidence. Which he fully expects to find."

"Even if you find a bunch of stuff out there—"

"Up to and including a burial site, of course."

Newman's exasperation began to get the better of his caution. "Up to and including the remains of Methuselah himself — how on earth will you persuade Parks to effectively hand over the resort?"

"I won't; you will. From what I've heard, you have some proven skills in this area. Bit of a reputation for turning sows ears into silk purses, figuratively, not genetically speaking we hope."

"I wouldn't know where to start with Parks."

"You underestimate your own abilities, Mr. Newman. And don't worry I'll give you all the support you need. We can rely on Fargo to provide anything else that might be required to tip the balance."

Newman was about to ask why on earth anyone would believe such a preposterous excuse for a land grab, when instead he asked:

"I suppose if I declined to help . . . "

"You're not seeing the positive side yet, are you. One way or another, your fish are not going to support this place for ever. In fact, Walker suggests the way these things work they are likely one-hit wonder, one generation and they're done. That sound about right? And look — there's plenty of marketing potential in the tribal angle for you, too. Could open up opportunities for whole new events and promotions in the longer term, once the fish have burned themselves out. And speaking purely selfishly for just a moment, if I may, I need you to run the place once you persuade them to hand it over. You're a natural. And surely you'd be a lot happier without the government breathing down your neck."

Newman immediately warmed to the idea of not having the government breathing down his neck, but he was weighing the implications of instead working for Fred when she continued.

"You know, you probably don't realize how important this is to me, Newman. I've made many plans, evaluated many potential outcomes. Spent a long time looking for a real opportunity to get additional funding for our people. The

Bay is maxed out; the lake has already shown its worth. So I have to say, and without wanting to sour our relationship, that the flipside is if you don't help us then Walker would be obliged to look more closely at your fish. I imagine he could forge an entire career on studying, investigating, and publishing about those fish, don't you think? Or maybe he could get back to Ziegler and forge a career on not publishing? Either way, all fingers seem to point toward you; frankly, it doesn't look great for you Newman. Nothing personal, mind you. I mean, you see the spot I'm in, don't you? Neither of us really has a choice here."

Newman had already decided Fred was a formidable force, so from his point of view the choice was to have her as an ally or an opponent. He decided to swim with the current for the time being.

"Well of course I can see the synergy here between our two goals, Fred. I clearly want the best for this place and the people who work here, and always have. You want the best not only for Walker but longterm for your educational foundation and so on. I'm sure we can work together somehow. Of course I'll help."

"I'll leave it with you to come up with something then," was Fred's parting shot as she headed for the lodge, leaving Newman to stare out across the water.

He'd never liked feeling that he was being manipulated. But he'd also always been ready to look for the positive in any situation, to avoid "cutting our ears off to spite our spectacles" as Steve put it. This crazy scheme of Fred's could bring down the whole debacle, the low profile he liked to maintain with Parks would be raised, they'd come in and figure out everything and it'd all go to hell for him while

Fred just stepped back and worked on the next plan in her list.

But then he thought some more about it and saw some potential; it would just be a change of ownership really, less bureaucracy. And the new owner would be far less of a threat. And a crucial advantage was that he and Fred certainly did share a mutual interest in the legitimacy of fish and relics alike.

So maybe Fred and her recent relics were not so much to be feared as embraced. She was smart, she had plans, and they appeared to be on the same side; It would be good to have someone on his side. Especially someone as inscrutable as Fred. And now it would be a burden shared. They had similarly benefited, if not from fate, then from improbable provenance. This could be the first day of the next phase in the redevelopment of Glacial Lake. Newman gradually but successfully cheered himself up; it might even be fun to exercise his underused rhetorical skills once again. A fresh start to redirect a plan that for a moment there had gone a little sideways. He felt — what was it — yes, relief.

He decided he would put together a Parks negotiation plan to present to Fred.

But of course, he reminded himself, best not to abandon all caution.

No immediate need to burden Fred with the uncertain and potentially Hollywood future of those sterile fish, thought Newman as he prepared his presentation. She seemed so pleased to have thought everything through in such comprehensive detail that it was unnecessary to throw any wrenches in the works at this stage. Better to help make sure this new project meets with success.

So Newman set to and came up with an approach that he felt would give them the best shot at persuading Parks to agree on a plan to incorporate Glacial Lake into the Coldwater reservation.

It began with reviewing the geography of the area, describing the rivers that originally fed Coldwater Bay, and that disappeared after the formation of Glacial Lake. Setting the boundary below as opposed to above the lake was a largely arbitrary decision that divided the land of those original headwaters from the land they arrived at when they entered the ocean. A purely political rather than a more natural geographical line.

Then there was the issue of rangeland, which defines boundaries according to historical and habitual use. The recent discovery of relics in the glacial soils surrounding the lake suggested the original surveys may have been inaccurate, and boundaries drawn at that time likely restrict accredited tribal members from inhabiting their traditional hunting and fishing grounds.

Finally, and this one he felt was a brilliant if long shot, even ancestral remains may have been trapped the wrong side of that fence. There was the ongoing investigation into claims that the formation of the lake may have covered sacred burial grounds, given the Coldwaters' established oral tradition of stories describing resting places above the Bay in the river valley. Tribes of the Coldwater nation were, after all, establishing themselves here thousands of years before that glacier did its work, retreated, and dammed a lake with massive deposits on top of which — some twelve thousand years later — along came Parks to build a resort that lost money for decades. Oh yes, thought Newman, this last one could be the doozy that sealed the whole Parks deal for Fred.

He drove down the valley to the reservation, and arrived at the Museum of Tribal History to discuss his arguments with her. She was engaged in a literal head to head with Fargo, who was very animated and clearly excited about something or other.

"Mr Newman," she said, "thank you for visiting. I can't wait to hear what you have to say. And neither can Fargo; he's been working on some ideas for an extravagant — no no, I feel it is a little extravagant, Fargo, but perhaps as you say essential — an extravagant exhibit here at the museum. It will showcase the recent discoveries he has made, highlight new insights into our history, and at the same time put a stake in the ground."

Newman knew exactly what she meant by that. The stake would be one of many in ground well above the current resort; survey markers indicating the new extent of the Nation's sphere of influence. Fred continued.

"Let us three meet in my office and discuss how we plan to handle Parks."

Just like the three witches, he thought; we'll spread a few half-truths. And truth be told, Newman was enjoying the conspiratorial side of all this. Part of his frustration with circumstances, and with Steve's sanguine delivery of potential bad news, was his sudden lack of agency. He felt he'd lost control, and now all he could do was wait around to see how things worked out. This wasn't how Newman had been used to operating, but here was an opportunity to get back in charge and have some sort of say in the way things would unfold.

Fred's office was appropriately stark. It contained a desk, a conference table, a topographical map of the coast, and along the wall beside the conference table was a variety of weaponry associated with each of the tribes comprising the Coldwater nation. Tall, businesslike and just a little threatening, Fred looked perfectly at home as she took her seat at the head of the table.

"So what you got for us, Newman?"

"I have written up a packet for you to review. If you like it we can have you and whoever you need sign-off on it, and I'll get it to the Parks management. The gist of it is that the land occupied by the resort must be incorporated into the Coldwater reservation. The fact that it's currently under government control is the result of historical error, and new evidence, if ignored, will only compound that error. It's only a matter of time before the land reverts to the nation, and there are clear advantages to all concerned if that time comes sooner rather than later."

"Yes yes," said Fargo, impatiently. "But they don't sound like our words, they sound like government words. How can we change their minds using their own words?"

"I think we have to go in strong, with a demand they understand," said Newman, "then we can include some facts justifying our claims — geographical, historical, physical and so on — while we introduce a little of our own stuff, some cultural leverage."

Fargo turned to Fred. "Do you follow him?"

"Main thing is for Parks to follow him," said Fred. "Cultural leverage sounds like it may be up your street, Fargo. Explain, Newman."

"Well I think facts alone may sway their rational side,

but there's the political side that's probably even more important. There are some essential block votes that may be influenced by the outcome of this negotiation, after all. So while we're arguing the facts of the case, we maintain the pressure from the moral side, the imperative for them to openly and publicly do the right thing, not shirk their responsibilities toward indigenous people. We should convince them that there is good reason for them to adopt our point of view, and no reason for them not to. We pit a money-losing resort against a burial site, vacationers against hunters and fishermen, a relative newcomer and largely absentee government custodian interested in postcards and meager tax revenue versus an entire nation with spiritual claims and a deep, one might say genetic connection with this sacred land."

"Here we go again with the biology, eh Newman?" said Fred. "But I like it. Fargo?"

"Tax revenue is meager, you say?" said Fargo, in an unexpectedly pragmatic response. Fred fleshed out his thought for him.

"Along with the return of the lake to its rightful home, the council needs to be clear that with the ensuing responsibility comes the potential for significant reward."

"Oh yes. Over the years the place has been operating at a considerable loss. It's only with the arrival of the fish and the changes we've made that things have started to turn around, but if we take, say, a ten year average they may recognize the place as a burden and it'd be in their best interest to seize this excuse to get rid of it. But what we don't tell them is that in our hands, the potential is tremendous. The fish will just have been the beginning, and this transfer alone will do wonders for securing our place on the map. This won't be just a nice place with good looking fish; it'll be the site of a cause, a focus for renewed interest in the spiritual, a retreat for the spiritually impoverished, a —

"Alright alright. And they'll pay for it?" said Fargo.

Fred jumped in. "Yes, Fargo, they'll definitely be prepared to pay for it. It's what outsiders do; they work hard for money so they can buy a life that they can pay someone to teach them how to enjoy. I think it was you who said that."

Newman was pleased to have Fred behind the plan, but he couldn't help wondering why he was so trusted to do the right thing when he dealt with the government. After all, it would be very easy for him to undermine the entire deal with just a few carefully chosen words, such as — oh — the dangers of historical revisionism in redefining boundaries; relics and artifacts requiring further expert interpretation, and spiritual legacies being by nature divisive and partisan. Fred must be very sure she's correctly identified the source of his motivation, but in truth it was a simple choice for him, as he saw any opportunity to distance himself from government involvement in his project as a good thing. His current responsibilities as licensee required a lot of monitoring and associated paperwork in connection with the lake and its contents, and Newman was thinking that a change of ownership might lessen the oversight and the number-juggling that would otherwise be required as even the happiest of potential futures unfurled.

"The Bay and the lake will be a complete package," he said. "Vacation, retreat, recreation, spiritual renewal, history, art and crafts, you name it — you can provide it. Coast is coast, but the lake gives the whole thing a unique focus."

It was resolved that Newman would get things started with Parks. Meantime he was confident, Fargo was not completely dissatisfied, and Fred seemed almost excited as she rapped a knuckle on the desk, got up, and suggested a visit to the museum bar.

Fargo had immediately implemented his plan to behave as though the "inclusion" of Glacial Lake was complete. In fact, his museum made no reference to it ever having been part of National Parks, and once the remaining Parks-related tchotchkes had been flushed out of the gift shop it would only be the mandatory selection of tourist literature in the lodge reception area that would need to be replaced. Fred's popularity with the council and with almost everyone she met on the reservation had never been more evident, and she decided to leave Fargo's premature revisionism unchecked.

"We have been pushed down, overwritten by the outsiders. They would prefer we didn't exist," he had announced at a council meeting. "Now we must begin the process of erasing that period. We must heal a rupture in our history and leave no scar."

If it wasn't for Fargo's otherwise complete indifference to logistical or political affairs, Fred might have feared a competitor for her council chair. But as it was, she felt confident riding a new wave among her electorate of almost jingoistic confidence in her plans and her abilities to execute on them.

Newman had been similarly energized since their decision to start negotiations with Parks. He, too, thought it best to proceed on the assumption that all would go ahead as they had planned. He had engaged a legal firm and much paperwork had been exchanged, evidence provided, and precedence cited. Steve was a regular visitor these days, partly because he was retired, lacked the physical co-ordination for golf, and so had little else to do. Although his townhouse gave him easy access to all the city had to offer, he found the unfolding drama at the lake much more entertaining. And he had difficulty containing his excitement when Newman described the latest stage of the journey toward independence.

"You have to get some face-time with them, Newman," was Steve's advice, "you need to work your mojo, and you can't do that through lawyers and faxes or whatever. You need to get in front of someone who's opinion counts, and do that thing where you demonstrate the advantages of doing what you want them to do, or the disadvantages of not doing it."

"They plan to send someone. Have a look around, meet with us, with Fred, see what we're talking about first-hand."

"Better be someone who counts for something, eh. Don't want the sort of powerless flunky we'd have sent in similar circumstances. I mean, I know you could run rings around the best of these government types, so good to make it worthwhile don't you think?"

"Oh it sounds like they're sending someone significant alright. Chief Negotiator. I think they're as confident as you are Steve — they expect to shut this whole thing down with a bit of on-site arm-bending. That's what I'd do."

"But what about those relics that wotsisname dug

up?"

"OK if I were Parks, I would argue that even if there is evidence of tribal remains of any sort up here, this supports only range rights, not a change in boundary. Kind of like giving them the key to the city, all very ceremonial but doesn't really mean much. They can walk about wherever they like, maybe catch as many fish as they want on designated days, hold a ceremony or two now and again, that sort of thing. But ownership? No chance."

"Alright," said Steve, "I'll bite. So if I were Fred at this point, I might say that's not good enough, it doesn't correct the arbitrary division between the coast and the inland lake, and it doesn't satisfy the spirit of the Reorganization Act, when the tribal folk living round the lake should have been consolidated and their land reverted to the tribe."

"The Reorganization Act?" said Newman. "You have too much time on your hands Steve."

"Oh yes, Mr. Parks, I don't see any distinction as to whether those people were living there at the time, or dead there at the time — any way you look at it, they were there, had been given individual rights, and then were reorganized into a single reservation. I win."

"Geez I may have to bring you in if the lawyers can't hack it. Anyway you may have your chance to make your lunatic pitch sooner rather than later, the negotiator's here next week. Trefor Evans. Trefor with an 'f'. A bona fide Welshman by the look of it."

"Welsh, eh? Well salt of the earth and all that — but certainly no pushovers, if their rugby team is anything to go by. Keep me informed, Newman, keep me informed. I haven't had this much fun in a long time and I intend to make the most of it before it all goes to hell and we have to run for cover."

Trefor Evans arrived without the sort of pomp and ceremony that might accompany someone with such an elevated title, the exact nature of which being Chief Negotiator, Office of Legislative and Congressional Affairs, State, Tribal, and Local Planning Directorate.

Newman spotted the official vehicle pulling into a visitors' spot in front of the lodge and rushed out to greet him. After a couple of attempts the car was aligned with the outlined parking space to the driver's satisfaction. Newman waited til the door half opened and a small man in a smart brown suit squeezed out, avoiding touching the car next to him while navigating himself and his sizable briefcase through the gap.

"Welcome — Mr. Evans, is it?" asked Newman. "Newman; I'm the licensee."

"Trefor, Mr. Newman, please. Is it OK to leave my car here? I'm not strictly a visitor. Should I move it to a longterm spot? But then, I'm not sure where I'll be staying. Oh by the way I'd like to stay a day or so, if that's alright Mr. Newman? I expect you're busy this time of year. I should say I know you are, of course I've done my research. I'm not trying to be disingenuous, you understand."

"Of course Trefor, not at all, actually we have a room in the lodge or you could take a cabin if you prefer."

No-one would have guessed Trefor Evans had likely just spent the best part of the day in his car. He looked, thought Newman, as fresh as a daisy; no wrinkles in his suit or nascent whiskers on his face.

"I did stop on the way to freshen up," said Trefor. "At the Överlappa Caféet just off the highway. Very nice woman, unexpectedly good tea. Whatever you think Mr. Newman, I can stay anywhere handy for our meetings. A colleague told me that the president of the tribe — a Mr. Many Branches I think — had offered me accommodation in a longhouse."

"Oh that's the president's assistant. He's a bit of a traditionalist, but I'm sure you'd be most welcome there too."

"That's alright, Mr. Newman, the lodge room will work perfectly. Might be easier for me to keep in touch and converse with my team back at HQ. You have wireless in the lodge?"

"Oh yes, we have all the latest mod cons here Trefor, don't worry! And I can let the tribal council know you prefer to stay up here; I'm sure they'll understand. How about a drink in the bar?"

Newman was pleased to see Trefor was troubled by having already done something that needs the tribe's understanding. The negotiations have begun, he thinks, he's barely out of the car and he's on the back-foot.

"Ah, no, thank you, a little early. Perhaps you could direct me to my room?"

"Doris in reception has that all set, Trefor. Let me get your suitcase."

As they entered the lodge, Doris was determinedly leafing through her book and appeared not to notice them.

"Doris this is Trefor, he's from Parks, he'll be taking a look around and getting to know the place. We have a lodge room overlooking the lake?"

Doris slammed the book shut and swept her eyes upwards in time to see Trefor jump.

"Ah! Yes, Mr Evans from Parks? I've made some preparations for your arrival. You have room four. If you look out of your window, you have a perfect view of the lake. Follow the line of hills down to the east and you can see where the valley continues down toward Coldwater Bay. Sign here."

Trefor signed there, and Newman walked toward the staircase with his suitcase.

"I'll show you where, Trefor. My guest for dinner later?"

"Oh yes, early evening OK?"

"Certainly. I'll alert the dining room. Six?"

"Thank you Mr Newman," said Trefor as they climbed the stairs to his room. "I think I'll take a walk around the grounds before dinner if I may."

"Make yourself at home, Sir. After all, it's what we've all already been doing for the last couple of hundred years here, eh?"

Trefor first smiled, then looked serious.

"You could say my home is in Wales, Mr. Newman, my name is a bit of a giveaway you see. So it'll be difficult to make myself entirely at home, won't it, unless of course you've also found coal in these valleys?"

Score one to Trefor, thought Newman. Maybe Steve's right; he's not going to be quite such a pushover.

Trefor decided to take an hour to walk the grounds before dinner. He was more at home in a Parks conference room than he was at an actual park, he'd never been that out-doorsy. But he could appreciate the beauty of the huge expanse of mirrored lake as he walked down the lawn toward the beach. A slight haze blurred the hills on the far side into a pastel palette of blues, purples and greens. A cool afternoon breeze was coming in off the water, and he noticed that, without having had to talk himself into it, he was nevertheless feeling a little more relaxed, a little more clear headed.

"Aha Mr Evans, I presume?" The sound of the small man's greeting immediately revealed him to be a Scot. He had appeared from nowhere, taking Trefor by surprise. Trefor checked his watch.

"Time for dinner already, is it?" he asked.

"Eh no, sir, my name's Robert and I'm the handy groundsman, I like to say. I'd make a poor maitre d' I can tell you that! I recognized you by the suit, you see. I was told to prepare the top cabin for your arrival — you are the Welshman from the ministry?"

"Well yes, from the Parks department. Trefor. Pleased to meet you, though I'll be staying in the lodge tonight. Thanks for your efforts though."

"Oh not at all, not at all. But you don't sound that much like a Welshman, I might say. Been away a while have you?"

"I've visited just twice myself. My mother and father were both Welsh, but I was born over here. I'd guess you're a more recent local?"

"Born in Ayrshire, I'm told, then here for the rest of my life. Parents bequeathed me my accent. Never felt the need to lose it. Mind you, maybe it's the accent that makes almost every American I meet feel they should tell me they're part Scot. D'you know, I heard even Jimi Hendrix claimed to be part Scot? Part native American too. Roots, eh."

Trefor wasn't really in the mood for a discussion. He very seldom was. But on this occasion he thought it best to make an exception since he was, after all, here to conduct due diligence and find out a little more about the place and the people.

"Don't get that so much, not sure whether it's not having much of an accent or just because Wales is less famous with Americans. They do struggle with the spelling of my name though. With an 'f'."

"Ah you Welsh need a thing, a gimmick to be more irresistible to them. We have several. Kilts, pipes, haggis — plenty to latch on to. Why have you no gimmicks down there in Wales?"

"Well we sing, you know. We are poets. And, of course, we dislike the English."

"Well I'm with you there, Trefor! There's something the Scots and the Welsh can rally around, eh! Though I haven't yet heard an American say anything like 'You're a Scot? You know, my family dislikes the English, too!' Have a seat Trefor, let's take in the evening vista here for a moment or two. Have to find something to do before the bar opens, eh!"

They took a pair of Adirondacks, Robert dropping heavily into his with an "aye". After surveying the lake for a moment, he said, "Funny, though. Americans, Scots, Welsh — we're each very keen on our independence, are we not. None more so than the Americans. And we've all had our fair share of issues with the English."

Maybe it was the air, the light, or the relief to be out of the car, but Trefor was definitely feeling like he was loosening up a little. He wasn't even thinking of getting up, walking away, and avoiding Robert for the rest of his stay — which, he thought, was uncharacteristic. He was even moved to join in with the conversation.

"I suppose so. The Welsh have been fighting with the English since the fifth century. Fighting to hang on to what they already had. Stop the English taking it from them. Probably why they wouldn't give up."

"That's about how the Scots saw it too. It may be easier to fight to keep your independence than it is to take it from someone. I mean even the Yanks saw themselves as independent, told the Brits so, and were prepared to defend it. Now who was that poor bastard the Brits sent to argue the toss with Washington?"

"I think there were a number of poor bastards," Trefor said. "Although in the Welsh case, we've ended up with something similar to what those poor bastards proposed to the Americans; self-government, seats in the British parliament and the like. But we still pay our taxes to the crown."

"Our taxes?" said Robert. "Sounds like there's still a Welshman deep down there somewhere, Trefor!"

Trefor was not comfortable being the subject of a conversation, especially not one he's involved in.

"Well no man's an island. No island is an island any more, come to think of it. Global economy, transnational corporations, citizens of the world. I'm not sure how much room there is for jingoism these days."

"Ach we all need a sense of belonging, do we not. To other people, to the place we live, even the language we speak. I don't think global economics will ever take that away. I see a lot of visitors come and go here, Trefor. I came here, to this lake, and the first thing I thought to myself was 'what a wonderful place to live'. And here I have lived for quite some time now. I feel comfortable here. I love it, you might say. But I don't belong here, you know. And it doesn't feel like it belongs to me. It makes me very welcome, but I'm a visitor, just like the rest of them."

Trefor pushed himself out of his slouch and back into his chair. "Oh, I don't know Robert. I only have to leave and come back a few times to anywhere and it pretty much feels like home."

"I can see why they're happy paying taxes to the English if all Welshmen are like you Trefor — where's the Celtic pride man?"

"Hey — the Welsh go back further than anyone else in Britain, including the Scots! Old, old genes inside me Robert, going back way beyond your pipes and your kilts. They say the first Welshman arrived in Cardiff Bay when the rest of Britain was grass and rocks. So let's just say we'll put up with the English for as long as it suits us and not a moment longer!"

"Fair enough, I'll grant you that. Well well, much as it pains me to tear myself away from this beautiful view, I must perform my daily quality check on the malts in the Rainbow Bar. You up for one?"

"It's almost six — I'm due for dinner with Mr Newman. But thanks for the chat Robert — and I may well take you up on your offer before I leave."

Doris was surprised when Newman invited her to join him for dinner with the man from Parks. Through judicious overhearing, careful questioning, and a small network of trusted staff prepared to keep an eye on Newman and report back, she was always in the know about what was going on with the Coldwaters. But what she knew included the fact that Newman was keeping some of his cards very close to his chest.

For this evening's event she chose a dramatic shawl with colorful metallic swooshes over a full length black dress, and she felt she cut a suitably metaphorical attitude as she swept around a room dedicated to those wonderful fish. Those fish that even now swept through the depths of the lake, occasionally breaking surface to make themselves shimmeringly apparent to diners gazing through breathtaking picture windows.

Doris stood wi th Newman, who she felt was dressed a little casually for the occasion. She nodded to guests who recognized her, and referred to reception those with questions or observations (and one, it has to be said, who just wanted to say "hello"). Trefor appeared, looking very sharp, and though she noticed he was wearing the suit he had arrived in, it still looked like he took it off the hanger only a moment ago.

"I invited Doris here," Newman said, "she more than runs the place, she's the heart of it. I always say until you've met Doris, you haven't met Glacial Lake."

When Trefor had checked in earlier, Doris's intention, as it was with all guests, was to be unsettling, even to induce a slight sense of alarm. Now, she thought, as she offered him her hand, maybe she should cut him some slack. He seemed a little nervous. As he performed a firm if brief handshake, he said "Oh yes I did meet you earlier, didn't I? Trefor. Sorry to be a bother with all this — hate to make a fuss."

And that was it; if Trefor had been trying to get into Doris's good books, he couldn't have taken a more effective approach. One thing Doris appreciated in a guest — and in any man, for that matter — was avoiding being a bother.

"Not at all Trefor, I'm eager to hear what you make of our little spot here."

They took a reserved window table and ordered drinks; gin and tonic for Doris, single malt for Newman, and a small beer for Trefor. Doris decided to break the ice.

"You know Newman hasn't told me much about you, Trefor. Man of mystery. Are you here to take stock, see how well we're doing? You know we were struggling for a while."

Newman stepped in.

"I haven't given Doris all the details, so please feel free to fill her in."

"Oh heavens — just give me the gist."

"Of course. You see, I'm here to take stock in light of the frankly unprecedented joint representations from the licensee," a nod toward Newman, "and the local tribes. There seems to be so much agreement on the ground here about the proposed boundary revision that the department decided to send me to see what's going on. We get administrative requests and complaints all the time, some trivial, some, like this one, more revolutionary, and my job is to make a recommendation. Most are settled these days by a bit or research at the office and a standard e-mail. If they send me out then it's because there's no cut and dried resolution."

Trefor seemed satisfied with the extent of his filling in, but Doris wasn't done with him yet.

"But what are your immediate thoughts, Trefor? First impressions are so important, aren't they? What do you feel now you're here?"

They paused to place their orders. Newman pointed out that the halibut, appropriately perhaps for Trefor, had a topping made of shredded, flash-fried leek. They made their choices.

"Oh I couldn't say. Since Mr. Newman took the license we were pleased to see the resort on an upward trend, but there've been many years when this place was a money pit for taxpayers, and visitor feedback was almost comically bad. And between you and me, we're always looking for high profile opportunities for a political win-win with regard to the indigenous Americans. I'll have a better feel for things after I've met with the local tribal council tomorrow."

Doris pressed him.

"Well that sounds like how the department feels, but what would you think about this place, owned and operated by the Coldwater Nation and not the National Parks?"

"Well, off-the-record of course, here's what I think." Trefor adopted a serious look, signaled by a slightly furrowed brow. "I think we're all visitors, aren't we? We have a duty to look after the place for future visitors. That's kind of the Parks mantra, you know. Even as custodians, we're only here for a while to take care of things. So, the question is — who is likely to do the best job? The government? The indigenous people? On the one hand, before you showed up, Mr. Newman, this place was falling to pieces. And that's no reflection of you, Doris, and your crew; Parks had disinvested and as you very well know there was a laundry list of renovations that went unfunded."

Doris would certainly have jumped in to make that point herself had Trefor not made it on her behalf.

"They expected the lake to carry the whole thing, and beautiful though it is, it can't make up for rotting cabins, unworkable plumbing and food that was — how did one guest put it — 'emetic'."

Trefor's very slight Welsh accent made the word even more effective.

"I've looked at the budget. It's surprising you were able to keep the doors open let alone provide any sort of service. Anyway, on the other hand we have the Coldwater people who have been pressing their case repeatedly for many years now. By all accounts their facilities at the Bay are first-class; they seem to make the most of what they have down there. People love it. Over the years they've sent us reams of detail on what they do and how they do it, tourist stuff, education, residential retreats, the museum, their environmental efforts — it's no wonder they have no cash left over to hire decent acts for their casino. But the bottom line is, I'm inclined to think they would be good for this place. Of course that's a separate issue from whether or not Parks will give it up."

Trefor paused before asking Newman, "But what do you all think about it? I'm interested in why you support the whole reorganization and what you think would happen. The former licensee really didn't appear as though they'd care one way or the other."

Doris looked at Newman. Newman began with a sigh.

"Well you know I'm a relative newcomer here but my overall thinking is that change is good. The resort was in a rut, and the discovery of the fish shook things up a bit, created a whole new set of ideas for marketing the lake, and whole new varieties of visitors. To be honest, Parks wants its paperwork filled out and on time, and that's about as far as their interest goes. But there's a commitment, even a passion developing among the people working and visiting around here that's a better match with the tribal folk than it is with the government."

"Plenty of passion around here these days. Then there's their ace in the hole," added Doris. "Or I should say aces in the holes they've been digging on the lakeshore. What do you think of that?"

Newman looked sideways at Trefor, almost defensively, as though expecting an explosive response.

"Well that sort of thing can be a no-brainer for deciding on development projects and the like. Mainly canceling them, of course. I don't think it's ever been used as a reason to move park boundaries though. But it's an important piece of a whole bunch of evidence for prior claim; hunting and fishing, living and dying here — as far as precedence goes they seem to be creating a historical argument going back to before the ice-age."

Doris was pleased to see how reasonable Trefor appeared to be. In her view a reasonable man offered far more opportunities for management, could be altogether more malleable, than a regular man. Of course, a reasonable man was also much more of a rarity.

"You'd better take a chaperone when you visit Fred tomorrow. She'll have you signed up and working on the dig before you can say 'partial sovereignty'. Then there's her man Fargo. Ever smoked a pipe before, Trefor?"

Conversation lapsed as they watched activity on the lake. Cooler evening air brought out a squadron of kayakers, and Ranger Dave was out on the water, looking like he was reminding some boisterous young boaters of the noise ordinance. Eventually dinner arrived, the presentation received compliments, and every dish was deemed delicious. The rest of the evening was spent speaking of memorable events at the lake, starting with Doris's tale of the flood that caused mice to seek refuge in the cellars and nibble through the beer lines, through Newman's part in discovering the unique strain of trout, to Trefor's recollection of Robert's observations on independence earlier that evening.

Dessert menus arrived just as Doris was seeking clarification on precisely what the difference is between Scotland and Wales.

"Oh, about four hundred miles and a hell of a lot of history. Some say the first Welshman must've been Adam's big brother. Compared to us Welsh, Scots are relative newcomers," said Trefor. "But I met Robert this morning, and no doubt he'll give you an argument."

Newman had been relatively quiet that evening. Doris noticed that he often seemed pensive when he was looking intently out across the lake. He must have a deep affection for the place, she thought, but that may have been a reflection of her own recently developed sense of enlightenment. She was starting to believe there may be something Buddhists know that may be worth knowing, despite her previous opinion that it was all mostly fuss and nonsense.

Newman was suddenly brought back into the moment.

"What's the plan tomorrow then Trefor? Do you have an agenda you want us to work to or what?"

"No, I'm here to listen. Parks is expecting me to give

them an informed opinion, so I'm looking for information. I'm also looking forward to meeting the president of the council; I gather she's now planning to come to meet us here, with her assistant."

"Well we have our meeting room ready and we plan for a working lunch — any particular sandwich preferences?"

"We have ham and cheese," said Doris.

"I think I'd like ham and cheese, if possible."

They agreed to skip dessert and ordered coffee. They exchanged a few casual observations on the setting sun and the long shadows cast among the hills. They debated the likely species of flies that must be gathering as increased numbers of fish jumped and flashed from the shadows. Midges? Mayflies? Maybe as unique to the lake as the fish. Who knew. Newman said the discovery of a new insect would have been a tougher sell to potential visitors.

Doris had high hopes for the following day's meeting, and also for Trefor. She'd dealt for many years with government people to do with accounts, forecasts, maintenance, promotions and so on — always with less than positive outcomes. She felt she could work with Fred, and the tribe was in tune with her new way of thinking. And now here was a man that had the power to bring about the change and who seemed like he may be inclined to do it.

During a lull in the conversation Trefor declined the offer of a single-malt nightcap, made his apologies, and got up to leave claiming it was time for him to retire. He said he needed all the sleep he could get to avoid being railroaded in the morning.

Newman didn't really daydream any more so much as

ruminate. Now, as he stared out of the meeting room window, it was the contrast between the lake's placid surface and whatever might be unfolding in its depths that put him into a state of very mild but persistent anxiety. He alone had all the pieces of information and could anticipate all the potential outcomes, and he sometimes felt that the burden of that responsibility now denied him the pleasure of a pure, unadulterated daydream.

He was early. He had time to think about the day's diverse web of potential outcomes. He was at the very least hoping for a change in the status quo. Steve was arriving sometime that afternoon, and Newman wasn't pleased about that. He felt Steve's presence increased the overall negative potential; that, longterm friend and colleague though he may have been, he was somehow tainted by bad news and tilted otherwise even odds toward the undesirable. Maybe Newman had been hanging around the Coldwaters too long; after all, this was a fairly straightforward equation, driven by quantifiable data, so the outcome should have been relatively predictable.

Who was he kidding? It'd be almost entirely subject to argument, outcomes determined more by rhetoric than by fact. Lots of talk and a very small amount of action. Politics.

And funnily enough, that was what had struck him when he first got into the genetics business. Here, he remembered thinking, we have identified biological destiny in the form of strings of inescapable numbers comprising life. What could be more hard-nosed, matter-of-fact than this intersection of mathematics, physics, and biology? But along with that pure scientific determinism came its flip-side; opportunities to intervene and shape fate to be more to our liking. We are like time travelers; we can predict the future and then debate whether that warrants intervention in the past. We can debate, argue, cajole around whether or not to interfere. We hire artists, lobbyists, filmmakers, writers and professional communicators to make our case. In the end the science is just the start of it, it's settled and all that remains is a matter of opinion. He thought this was the closest he'd come to a daydream in a long time. Hmm. Wonder if there was time to visit the bathroom before they started?

Just then the door opened and Doris ushered in Trefor.

"Ready?" he said.

"Yes — Coldwater party due here any minute. They didn't request any equipment, so I assume we're in for a straightforward chat."

"HQ wanted me to conference in the boss. I told them technical impossibility, but I would like to record the proceedings — that OK?"

"OK by me, but Fargo may consider it stealing words, you know."

"Really?"

"No not really. Relax, Trefor."

The door opened again, this time Fargo entered the room, carrying an unwieldy flip-board, and followed by Fred. He looked at Trefor.

"Hello."

"Hello — Trefor Evans, from Parks. How are you?"

"Good question," said Fargo, struggling with hinges, legs, and unruly paper to erect the flip-board. "I can tell you where I am and why I am here, but how? How is always a tough one."

He got the flip-board arranged to his liking.

"You sound like something out of *Alice in Wonderland*, Fargo!" Fred said. "Don't mind him, Mr. Evans. He sometimes over-thinks things. Fred. Fred Jesperson, doing fine thank you. Good to meet you at last, we've exchanged a fair amount of paperwork, haven't we."

"I can certainly say I've received a lot of paperwork! Good to meet you at last. I suppose this is also my opportunity to put the Parks' position, but I'm very happy for you to run the agenda."

They all took seats at the table and Trefor looked apprehensively at Fargo, and asked if he could record the discussion. Fargo shrugged and Fred said, "Sure. Can we get a copy for the museum? Future visitors might find it interesting."

The meeting began with Fargo displaying a hand drawn picture of a historical timeline of the region. The line represented about forty thousand years, and extended to the present day. The line, he said, shows the period indigenous Americans have been here. A shorter segment represented the glacial period, and within that a shorter one for the period of the lake's existence. Then within that there was the creation of the Coldwater reservation, and finally a single dot that represented the hundred years or so the Parks service had been around.

Instead of spending too much time talking, and without regard for Trefor's recording, Fargo simply flipped to successive pages and at every flip, stared at each person individually with a knowing gaze, sometimes accompanied by a slight nod. "You see?" he said as he showed a collage of photographs from the dig. And "There you are" after they'd looked for a while at a list of educational activities planned for the lake. In fact, Fargo's entire presentation was designed as though the lake were already fully integrated into the cultural, entrepreneurial, spiritual and historical life of the tribes. It was less a proposal than it was a review. He ended it with a final chart showing a map of the entire reservation, including the lake, with the resort appearing as a natural extension of the Bay, and as a very small part of the overall parkland. That one was accompanied by a nonchalant shrug, and applause from around the table once everyone realized that he had finished.

Fred said a few words about the unanimity among the council members, and about the many years' preparation they had made for this occasion. She claimed the time had now come for the transfer, that there was an inevitability about it; people felt that the recent discovery of a unique strain of fish, and the discovery of new historical evidence for tribal occupation of the area were exceptional circumstances that warranted the Park service making an unusual grant for the Coldwater Nation to take back sovereignty over the land. She asked Newman if he had anything to add.

"Well I've sent you thorough documentation of the evidence I have in favor of the transfer, Trefor, and the legal folk have included relevant precedent and process. I do feel that for all Parks has invested in this area, all it has done to develop it and to make it available to the public, the Coldwater Nation will do all that and very much more. Let's face it; the resort has been a losing proposition for a long time and the government has shown little will to invest in it. Doris, on behalf of the previous licensee, has a huge amount of documented communications asking for infrastructure improvements, development and environmental work, promotional support and the like and this has consistently met with unexplained rejection if it's not been simply ignored. So as the current licensee, I do feel that it's in the interest of not only the tribes but also the Park service and of course future visitors to reassign the resort land inside the boundaries of the reservation, and grant control to the Coldwater council under Fred here. Of course there will be representation for Parks and all decisions regarding future development of the resort will be subject to due consultation and so on and so forth."

Nods from Fred and Trefor, a grunt from Fargo. Newman felt he'd said enough. Trefor had heard most of it before anyway — except perhaps Fargo's point about the clouds migrating up from the bay through the valley and over the lake, which seemed to have Trefor nonplussed. Newman could see how he might have confused some sort of spiritual claim for a more pedestrian meteorological observation.

"Unless you have anything to add Fred, Fargo — I'll hand things over to Trefor."

Trefor thanked them for the thoroughness of their presentations. He began by reviewing his duty there, which he regarded as collecting and summarizing argument from both sides, to help the Parks people evaluate them and arrive at a decision.

"I do feel when all is said and done, the central issue here is precedent. You have offered very strong arguments of the sort used successfully in the past to influence construction and development plans. It's a tougher proposition to move boundaries though; boundaries are the one thing that tend to persist while activities either side of them can be redefined. I wonder why you are looking to extend the reservation, rather than to simply take over the license and perhaps take greater control of the function and development of the resort?"

Newman sat back to make it clear it was up to Fred to handle these sorts of questions but before Fred could answer, Fargo said:

"I'd rather be allowed to buy my own hunting boots than have the government lend me a pair of loafers."

After a brief moment during which Fargo looked around a clearly baffled table for confirmation that his point had hit home, Fred said, "That's a good point, if a little condensed — let me unpack it for you, Trefor. We feel that effectively licensing the land from the government would neither satisfy the cultural, historical and geographical imperatives we've described, nor would it enable us with confidence to make the sorts of investments we plan." Fargo slapped the table and held out his hand in a 'there you have it' gesture. "For the whole area and for future visitors to fully benefit from our efforts, we cannot be simply custodians in the sense of government lessees. We must be custodians responsible only to the land, to the hills, the lake, and to the creature inhabitants. I understand that this may be a little hard for the administrators to digest, being an unusual mix of cultural, political, and economic imperatives. But I have complete confidence that with your help they will be able to see the overwhelming advantages to all in moving forward with our proposal. After all, it's been many, many years in the making and we do feel we have arrived at a very comprehensive and fully justified argument."

"Can I add something?" asked Newman. "You can see

how well the Bay has been run, and you can expect nothing less of the resort once it's under the control of the Coldwater people. I have here the mission statement of the National Parks Service. It is not to own land, to lease or license it. It's not to maintain boundaries either. I'm sure you're familiar with it Trefor, but for the benefit of the room let me repeat it: 'Our mission: to preserve, unimpaired, the natural and cultural resources and values of the National Park System for the enjoyment, education, and inspiration of this and future generations.' Now, I can't think of a better way to fulfill that mission — especially given the Parks' disinclination to invest in it — than to incorporate the Glacial Lake resort into the reservation, and have the Coldwater Nation do that work on all our behalf."

Trefor was smiling the sort of smile, Newman thought, that betrays a hint of resignation. He felt confident that he hadn't left Trefor much room to query or amend what had been said. In the past he would have taken a similar approach with an internal Ziegler competitor, or with a senior manager otherwise intent on reorganizing or defunding his project. He would have covered all bases, combined sweeping and powerful generalizations with inarguable detail, attacked on far too many fronts for them to know where best to defend. He would leave them only two options: ignore him completely, which would require them to take on a generally unwelcome level of personal responsibility, or accept the inevitability of his request and let him go ahead. They could then either claim the idea as their own, characterize it as a considered investment, or begrudgingly give him enough rope to hang himself. In the end, he didn't care how they justified it to themselves and their peers as long as they did what he wanted.

And in this case, what he wanted was for Trefor to be genuinely on their team. The fact that they'd sent him at all had been a good start, and he seemed to be a reasonable person, or at least open to Newman's line of reasoning. Newman had high hopes.

The meeting concluded with a request from Fred for next steps; what was going to happen and how soon. Trefor said he'd take the following day to prepare a presentation for his superiors, and once he'd met with his department a decision would arrive very quickly. This whole business had already been taken up by the national press, and in a period when funding was tight the most favorable outcome for all, including Parks, was for it to be resolved as soon as possible — one way or another.

Trefor was never one to go unprepared, and in this case he took a leaf from the obituary writers' book and had something ready ahead of the event. He had already put together a framework report that he could tip one way or the other in a few hours given that, after reading all the available materials before he'd visited the lake, he'd ended up on the fence. But he felt more than qualified to make a judgment, and he enjoyed the full confidence in doing so of the Office of Legislative and Congressional Affairs, State, Tribal, and Local Planning Directorate.

He got up early and dressed uncharacteristically casually in the other outfit he had brought, one that featured a Coulee Dam t-shirt, a pair of desert boots, a straw hat, and classic pants of the sort hikers might have worn before outdoor recreation became an industry.

The light was clear, the air was cool and fresh, and fellow early risers' voices sounded muted, as though everyone was showing respect for the arrival of a perfect new day.

He strolled through the gift shop to get a complimentary morning coffee, and realized he was smiling for no apparent reason. He didn't get many chances to be out of the office, and that just made him all the more appreciative of this one. He had a whole day before he intended to return to make his recommendation, he had no meetings to attend or calls to make, he just had to come to some conclusions.

He saw Doris down at the beach, interrogating a small child who looked like he was wearing an inflatable duck. Trefor arrived just in time to hear her ask whether the boy expects her to stand there and watch out for him or if he will go and find a parent to do it. "You never know what will happen out on the water," she said as he struggled to run in the duck back to his campsite.

"Mr Evans, I presume," she said in what Trefor assumed to be a crack about his safari-esque wardrobe. "Doing a little more exploring today?" she added, as if to confirm it.

"I'm here just for today then off again back to the office, so I'm determined to make the most of it. Wish I could take a leaf from your book and call this my office."

"It's a great view isn't it," said Doris. "You know, I went to visit Fargo when he was working on his dig over on the other side. He says he has no word in his language for anything like 'office'."

"It would suit me to never have to go back, but I'm a little way off retirement. Though I suppose I may be closer than I think, depending on the outcome of this deal with the tribes."

"How come?"

"Well between you and me I believe this is much more a political thing than it is anything else right now. The department is fighting public relations disasters on all sorts of fronts what with the pipelines, the water tables, the mining, fishing and whaling — they feel beset with what they call 'unresolved native American projects'. This one seems like an easy win for them — there's no corporate interest to pander to, no environmental consequences I can see, no protesters on either side making the headlines. Nevertheless, I've worked there long enough to know they will pin any negative outcome squarely on the negotiator whose recommendation's at the root of it."

"Negative outcome? What do you think could go wrong if the tribe takes over? I mean I've considered that, but only from my own point of view. I'm pretty sure it'll be more interesting round here and less of a grind without Parks involved. I'm not ready to retire yet either — and even if I was, it'd probably be to live here anyway."

Trefor had thought about that too, and was similarly concerned for his own welfare. It was unlikely the Coldwaters would do anything that Parks wouldn't have done if they'd had the resources, but there was the precedent issue.

"Oh, I don't know. We have to be careful not to create a precedent that encourages all sorts of new litigation. That would probably be the worst thing that might happen — further demands on Parks' meager budget traced back to decisions made today. By me."

Doris looked surprised.

"I'm surprised. I mean I know it's probably your job as negotiator to anticipate the good and the bad, but you're sounding a bit over cautious maybe."

Trefor smiled.

"Maybe. But you know — right now I think I'll throw caution to the wind and take out one of your motorboats. Have a look around."

"Be my guest — well, I suppose you already are — and take my advice too; if you can swim at all don't bother with the lifejackets, they're less than sanitary. Another area where I couldn't get anyone to pay for an update."

Trefor sauntered down to the boathouse where he disturbed the fresh-faced attendant's phone-poking for long enough to rent a small boat, and he was soon heading out across the water. As far as he could see, he had the entire lake to himself. He reached what he judged to be the middle of the lake, cut the motor, and as the boat drifted to a halt even the sound of water lapping around the sides stopped; the lake was completely still.

He looked down into the depths of cold, clear water and could see nothing. He looked up and across towards the hills where smoky remains of morning mist still hung mid-air. Somewhere between here and there an occasional splash was the only sign of life. He was reassured that he wasn't the only soul alive on the lake this morning, and rather than being threatened by the huge thousand foot chasm beneath him he imagined all its varied inhabitants going about their business, each with its own plans and obligations for the day ahead.

It was starting to get a little hot; it was now a cloudless blue sky and there was little or no breeze to help with the heat from the rising sun. Trefor started up the motor and enjoyed the cooling feeling of moving air and splashing water. The smells of fresh lake and outboard motor took him back to childhood vacations and as he approached the far shore he was surprised by what looked like tree tops looming up toward him from deep in the lake. Thanks to Fargo's detailed documentation he realized this must be a part of the shoreline where masses of glacial soils slipped down to create a shallower shelf, taking grass, rocks, and even trees along with them. It was as if he were flying above those treetops, looking down through history toward the ground beneath the water. He looked up and saw a group of people on the shore, a couple of tents and an awning by the look of it; one of Fargo's digs, looking for disclosed evidence of prior inhabitants.

Trefor thought: what did the government know or care about any of this? This was all acreage on maps, numbers in calculations of value, calculations captured on spreadsheets. The jealousy with which government control of land was defended seemed to diminish the further away it was from anything of political, economic, or military value. This place was a long way from the White House. There wasn't likely to be any oil. Nowhere to point missiles at from here. Trefor edged the boat along the shoreline, and as a canopy of surprisingly well-preserved trees glided beneath him three dark figures spurted out from among the branches. He turned suddenly to try to follow them as they passed under the boat, and was startled by a glimpsed flash at his side as one of them momentarily abandoned the lake for the bright morning air. A splash and it was once again a powerful shadow beneath the surface, merging, disappearing, gone.

That was a shock. Much closer and it might've been

in the boat, Trefor thought. He was wet — that thing had raised a fair amount of water, and it certainly wouldn't have won too many points for re-entry. He supposed it was uncommon for visitors to venture around this side of the lake shore. Fish were easily startled. He was an intruder. Maybe that was a warning; next time we'll be in your boat and setting about you — watch out!

Trefor continued to follow the shore around the lake, taking in the scenery but keeping an eye on the water around the boat. He didn't know much about fish and he'd never tried fishing, but he felt he'd learned a lot from reading reviews of the resort from fly-fishing vacationers. From what he could make out, if anglers were by nature prone to exaggeration then the fish in this lake will probably frustrate them. Their size and ferocity resisted hyperbole; by all accounts, that's just the way they were. They were indeed big, and they almost invariably seemed to get away. Of course, the barbless hook law made it a tougher proposition to land one, but there were pictures he'd seen of fish comically out of proportion compared to their captors, and ranger Dave had made a few videos of his own that demonstrated, among all else, the many opportunities for personal injury there were between catch and release.

Even after the hours he'd spent studying the area in his office, from his boat the lake seemed bigger than he had ever imagined.

He decided to cut back across to the resort in time for an early lunch, then write up his recommendation before taking off the following day to head back to the office.

When Parks' response came, it came swiftly. Trefor made his

presentation, and the review board had arrived in very short order at a verdict. It was by no means unanimous, but their voting rules were designed to tolerate an apprehensive minority. Dissent came from many directions, though Trefor was surprised to see the expected political and geographical arguments supplemented by thinly disguised racist assertions that the locals didn't have the capacity to manage the place. This had, in fact, brought about the reverse effect of reinforcing Trefor's argument that the transfer would further the progressive mandate of the service and be a big political win, raising visibility in a positive way at a time when it was accused of being dominated by political fossils with outdated ideas that did little or nothing to justify the taxpayer investment they enjoyed.

So the transfer would go ahead, with the most significant caveats to be outlined in a followup with the transferees in a few days' time. Trefor called Newman and conferenced in Fred to talk about the results.

"Go ahead Trefor, we're ready."

"OK. I decided on balance the place is in safer hands with you than it is with Parks", Trefor said. "And they bought it. So it's yours, pending the production of a few trees-worth of legal garbage of course."

"Good," was Fred's response.

"Good lord," from Newman, "I thought you'd back us Trefor, but I had my doubts they'd agree. Well that's that then — fantastic."

"Mmm . . . there are a few minor caveats and one that you may feel is more of a major one, Mr. Newman."

"Oh yes?"

"Well there's some merchandising stuff, they want a

cut of visitor passes and so on. But they also — and they say this is for legal reasons — they also insist that the manager of the place, the person currently doing your job as licensee, Mr. Newman — they insist that that person be a member of the Coldwater Nation. Something to do with mandates around concealed controlling influence, misdirection of gains; legal stuff. They seem above all else to be concerned with avoiding any scandal that may occur whenever land is transferred out of the public trust, you see."

"I do see," Newman said, "but it sounds like it's just my position that's the issue then — everything else is purely up to Fred?"

"Yes."

"Well I can find something to do round here perhaps; there's always burgers to flip. Or I'll be Robert's apprentice handyman."

Fred picked up the handset and took the phone off speaker, sounding suddenly present in the conversation. "Well of course I don't know much about federal legal shenanigans, Trefor. But I think this is all good news, and we can handle these little ups and downs in the process I'm sure. Trefor: I want to thank you for your efforts. You should come over and take a non-working break as our guest. Will you come? Looks like there's an Indian summer ahead."

"Oh — yes, well, I mean of course I tried to do the right thing you know. For all concerned. But I suppose it didn't take too much effort on my part except for reading the reams of material from Mr Newman. Oh and I'm not sure I'll ever be up to understanding everything Fargo sent me. But I'd love to come down and enjoy the last of the summer with you, that'd be great."

They fixed a date for Trefor's visit, and Newman asked Fred if she'd join him and Steve for dinner. He hadn't been looking forward to another of Steve's visits — they were usually accompanied by bad news that he, Steve, nevertheless found hilarious — but with the generally positive outcome from Parks he felt a new surge of bonhomie that extended even as far as to include his former boss.

"Steve's retired, and our unfolding story here is now his principal occupation it seems. Can't keep away from the place. I imagine in future he'll be as much a fixture here as Doris. Or even the fish."

"OK thanks," Fred said, "see you later then, Newman. Can't wait to get plans in progress — it's all turned out as expected, eh. Apart from where you fit in, it sounds like. But don't worry; we have a plan for that, too."

Fred dropped off the call to go and deliver the news to Fargo and the rest of the council.

More plans, more progress, more expectations; Newman was both pleased and a little apprehensive. But Fred was clearly competent, and he felt that, unlike many of the competent people he'd met during his career, he could clearly trust her. Surely he could. So above all else he was excited to see what would happen next. Of course, he would have preferred to remain in control of the place as he had been as licensee, but on the other hand, maybe this was his opportunity to slide into retirement. He could join Steve and enjoy some irresponsible levity— they could together haunt the place like a couple of lakeside dinosaurs.

Newman called Doris.

"Doris — it's on. Trefor came through for us, so stand by for a change of ownership around here! Dinner at seven?"

8: The joining

FRED ARRIVED AT the resort as the sun mellowed and the atmosphere around the lake calmed down after a busy day. The cabins, campsites, and RV park all looked full to capacity; it was getting toward the end of the season and the place had acquired a kind of patina from many weeks of hot sun, groomed and re-groomed grounds, and legions of energetic visitors. She saw a small group of people gathering for Dave's evening lecture down by the water, and she was reminded to meet with him about some new material she had in mind.

The meeting with the council had been more like a party. She'd never seen Fargo quite so enthusiastic. Almost euphoric. It had been a personal goal of his to see this happen, but nonetheless she'd never seen any traditional dance performed in the council chamber before, let alone on the desk, and without a full complement of clothing. Fargo seemed transformed.

Fred saw Doris behind the reception desk and waved. Doris handed off her duties to an assistant and walked across to join her.

"Fred! Congratulations! Big day. Newman and Steve are already in the restaurant; shall we join them?"

On the way Fred thanked Doris and took the time to make sure she understood that things would mostly stay the same, and she was relying on her to keep things going during, and following, the transition. "You are at the center of the dreamcatcher," she said, immediately regretting the association with spiders and webs that might have been more appropriate for the old Doris. But Doris seemed pleased with the image and thanked Fred for having faith in her.

Steve and Newman rose as they arrived at the table.

"Alright!" said Steve. "Looks like the band is back together then!"

"Heard that before, Steve. Fred, this is Steve," said Newman, "longterm friend, colleague —"

"And partner in crime!" added Steve with a wink. "I have to say off the bat Newman's told me what's going on and I couldn't be more delighted. He's done wonders with this place, hasn't he? And as far as I can see this just guarantees it a rosy future."

Fred thanked him for his good wishes as they took their seats.

"You know Steve you're right; Newman's a real magician isn't he. And I have more news. Walker — he's my nephew — Walker's doing a block release internship from Yale. At Ziegler. That's the old stamping ground for you two, isn't it."

"Oh. Wow," Steve said, "what division? Not drugs I hope."

"No, he's working in Food. He has a project to do for his degree, and he also hopes to get a job at Ziegler when he's done. Working for Geoff someone or other. Having a great time by all accounts."

Fred saw Steve glance at Newman. Newman did look a little surprised there, but just for a moment, before he said, "He's a bright boy isn't he? And only the best get into Ziegler, we can be sure of that. You know a Geoff at Ziegler don't you

Steve? Surprised you didn't get wind of this."

"Yes, I'll have to give him a shout — can't be too many Geoffs in Food. In good hands then, Fred. Fast moving business; can't wait to see what he comes up with."

"Red or white?" said Doris, offering the wine list to Fred.

"Oh, Champagne, surely!"

They ate, they drank, and they were appropriately merry. After a while, Fred turned to Steve.

"I heard from Walker that this Geoff has been promoted to some sort of analyst position. Holds a fair amount of sway I gather — I'm hoping his rising tide lifts Walker's boat, too. What do you think?"

"Well in my day it was the analysts who were responsible for scoping out the commercial potential of schemes proposed by the technical people. So it sounds like he's become what the technical people call 'overhead'. Always a good thing, eh Newman?"

Newman didn't appear to be listening.

"What say Newman?" Fred asked. "Think Ziegler's a good bet?"

"For what now?"

"For Walker. Working for Geoff. Keep up now Newman."

"I'm sorry, I was miles away. You're asking two people who chose to leave, you know."

"Well I'm sure you had your reasons and they probably don't apply to Walker at his time of life. As a matter of fact he tells me the work they do there will help shape the future."

"Have to agree there," Steve said, "central to pretty

much all our futures I'd say. Has been and will continue to be with a bit of luck."

Fred looked at Newman. "Speaking of futures, I mentioned to Doris that the plan is to keep things pretty much on the same path. Doris continues to run the place, Robert patches it up and keeps the bar in business, Steve is of course a regular. And Mr Newman — we'll need to maintain your guiding hand around here."

"Well I'll be here anyway I expect, though maybe you wouldn't like me so much as a customer rather than a colleague, Doris."

"I can still deal with you Newman. Different method; same result. Don't worry."

"Another thing. We will need someone to work with Parks. Once they become a neighbor rather than landlord, we will need to work with them. Plus, they get a cut of our visitor passes — they feel we benefit from the overall Parks association so we should pay for it."

"Oh well that's easy," said Doris, "Trefor's your man."

"Trefor?"

"He loved it here. His face dropped each time he talked of going back to the office. He'd be a pushover — and who would know better than Trefor how to get the best out of any sort of relationship with Parks?"

"Doris!"

"Fred? What? Don't tell me you can't recognize a good deal when you see one."

Steve snorted. "Sounds like you're the one setting up a deal, Doris. But fair play and all that."

Newman said, "Better check your book Doris, see if Steve's due to go home this evening, eh! His room may have suddenly become unavailable."

Fred said she thought Trefor sounded like a great idea. She definitely felt she'd need a buffer between herself and Parks as things unfolded.

"What do you think, Newman," she asked, "how much ongoing negotiation do you think we'll need to do? I gather we pretty much control everything that doesn't affect the surrounding park. I mean, it's up to us what goes in and what comes out of the lake isn't it? How we choose to develop it?"

Newman's brow furrowed as he considered the question.

"Yes I believe it is, now. Including all commercial, mineral rights, probably. Water, oil, gas, fish. All yours. But I imagine Trefor would have his work cut out dealing with Parks if you decided to drain the lake and drill for oil."

"No plans to do that, exactly. But it's good to know precisely where we stand. I think we should get in touch with Trefor and feel him out. I got a sense he would fit in well here as soon as I met him. And even his suit looked more relaxed by the time he left. Let's see; can you do that Doris?"

"What say Doris?" asked Steve. "Can you feel Trefor out?"

"That's it; where's my book?" said Doris. "I'll throw it at him. But I'll have to call Trefor anyway, they found he'd left something behind in his room."

"Uh-oh — what was that? Very psychological I'm sure. May be a clue as to his likely decision there," Steve said.

Fred had decided Steve was an oaf, but an affable enough oaf.

"Yes," she said, "what did he leave behind?"

"A book. Poems. Wordsworth and others I'm told."

"Oh god the Lake Poets!" said Steve. "He's a gonner. Take my word; you won't need to offer him much to have him back here. I'd start off with a campsite, a glass of beer, and a pickled egg and move up from there. That should do it. May have to throw in another egg."

Fred smiled and signaled the end of the meal by pushing her chair back with a "Well!" Before leaving, she arranged to meet with Newman the following day. "Let's talk logistics," she said. "Tie up the loose ends before we put plans in motion."

A number of things had by now joined the fish to disturb Newman's peace of mind. He was meeting Fred to discuss what she had called logistics, a meeting she'd said should happen before she "put plans in motion". He may be about to lose his job, and among other things that would probably mean spending more time with Steve, which he wasn't sure would be good for his longterm wellbeing.

In addition to that, there was ranger Dave. A fish he described as "a real corker" had been reported to him recently. He'd been asking anglers to report on fish sightings when he issued their fishing permits, and he'd noticed an upward trend in size estimates that was surprising even to someone familiar with the exaggerations of the fly-fishing fraternity. "I'd be loath to get one stuffed today," he'd told Newman, "in case an even bigger one is hauled in tomorrow." Already, an unfeasibly hefty specimen adorned the reception area, a shiny, glassy-eyed reminder to Newman of his potential folly every time he passed by. He was thinking that, so far, reports of record-breaking fish had only been good for business, but he feared there may be a point at which every fish was a record breaker and the sense of a challenge among visiting anglers might give way to one of anxiety.

He'd taken to using the radio to wake him up, and every so often that was another thing that gave him cause to question his sanity. It was set to National Public Radio, and as he snoozed he sometimes mixed up what he was hearing with what he had imagined or dreamed. That morning a weight loss doctor was being interviewed and he'd found himself debating the health risks for fish that are too heavy. But he couldn't seem to get a word in edge-wise; someone was always talking. He wanted to talk about his own weight, which was, oh, let's see, how many pounds are there in a stone? Ten and a half stone? No that was his shoe size, ten and a half at least the European size. Get them shipped to your home many happy returns how old am I? No questions asked and now traffic is heavy on the freeway. Freeway. Friday? Tuesday. Oh god it's Tuesday. That's right, Tuesday, so Fred's coming. Better get up.

Newman arrived, not fully rested, in reception. Fred was already sitting enjoying a cup of coffee.

"What's up Newman — hope you didn't overdo it with Steve last night."

"I've learned to watch it with Steve. Complete disregard for wallet, liver, and if you're not careful, carpet. No, I took off early for a change and tried to get some shut-eye. A bit tough with all that's going on, though."

"Let's get down to it, then. You alright talking about this in reception?"

"Yes of course — no secrets around here."

Newman looked for any indication from Fred that

there may have been secrets on her side, but didn't see any.

"Good. I did want to say that everyone involved regards your continued direction here as absolutely essential. Can't imagine the place running without you."

"And I'm keen to continue of course."

"But it sounds like Parks is picky about that requirement that it be run by someone from the Coldwater nation. So." She paused. "So I had Walker work with Fargo to figure out precisely what that means. Turns out that there's some sort of reconciliation between the legal paperwork defining our sovereignty, and the genetic mumbo-jumbo that determines to their satisfaction who we are."

Newman said, "Shame it's not just a club I could apply to join, eh. Just get the dress code right, do the special handshake and I'm in."

"Well it turns out, Newman, that to all intents and purposes you may already be in. Walker's done some analysis, you see. Depending on which way you look at it, gross invasion of your privacy or an opportunity for you to become enlightened. Either way all free of charge."

"What are you talking about — what do Walker and Fargo have to do with it?"

"You're a native American, Newman. Or, at least, a significant enough fraction of you is. And before you start bragging about it, that's not very much."

"What? I thought I was a Scot?"

"Well you may be, Walker wasn't interested in that. We used to use fractions of blood lines — very messy. Now we have the opportunity to go hi-tech and we can figure things out in much greater detail. And complexity. And, perhaps, controversy. But overall, we can figure things out well enough to count."

"So you're telling me I am definitely a native American, Fred?"

"Definitely is a very strong word, Newman. Thanks to Fargo and Walker, it appears you would definitely qualify as such per the sovereignty rules that Parks are applying in this case. But definitely definitely? I've been talking with Walker, and although genetics and all that DNA stuff suggest certainty, here we should think of a sort of continuum of probability. Especially since Fargo is also involved. So very probably. Probably enough. I'd say probably conclusively, Newman."

"But how—"

"Oh, a used wine glass, strand of hair, spittoon — something like that. You've seen the TV shows. They must've thought you'd never go along with it or something. Who knows; but there it is. At least, I imagine that's how it might have gone."

Now Newman saw what he was looking for a moment ago. There were secrets in the room somewhere; Fred was glancing around as she spoke. She appeared to be looking for something she could pull out of thin air to help explain.

"Well that's very convenient, I must say. Can I assume my continuing resort director resume just became a lot more viable?"

"Certainly. It's a happy coincidence, isn't it? Everything coming together. Now you can join us on the reservation whenever you want. Fargo can provide you with suitable ceremonial garb and so on. You could probably even live down there if you like."

Newman felt a little manipulated, painted into a

corner even. And in those situations, he typically came out fighting. Or not so much fighting, as maneuvering with humor. "I'll have to pick a traditional name then, like — oh, how about Fred? Oh no - that one's taken. Something that suits my new status."

"I think Newman's appropriate enough, Newman. Stick with that. And we'll take care of clearing the hiring process with parks. Look better that way."

"Suits me, Fred. Thanks — I guess."

Newman was still a little disconcerted about Walker and Fargo even thinking of making free with his DNA.

"Still, I'm a bit concerned about Walker and Fargo messing with my DNA behind my back, as you might imagine."

Newman was surprised when Fred laughed.

"Oh, don't worry. Doesn't seem likely either of them would do something like that, does it. Anyway, and speaking of suits. First task for your new old role: can you take care of hiring Trefor?"

"Certainly. Doris's probably already called him. If he's ready to play ball, I'd work with him to come up with a job description, salary and everything. I'm thinking Parks would be happy to work with him here, too; at least, that's the way I'll spin it to them if they balk at letting him move."

"Let me know, Newman. See you later."

Once Fred had gone, Newman walked across the lobby to the reception desk. Doris was waiting for him. By the look on her face, she hadn't missed much of his conversation.

"You have a strange new gravity, Newman. Hadn't noticed it before but between you and Fargo! Well, you're like two peas in a pod, aren't you?" She beamed at Newman. "And by the way the answer's yes; I called Trefor and he sounded very keen. Relieved almost. I can't see it needing much negotiation, he sounds about ready to turn up here tomorrow."

"Alright, thanks Doris. I'll set things up then, get him back down here to finish sorting it all out. It's a weight off I can tell you not to have to deal with Parks any more. I think Fred's a far better option."

"Well you certainly seemed at home working with her."

"Despite your joshing me, Doris, I'd say yes. Yes I think we understand each other. I think we can work together."

Newman looked out of the window for a moment and across the lake.

"I think so. Sure of it. It'll be plain sailing from now on."

Trefor took up his new role with gusto. He understood that he was to instill confidence in Parks that everything post-transition was running as expected, to the point where they felt no need to pay much if any further attention to the matter. Their main interest was in their share of the revenue, which thanks to Newman and Fred seemed to increase in value almost daily. Newman had made a list of proposed investments, may of which had been repeatedly postponed or right-out rejected by Park in the past. And now Trefor was pleased to report renewed interest in those projects from the new owners, accompanied by significant investment to develop them. Trefor was no accountant and he wasn't involved in where that funding came from, but he could assemble impressive spreadsheets demonstrating the beneficial effects on the overall profitability of Glacial Lake.

He enjoyed taking part in what Newman called his Cabinet. They would meet weekly and ad-hoc to deal with particularly urgent issues and ideas. Newman as overall director, Fred representing the Council, Fargo as cultural officer, Doris was now Operations Manager, and of course Trefor as liaison officer for the outside world, meaning Parks. The committee wasn't the sort of bureaucratic dead-weight Trefor was used to. Meetings were as productive as they were short, particularly when Fargo was absent or otherwise engaged; proposals flew, debate was vigorous, decisions made, and progress reviewed.

Without doubt one thing that made the committee so productive was the amount of money that Fred was able to make available to fund those decisions. In no time at all they had built a new boathouse complete with motorboats, life jackets, kayaks, and all the trimmings. They had redesigned the reception area to better reflect the Coldwater brand (and remodeled the visitor center down at the Bay to match). Cabins were brought up to authentic historical spec, but with the addition of luxuries tourists require but for which, in the past, Parks had not seen the need (such as locks on the doors, effective showers, rust-free tubs, and reliable hot water — yes, hot water "at any time of day", as Robert proudly exclaimed). The restaurant now offered gourmet options and was overseen by a world-class Chef de Cuisine brought in at considerable expense from Seattle. And to top it all, a new auditorium and Executive Briefing Center was planned that would attract renewed interest in the resort — and provide low-season income — as a corporate retreat and Customer

Engagement Facility.

Trefor also enjoyed the lake. He would take a rowboat out in the early morning, or in the evening when the daily excitement had died down, and drift past the steeply rising rocks edging the less traveled backwaters. On one such occasion he'd become an unwitting hero, rescuing an angler adrift and without the means to return to shore. Trefor recounted the story to ranger Dave over a latte in the freshly remodeled Mochas Inn coffee bar.

"I was over at East Cove, just drifting and enjoying a little snooze when I heard shouting and saw a rowboat and some splashing about. I rowed over and found a guy fishing. Actually swearing, really, not fishing. He had been fishing, but he said his gear had been yanked out of his hands and dragged over the side."

Dave laughed. Not the first time he'd heard of that. Usually a beer or two involved.

"Not supposed to drink in charge of a watercraft," he said.

"No evidence of that. Anyway, without thinking he dug down into the water with an oar to see if he could hook the line on the way down. I think that's when I heard the shouting start. He says the oar was just pulled out of his hands and away from the boat, disappeared for a bit, then popped up fifty yards away. I had to go get it for him."

"You sure he didn't nod off, drop gear and oar over the side, then wake up wondering how to get home?"

"Could have I suppose. But then, that wouldn't be as good a story would it? I prefer to think of myself sweeping in, oblivious to the danger, to rescue a fellow mariner from who-knows-what out there. He seemed very rational and collected to me. If what you say is true, I think he'd have said something like 'give me a hand will you? I nodded off and dropped the oar over the side'. Instead, he came out with string of words I'd be surprised to hear from a real sailor. And anyway, if I'd questioned his story he may not have bought me that pint in the Rainbow Bar when we got back in."

"Maybe he was drifting quicker than he thought, and the gear got snagged on a submerged branch or something? Or he could have dropped the gear when he thought the oar was sliding over the side and ended up losing both of them?"

Trefor thought Dave was a bit too keen to re-cast his story in more mundane terms. Or was Trefor right in thinking Dave looked a little concerned about it, a little too keen to find an explanation for what otherwise looked like an aquatic mugging.

"Could have been Davy Jones reaching up from the depths to grab another soul and ending up with just a paddle too, eh? I dunno Dave. He was a little rattled, I can tell you. Even after a couple of pints."

"Alright well I'll have to run a patrol over there tomorrow anyway, see if I can find that fishing tackle — don't want it showing up wrapped around some kid, or worse a protected lake fowl."

Trefor saw Dave as a practical man, firmly rooted in the matter-of-fact here-and-now. He considered Dave's pragmatism to be the flip-side to Fargo's metaphysics; each provided the overall balance for the other, although the alternating yin and yang could often lead to mutually baffling exchanges between the two ("Well of course I wouldn't have been hiding with my shotgun at two in the morning if I'd known the wolf in the night Fargo was on about was not a regular wolf at all. Now he says he was in fact casting as a wolf some sort of fearmongery he thought was being spread by Parks to undermine the transfer. I've already made my apologies to the guests who discovered me in the outhouse.)"

Trefor had initially wondered where he would fit in; what part he would play in the overall pattern of the place. There was Dave and Fargo, and then Doris's hands-on day to day management playing against Newman's grand plans. Maybe Trefor, representative to the outside world, complemented Fred's role as representing her people. He liked that idea, the responsibility, each of them facing outward, representing, defending, and singing the praises of the lake.

Trefor would, from time to time, find himself thinking like this. He put it down to his Welsh roots; a sneaking fondness for lyrical recollection and a slight tendency toward the melodramatic. He had spoken with Doris about this when she talked of her own enlightenment as a result of the gifted book. "Who'd have thought it," she had said, "I always thought of that sort of stuff as self-help nonsense, irrelevant to my life here, which was mostly just my job." She told Trefor that her job used to define more or less who she was, but now "the dog is definitely doing the wagging". He felt he understood when she talked about regaining a sense of control, of days making sense that used to be at best endured. "I used to have a laugh now and again, but I wasn't getting much out of it." She still did have a laugh, of course, and she wasn't above occasionally taking pleasure at a visitor's minor expense. But now it was all in service of something bigger, more important — at least, that's how Trefor interpreted it.

The lake made everything, somehow and regardless of how otherwise small and insignificant, seem worthwhile. And he was glad to be a part of it.

Newman could hardly remember an idea to improve, enhance, develop or re-develop the resort that Fred didn't think was a good one. Plans, however grand, could always be grander after a little brainstorming. In all his corporate years he had never known smoother or more rapid transitions between vague if enthusiastic hand-waving, multicolor whiteboard scribbling, and fully funded deployment.

"Where are we going to find the funding for all this?" he asked, after a particularly productive Steering Committee meeting. "I hope we're not involved in anything like the sort of stunts Steve would pull in the old days to conjure up cash."

Fred had created a general fund, and projects that once required protracted haggling with Parks before eventually being rejected or canceled could more often than not be covered by petty cash these days. She seemed uninterested in the subject of funding, and would refer only to her accountant back at the Bay who handled everything. "Don't worry about that, Newman," she'd say, "you'll just age prematurely. Micky's got it all covered for us, and in case he hasn't, Fargo's working up a great magic act for the ballroom."

The last time Newman had encountered anyone quite so sanguine about future finances it was Forbes, a friend of Steve's, who was shortly thereafter put away for insider trading. Come to think of it Steve, like Fred, had been similarly vague about that whole affair and would say only that it was another example of the advantages of demonstrable ignorance. "Bear in mind the rules: see nothing, hear nothing, do nothing. You only have to stick to any one of 'em and you'll be alright. Old Forbes broke all three."

Newman had both seen and heard about the thin financial ice they had been skating on for years down at the Bay. It was one of the things that had made him a little apprehensive about the transfer of the resort; despite Fred's plans, he thought the split from Parks might have been a choice between financial frying pan and fire. But it hadn't been long after the paperwork was all signed and sealed that checks began to be written, and now the pace of development was such that Newman was beginning to think it might be best to distance himself from whatever Fred might be up to.

But whatever she was up to Newman was, in fact, happy to see her succeed. And he was beginning to think he couldn't have planned it better, or at least in a more clandestine manner, himself. It's a fine line between quaint and shabby, and the resort had been inexorably sliding toward the shabby. Visitors appreciated the history of the place, the sense of permanence that extended from the ancient hills, across the lake, and into the fabric of the grounds, the cabins, and the lodge. But not at the expense of clean, convenient, and comfortable.

History, it turns out, doesn't smell so good when it's a defining characteristic of your bathroom or your kitchenette. Likewise, the brand new restroom and shower facilities Fred had installed in the campground could be forgiven a little overly-chic Scandinavian anachronism when compared with the dyspeptic frontier plumbing they replaced.

Fred would regularly walk the grounds and report back to Newman what she'd heard and seen. She would seek out what she called "vox pops" in an attempt to discover visitors' real opinions. Newman assigned Robert, whose regular duties had diminished in proportion to the various upgrades to less maintenance-intensive facilities, to shadow Fred and take on more of a high-level, property management role. In exchange for significantly increased remuneration and the assurance that he wouldn't have to wear a suit, Robert had taken on the task with uncharacteristic enthusiasm. It turns out despite his regular expressions of contempt for management of all sorts, management was something he supposed he could "get to grips with if I have to", and when Newman hired an assistant for him Robert even began to refer to himself as an entire department. "The property management department will be needing some sort of a website or other to keep track of things, you understand," he had said. Clearly he had been listening to his assistant, who Newman had hired to take care of just these sorts of requirements, filling in those areas where Robert's mid-century expertise fell short. Where once he fixed coin-operated electric meters, now Robert was responsible for computerized energy auditing; simple plumbing jobs had given way to automated hydraulic systems, and it seemed there was nothing these days that broke that could be fixed with anything found in his shed.

"I used to spend my time in the field — literally in the field, you understand — but now I coordinate, so to speak," he had told Newman during his departmental review. "I coordinate and brief the experts we have on hand. I keep very close track of how things are supposed to work, and I call whoever we have on file to replace them when they misbehave." These days Robert dressed a little more sharply, and his old overalls were reserved for days off, fishing or working in his greenhouse. He became much more outgoing, and for the first time engaged with guests rather than avoided them. "Robert, property," he would say, leading countless guests to remember him as Mr. Property, that dapper little man in the bar with an unusual interest in the facilities.

"Well. Fred. You've brought us into the 21st century," Newman said as he walked the campsite with her. "This place is a little jewel. Outshines what you have at the Bay, I'd say."

"Thank you. But I don't see it in quite those terms. The Bay is key to who we are, just ask Fargo."

Newman was still struggling a little to count himself among the "we", in however small a part.

"This place up here is very nice, but it's more than a pretty face. It's also the top of the funnel bringing cash into the council coffers. You know, the Bay is a great place to visit but it doesn't generate much capital for us. This place can be different."

Newman was delighted to see the lake become self-sufficient, but it was a stretch to consider it a significant earner for the Nation.

"Really?," he said, "a hidden source of support, like popcorn to movie theaters, or baggage fees to airlines?"

"I was thinking in less pedestrian terms; more like a patron of the arts, let's say the lake might play Peggy Guggenheim to the Bay's Jean Cocteau."

"Ah, I see."

Newman didn't see at all, clearly he didn't, and his look betrayed the fact that either the overall economics or maybe the Jean Cocteau reference had left him none the wiser. He was beginning to wonder how, even if the resort could one day be built into a massive revenue generator, Fred was keeping the lake's head above water today let alone making such significant investments without him knowing where it was all coming from. He was pretty sure he must be missing something, but since he was probably missing it, he couldn't be sure of its significance.

Steve arrived with Geoff in tow. Having heard he was taking a trip to the lake to meet with his intern's aunt, he had refused to let Geoff shake him off and insisted on carpooling. "An old boys' vacation", he had called it.

"Is it that time already?" said Newman, as Steve and Geoff checked in. "It seems like only last week you were here, Steve."

"I like to do my best to prop the place up. This is Geoff. Geoff — Newman."

Steve seemed very excited, even for him. He reminded Newman that Geoff is now Walker's mentor at Ziegler.

"You remember Geoff helped us out before, with the whole —"

"Yes, of course many thanks Geoff and welcome, welcome! Here to see Fred then," Newman said, before Steve could finish his recollection.

Evidently, Steve thought, despite the changes that have taken place there are still some areas that require discretion.

Marvelous.

Steve saw no reason to conceal the fact that a big part of the attraction of the place, for him, was the unfolding drama. Although he wouldn't admit it even to himself, he missed something about the corporate intrigue, the "inside, outside" culture where you either knew what was really going on or you didn't. After all, it had served him well and a large part of his success had been down to knowing who was who, where things were headed, and what his best next move would be. Now he was in an ideal position; he could enjoy the intrigue without having any particular role or responsibility in it, and all while being ostensibly on vacation. He was effectively grandfathered into the whole business, and he was loving it.

Fred, perhaps unwisely, wasn't available that evening. Tonight it was left to Newman, Steve, and Geoff to watch the sun set from the bar.

"So Geoff here's on the management track now, Newman. He's thrown in the towel and become overhead."

"Oh no not really," said Geoff, "not at all. I mean not that there's anything wrong with overhead. Management. I'm sure it's an essential skill in its own right."

"No," Newman said, "no, it's pretty much overhead, don't worry. I mean look at Steve. So what's going on then these days at the bleeding edge of food technology?"

"I'm not sure I'd know, I'm in a fairly specialized niche of course. I mean I'm still technical lead, but I do have a report, which on paper makes me management I suppose."

"Right, Walker is down from Yale isn't he. Got him working on something interesting then?"

Steve leaned a little closer on the bar.

"Well you must know he brought us the fish to look at, but they were of limited interest as it turned out. I mean we are interested in your fish of course, but we're more interested in where they come from as it happens." Geoff paused for a moment, and put his beer back onto the bar. "I assume we're sort of under non-disclosure here aren't we?"

"Oh yes," Steve said, "We're all still in the same non-disclosure boat here don't worry. Anyway, can't be much Newman doesn't already know about all this, eh Newman?"

"Exactly." Newman said, the confidence implied by his response fully absent from his expression.

"Ah good, of course, yes. Naturally you know Ziegler's always interested in unusual mutations, and we have a longstanding connection with Yale, so initially when Walker applied to the internship program with his project ... anyway, he wanted to look into the fish."

"And you said you are more interested in where they came from?" Newman asked.

"Yes, well of course working up a differential on the entire genome would have been out of the question, as we've touched on in the past. But there were definitely some immediately apparent unique traits going on, and well that caused me to take another look at what you had been doing, Mr. Newman."

Steve sensed Newman's growing alarm, and decided to intervene. "Back in the day? How important could that possibly be, Geoff? In this industry things move on, and fast. Nobody cares what you were doing last month let alone years ago, eh?"

"We had so many projects going on in Food in those days, I doubt there's much of a record any longer," said

Newman. "Is there?"

"Oddly enough, given the excitement around the early days of spliced fish and all that related experimentation I've heard about, there is little or no record as far as I know, that's true."

"Oh good. I mean, good that nothing's been lost, then. Meaning there was nothing to lose in the first place I expect."

Steve helped Newman out once more. "Things were moving so fast in those days I remember, we scarcely stopped for lunch did we? Let alone to document anything. Probably a little naughty from a logistical point of view, you think Newman?"

"Well don't tell but I've never been one for documentation — by the time it's documented it's out of date, we used to say."

"Not sure anyone cares about that." Geoff seemed immune to any humor. "The big thing now is, as the realtors say, location. We were immediately interested in the sort of wild location that could keep a mutation like that locked up. And it turned up in one of the scouting reports that came out of your organization, under Mr. Newman's direction. Now those reports are still available, and very thorough I must say — clearly Glacial Lake was already a candidate for field testing. A natural, proven container for experiments." Geoff pushed his glasses back up his nose and reached for his beer.

Newman took a lengthy swig of his, while looking at Steve. Steve stared at the bottom of his empty glass with a smile. Newman tried not to sound too relieved.

"We canned that idea. Parks would never have entertained the thought even for a moment. Can you imagine, hordes of protesters up here with their anti-GMO placards on the evening news, shouting about the government sell-out to big corporations?"

Steve almost choked on his beer and couldn't resist joining in with "And some poor bastard — Trefor probably — stuck in front of a camera to explain why taxpayers are funding armageddon."

"Yes. Well then. I was interested in the fish, but in so far as the interaction of environment and genome, nature and nurture you might say, in terms of how variations spread or are contained and so on, you know."

Newman certainly did know, and he was interested to see the spotlight off the fish and onto the lake. He could imagine Geoff, a little like himself, coming to see it as important to visit the lake now and again, to further his research of course, but also to enjoy the location. A growing enthusiasm perhaps fueled by Walker's connection. And what better than to have Walker on the books, an intern and mentee requiring guidance and overall corporate indoctrination, who would also justify regular field trips to the lake and its new owner.

Steve slapped Geoff on the back.

"Geoff I underestimated you. I mean you could have spent your time looking at disused reservoirs, underground storage tanks, flooded mines and the like — but no, your self-sacrifice and dedication leads you to Glacial Lake of all places. You're a martyr to the cause old man, no doubt about that."

"Hats off," added Newman.

"You're joshing me, I know, and it is a charming location isn't it. I can see why you retired here Mr. Newman.

The area reports and geological analyses I dug out said nothing about what a wonderful place this is — you kept that quiet. Can't say I blame you — wouldn't mind moving here too."

"So what's your itinerary while you're here?" Newman asked.

"Oh for this visit?"

"'Course. What's your agenda?"

"Visiting Fred. Walker's sponsor, you know. Wants to speak with me. I need to get some paperwork dealt with and so on. Going down to her place at Coldwater Bay, actually. Then, unfortunately, straight back to the office. But it won't be long before I'm back, I'm sure."

Newman was pleased to see Geoff turn slightly awkward again. Something of the old Geoff. But now even a little shifty perhaps?

"Oh I'm sure you'll be back Geoff — and you'll be very welcome," said Newman.

Fred came out of the council meeting in a good mood. The purchase of a pair of whale-watching boats was unanimously approved, along with dockside development and a tie-in to an updated hunting exhibit in the cultural center (aka the museum). She and Fargo had put together a long term plan to reduce reliance on casino receipts in favor of new development that aligned more closely with the cultural ambitions of the council. She called it investing in ourselves, extracting value from our strengths, and reducing reliance on external fads and fashions. She had presented her ambitions with gusto.

"We should turn back toward our heritage, nurture its

potential and harvest its many gifts. Everywhere there are opportunities offered to us by our history, the land, the water, the sky; for too long we have overlooked them in favor of what: entertaining outsiders. We have engaged in a fruitless struggle to succeed, where success is measured in reaching goals that are not our own. No more. Everything we do, all our efforts should be derived from, be connected with, and further the development of our nation and its identity. We will take from the world only what we need; we will give what we alone can give; we will grow and prosper in harmony with who we are and the people we have always been."

This wasn't exactly how Fargo's contribution was phrased, but Fred suggested that his whole "Yankee go home" angle — though it had the virtue of a direct, no-nonsense slogan — was perhaps underselling the scale of their ambition, or undermining the sophistication of their argument. But she admired the fact that he made no bones about his goal; close down the casino, build up fishing, crafts, and his cultural center.

The rest of her day was given over to meeting Geoff. That was enough, she thought. This would be the first time she had met Geoff face to face, and she might need to take some downtime to figure things out later; Walker had relayed what was going on with the whole business so far, but Fred was looking forward to getting some detail from Geoff on Ziegler's broader proposal.

She had arranged to meet him in the conference room upstairs in the cultural center. Visitors had to come through the center and up a central elevator, ending up directly above the main exhibition space. The room also enjoyed an elevated panorama of the lake through expansive windows. A docent ushered him in and they met either side of the long conference table. Fred was pleased to see that Geoff looked suitably uncomfortable, and made sure she exploited her considerable height advantage when she rose to shake his hand.

"Good to meet you at last, Geoff. You arrived this morning?"

"Hello, yes. Lovely place. Really marvelous. Yes, no I arrived last night actually, bit early, wasn't sure how long it would take to get here, staying up at the lake."

"Oh — you've met Newman and company then? Did he have anything interesting to say?"

"Yes I met Mr Newman for the first time, and I drove up here with Steve — do you know him?"

"Yes, quite a double act, aren't they? Did they seem particularly interested in your visit?"

"Not really, no. We spoke about Walker's project a little, and the lake generally, but they didn't ask about anything specifically."

"Good. It's a little soon after the transfer to get them involved, I think. Rather take care of things between the three of us until things are more settled at your end. Speaking of which, how is the third of us doing?"

"Walker? He's doing great isn't he — full of ideas. Initially I wasn't sure where an intern would fit in, but it was his work on the fish that got me interested. He did mention that Mr. Newman had graciously allowed him to bring the fish to the lab for study, and of course Mr. Newman is very highly regarded by his colleagues who are still around, at least those in Food. Turned out to be quite a star, and to be quite frank with you it was shortly after we hired Walker and he showed me his plan for the lake that I got given the entire project. So I suppose maybe you should rather be asking Walker how I'm doing."

"Doing OK in my book," Fred said, "at least, the business account seems to be fully funded, so things must be going in the right direction. Which is a good thing, as I have a number of projects that currently depend on it."

"Walker really is very creative. I mean I have some technical clout, but Walker's put together all the logistics. He pretty much built the internal presentation around the materials you sent too — I just had to deliver it. They loved it - talking about creating an entire division devoted to 'field and community alliance development' or some-such, with a senior position for me."

Fred smiled as she got up and walked to the window. "Walker is a smart cookie, for sure. Any news on the timescale?"

"Well we have had major components of the plans in place for some time, we were just waiting for the ideal location. So now we are just finalizing design proposals for the specifics of the development and testing labs, the research and business briefing center, and the residential accommodation. You saw those proposals?"

"Yes — I liked them."

"That's it? You like them?"

"That's it Geoff — it's the 'if they'll build it, they can come' principle. We need the revenue, and we want a sustainable income in future to fund our less profitable projects. We have no money; you do. We have the perfect location, you don't, but you have great plans. Your long-term is our near-term, so our timescales mesh. It's the perfect marriage. Or symbiosis, more like."

"I know the Ziegler people were surprised how quick they made progress. I mean, they were expecting negotiations to take for ever. I heard you seemed to anticipate their demands at times, and had your own positions already figured out. Or rather, perhaps Walker was pretty much spot-on in his assessment of what Ziegler might hope to achieve. Pretty impressive — you'd think he'd come from Yale business school, not the genetics department."

Fred turned from the window and looked directly at Geoff.

"Hmm, not sure about that. Walker is there to work with you, help move things along, but let's be clear though before we get carried away. The Nation runs things round here, and it suits us to let Ziegler make some hay while the sun shines. But the farm belongs to us, and will always belong to us. If a tenant needs to build a few hay barns, that's great. But the barns remain part of the farm, and remain so long after the tenant has moved on to pastures new."

"I think I get it. I mean I guess I think — I hope — the legal people get it. As you know I'm not one of the negotiators. From my point of view, I just want to be a part of a great opportunity here. Never been anything quite like it far as I can tell."

Fred sat down again. "Really? How so Geoff?"

"Well here's the deal from what I can make out. I get this from talking with Steve to be honest. The genetics business is a mix of science, politics, pure speculation, and public relations. The most important being public relations. Steve's point is that if public relations isn't working, then everything else will be much more of a struggle. When I took over Mr Newman's scouting work, I could see plenty of locations that satisfied one, two, or at most three of those requirements. Very few satisfied all of them, and if they appeared to, a closer look would reveal an issue of some sort."

"What sort?"

"Oh, we had a flooded quarry with the water conditions, development grants, tax advantages, all of that in a place represented by politicians desperate for some good news to own. Everything seemed perfect except a marketing organization confirmed that none of our target employees would ever want to work there. And we had another place. Beautiful naturally contained ravine with every conceivable advantage, an easy commute to a flourishing town with all the arts and entertainment our people would be looking for, and depressed housing prices — perfect. Except the local State representative was almost religiously set against anything smelling of genetics. History of local farms being sued by corporations over seed patents or something. But in this case — with the lake — we have everything lined up. Perfect geography, with an established genetic variation. Everybody wants to work here, who wouldn't? The politics would have been a showstopper, but that's been taken care of now the government is a minor beneficiary rather than a controlling influence. And the fact that you seemed decidedly in favor of the investment from the get-go — it's an unprecedented opportunity. Or what did Steve call it? A "slamma-damn a dunk-dong" I think is what he said. Reference to an old pop song. Seemed to amuse him. I looked it up."

"Right, well I just don't like corporate types feeling

too comfortable, that's all. We are sensitive to people taking advantage, you understand, and I've put a lot of work into this so I don't want any suited types swaggering round here thinking they're slam dunking any sort of a takeover. Because I'll shut them down soon as look at them."

"Got it."

"Good."

Newman sat in the lodge with his coffee and danish, looking at the fish Dave had installed above the door. It was without doubt a magnificent specimen, and whoever was responsible for mounting it had done a wonderful job. It wasn't just stuck up there, cold and dead, it had been captured mid-glance as it appeared to scan the surface for its prey, glimmering colors enhanced — not that they needed it — by a strategically placed spotlight. Newman considered how far a mouthful of fly would go to assuage the appetite of that monster. Bald eagle might conceivably get stuck between its teeth. "Wonder if the taxidermist charges by the pound?" he thought.

He'd been thinking about Walker's success at Ziegler, and Geoff's visit, apparently to discuss his project with Fred. How often did a manager — however middle — take a trip to visit an intern's relative in order to discuss his project? What was it he said? "Fill in some paperwork"? Newman hoped that paperwork was what he thought it might be. He expected it was. When he had suggested that Walker might be a great future hire he had also provided the candidate with some inside information he'd compiled years ago about the lake that he was sure would complement what he'd told Geoff, and enhance Walker's chances of impressing his new bosses. Nothing so much about the fish as about Newman's research on the local geography, the potential of the location. He'd sown the seeds of a few talking points that he thought would catch Geoff's attention, and now he was convinced that would be the reason for the visit.

"What the hell's he really down there for then, Newman? Geoff I mean."

Newman had just begun to consider Fred's options, and how Geoff might fare in dealing with her and Fargo when he was startled by Steve's customarily robust entrance.

"Beats me."

"I'm sure it doesn't, Newman. Middle management doesn't visit an intern's family unless there's been some incident. Like he fell in a fish tank, or shot himself with the gene gun or something. Eh? You know what's going on and you know I'll wheedle it out of you one way or another."

Newman ordered coffee for Steve. "Sit down. As it happens, I am feeling pretty good about how things are likely turning out."

"Knew it. Go on."

"When Fred told me Walker was diddling with the fish, I wasn't too worried. But I did wonder if there was any opportunity for us in having a link back to Ziegler. I mean, I'd gone it alone a bit with the fish and it might be reassuring to have them onboard in one way or another."

"A burden shared?"

"More a liability offloaded. There'd be much bigger fish to fry at Ziegler," ("Oh very good," from Steve.) "and then again Fred needed the income, and I knew the success of the resort couldn't rest entirely with the fish; they might peter out at any minute. And if they don't—"

"Heaven forbid."

"Right. So I let Walker know how important a new field location was to Ziegler, and how the lake was a prime candidate back when. The only obstacles had been political, otherwise this place would have been a prime candidate for considerable investment. All this of course not directly relevant to the furtherance of his education, but a potentially explosive jumpstart for his corporate career."

"Should he wish to pursue such a thing, of course."

"Of course. Many a successful mogul has flunked out of a great college. And I did let drop the sort of starting salary he might shoot for as one of the first hires in a new division. A new division just waiting for the right opportunity to get funded and have its people thrust into the fast lane."

"You're a bad man, Newman. And I mean that in the best possible way. So Geoff is up there thinking he could talk Fred into letting them in you think?"

"I think so. I reckon he must've been struck with insight while talking to Walker about the lake, and now he's up here sounding out Fred. Certainly didn't want to let on about anything to me when he showed up here, so that's a good sign."

Steve poured a final cup of coffee from the carafe. "Best outcome?"

Newman sat back, hands behind his head, and stared up at the spotlit fish as he spoke. "Fred extracts a huge amount of money for them to lease the lake, along with commitments to develop here or maybe even down at the Bay. Ziegler will insist on clauses to assert their ownership and responsibility for everything in the lake. I can imagine Donoghue and Stevenson sewing things up on that front — they wouldn't want Fred able to claim any sort of rights over any aspect of their business. So that suits me fine. What else, let's see. Oh and we get access in the bar, the cafe, the restaurant, even the damn coin operated restrooms to the corporate expense accounts of all those visitors flocking here for Ziegler's latest briefings from the leading edge."

"Oh yes. The trout swimming home to spawn. Ha! And I can see a dramatic improvement in the quantity and the quality of your visitors Newman."

"Well I wouldn't say that, Steve, I see it more as a cross-funding opportunity. There could be a dramatic improvement in the overall facilities here for everyone. We'd be generally making hay while the corporate sun shone and with a bit of luck and a good long lease from Fred it'll be shining on all of us for a while yet."

9: The unraveling

THE REPORTER ARRIVED without any booking. "On spec", he said, as Doris put him through a shorter version of her protocol for this sort of occasion. These days she had softened slightly, and no longer gained the pleasure she once did from prolonging the would-be visitor's uncertainty over whether he would have to get back in his car and look for somewhere else. So she made a few half-hearted attempts to disquiet him while she thumbed through her book ("well it's the busy season you know", "we have a number of re-bookings this week", "lot of people here for the fishing at the moment") before admitting that there was an available room in the main lodge.

"Here for the fishing, are you?" she asked. "I have to say, reports are that they're not biting at the moment. Wouldn't want to disappoint. Mr . . . ?"

"Call me Cooper. Cooper Black, actually I'm here to see if I can meet with your Mr Newman. I guess he still runs the place?"

"He is in charge, technically. I'll book you in twenty-three then — Newman generally pops into the bar for a drink before dinner, so you might want to see if you can catch him there around six-ish. He'll probably be on his own, hunched over, sort of a hunted look, at the end of the bar."

Cooper had not only arrived without prior booking, he hadn't told anyone where he was going when he left his office at the National Observer the day before. This could be the story that boosts his career out of the rut he'd fallen into. Could even be his ticket to national television. He'd learned the advantages of flying under the wire when his former partner blindsided him with that drug dealing dentist story. He had actually undergone a (not so minor) dental procedure in order to help find out what that guy was doing with his lab boxes, only to see the whole sorry story in full page print with pictures — police dogs, screaming receptionist, handcuffs and all — without even a shared byline. He'd decided then that if ever even a hint of a half decent scoop came his way that he could pull off himself then he'd keep it to himself at all costs.

So here he was, ready to meet with Mr. Newman, after amassing considerable circumstantial evidence about recent developments at the Glacial Lake operation. The sudden rise to fame of these fish that accompanied Mr Newman's arrival; his unlikely resume for a resort operator; the transfer of land out of the National Parks Service; the apparent revision of local tribal history. It was all an unlikely confluence, it had seemed to Cooper, as he spent the last few months gradually filling his computer with related information.

Doris noticed a *National Observer* luggage tag on the larger of the cases. "Shall I have your bags taken up to your room, Mr. Black?"

"Oh — no thanks I like to keep hold of them myself."

His luggage, more specifically his messenger bag, and in particular his computer case, seldom left his sight. Cooper suffered from a mix of paranoia and insecurity that meant he couldn't trust his vital data to any kind of facility that may be out of reach — no paper, no other person, no backup service, and certainly not his office systems — yet he was in constant fear of losing the one and only copy he had, held close to him on his computer or on a thumb drive on his keyring. After the drug dealing dentist incident with his former partner, a psychiatrist had told him that he needed to learn to trust again. Instead of taking this on board and moving on, he became unsure whether his analyst, paid for through his employer-provided health insurance, could herself be fully trusted. "What are you working on now?" and "Why don't you invite your old partner out for a drink?" were suspicious questions, and he even began to wonder whether the analyst's office might be bugged. The result was he had made excuses as to why he had to miss counseling appointments — didn't want to raise any suspicion — so he could get on with his story without risking anyone scooping him on it.

Perhaps he would return to his weekly sessions later, when it was all finished. He was doing fine on his own right now and anyway, maybe by then he wouldn't need it. That would show that therapist and all her conspirators at the Observer what he was capable of if only they'd get out of his way, stop interfering and let him do his job.

As he looked around his room in the Lodge, with its magnificent view of the lake and the hills beyond, he felt those insecurities dissipate as his confidence rose. He definitely knew there was something going on, he probably knew how it was going on, and he had a good idea why. Mr. Newman would be first in the firing line to help focus his suspicions into a story that would take the national news by storm and establish him as a journalistic force to be recognized.

* * *

"Evening," Doris said, "quick chat?"

Newman was in his office, winding up his day by attempting to complete the Observer crossword. "Sure, looks like everything is just about buttoned up here. Anyway, I have little or nothing to do these days."

Doris came in, closed the door, and took the guest chair. Newman could tell immediately she had something to say.

"I wasn't sure how best to broach the subject, Newman," she said, "So let me just say this. Ranger Dave might be the only one of us who hasn't figured out your damn' fish and Fred's damn' bits and pieces."

"Really?" said Newman. "What's up with Dave then?"

"Well he's all wrapped up in his public service presentations, stuffed trophy fish and the like — but that's not the point, Newman, and you know it. Come clean will you? We're all in the same boat."

"In the boat, Doris?"

"There's a reporter here checked in today and he's looking for you. Let's say he knows as much about what's going on as Dave. Well he's clearly here to find out. Why else would he be here? I have a hunch about these things Newman. And I don't want to be left knowing less than some reporter."

"Fish and bits and pieces aside for a moment, Doris, what makes you so paranoid about this guy?"

"Whenever reporters come here they announce their arrival and start asking about the place straight away — 'how long have you been here? What's the best way to see the lake? Who should I talk to about the fish? Is there a local historian I can meet with?' They try and get in my good books, hoping for some angle that's not yet been covered. This one was different. Didn't let on who he was or why he was here — keeping his cards far too close — I can tell you Newman he's up to something sneaky."

"And what about the fish, and Fred's bits and pieces?"

"The fish have been here about as long as you have. Fargo's relics are even more recent. Right?"

Newman sighed. "There are some things better left as rumors. I'm thinking it might be best for us all to join Dave in this — we should follow his lead, and become simple ambassadors of our good fortune, like you said. Show off the lake, the fish, the bits and pieces, whatever. If the reporter needs a new twist, he's out of luck. Or we'll let him talk to Robert. Don't think anyone's done that before."

"Sorry Newman, I'm not following Dave's lead anywhere. I've been following you. And Fred. And most importantly, the money. I won't beat around the bush; where did those toilets come from? And the new parking? The boats? We're doing better, but not that much better. And it all started after Fred took over, but it's no secret she's never had any spare cash. Something fishy going on Newman."

Newman sighed.

"OK. Between you and me, OK? Here's what I think is going on. That guy Geoff from Ziegler visited — remember him? Went down to visit Fred. So now Parks is out of the way, Fred's presented Ziegler with an opportunity to invest. Without any government roadblocks. Another one of her plans, basically. Used Walker to help set it up. He works for Geoff."

"Ziegler? Invest? In what? Why?"

"In the lake. I know for a fact it's the perfect spot for them. Opportunities for study and maybe even experiments, corporate boondoggles, Lots of PR on investing in nature, visitors appreciating the softer side of the global corporation — all that. When I was there I always said we'd take 'GMO' off the cussword list. That's probably got something to do with it. Plus I know that Stammbaum himself — the CEO — has a soft spot for this area and might see it as his North American pied-à-terre."

"How can this be good?"

"Fred's not going to give anything up, and certainly not permanently. Ziegler will invest a ton of cash doing the place up; they want pretty much what we all want here, surely. A beautiful place, great to visit, nature front and center and all that. And clean toilets."

Doris stared at Newman, or rather through him, for a moment.

"OK. I see that. I think. Thank you Newman. It's Fred we're dealing with too so I assume you don't have all the details but I appreciate your thoughts. And I do agree Fred wouldn't give up any of her hard-won spoils, at any rate. But a little corporate glitz would go a long way round here, especially if they're committed to the whole natural scene thing and not thinking of installing any sort of industrial plant. I don't want the place to turn into a laboratory."

"Not going to happen," Newman said, with a shake of the head as if to underscore his certainty. "I can guarantee that. Now. As far as this reporter goes, from what you say it sounds like he may have come here on some sort of a mission. With a few things he dreamed up himself for us to deny. What did you tell him so far?"

"I told him where to find you, in the bar. My bet is he'll be looking for you this evening. Let me know what you learn about him, will you? I like to know what I'm dealing with and this guy strikes me as a bit of a loose canon."

"No worries, Doris. If he's looking for any scandal, then between you, me, and Fred he may well have bitten off a little more than he can chew. Hell, if all else fails I'll let Fargo have him."

The figure at the end of the bar sat down and was served a beer without having to ask for it. Hunched over his drink, he cast his eyes from side to side as if anticipating an approach. Cooper Black decided this was likely Newman, and was pretty sure Doris would already have given him a heads-up. He walked up to the bar next to Newman and ordered a pint of beer and a whisky.

"Mr. Newman?" he asked when his drink arrived.

"Yes. How are you? Nice evening."

"Fine thanks. Doris was it on reception? She mentioned you might be here when I checked in earlier today. My name's Black. Cooper Black. Call me Cooper. And before you ask, no I'm not here for the fishing."

"Oh — how so then?"

Cooper paused and cast his eyes around the bar conspiratorially. "Well, if you have a moment. I'm a journalist, and your story intrigues me. Not much going on in town these days, I was getting a little cabin fever, you know, so I hunted about for something to look into. Spotted Glacial Lake. Fascinating. Sort of thing any journalist might be interested in.

"Ha. Where were you before we spent a small fortune

in advertising the place? You saying we could have got some free publicity?"

"It was partly the whole buzz you created about the new management, the upgraded resort, and of course the fish that got me interested. But you too, Mr. Newman — you caught my interest in particular."

Cooper took a swig of his beer, then a sip of whisky. Newman leaned back and directed a puzzled look directly toward him. Not getting any sort of rise from Newman, Cooper added:

"Not keen on your beer. Maybe doesn't travel well, eh. But the whisky's always good wherever it ends up. Well. So you took early retirement, from a very successful career at a big genetics multinational, to come here. Longstanding dream they said."

"You're a reporter?"

"I am, for my sins. Not just a reporter. Investigator, writer. Creator."

"And you came here to wash down second-rate beer with first-rate chasers, and reminisce about my career?"

"Ah well that's where reporting stops and investigation starts, isn't it. I have it on authority that you didn't so much discover those fish, as disclose them. So what was said to be a stroke of luck may have been more a triumph of logistics, perhaps. It was like you introduced them, wasn't it Mr. Newman, like a master of ceremony with a brand new act. Remarkable, isn't it? Some sort of conjuring trick. In fact, that gives me a great start for my story: 'The Great Newman, Fish-Conjurer, brings Miraculous Transformation to Otherwise Lackluster Lake.' Bit long for a headline, perhaps."

"I think you may have skipped the investigation and

the writing and be well into creation, Mr. Cooper."

"Black. Cooper Black. Don't know about creation, but I was confident enough in my guesswork to confirm a few points with some folks from the labs where you used to work. The gist of it is that a Mr. Walker is analyzing the genetics of fish from your lake. I'll spare us both the jargon — wouldn't like you to think I was misleading you, Mr. Newman — heaven forbid that. Of course I don't know anything about genetics, but I can spot bullshit when I see it, especially the corporate variety. Dealt with a fair bit of it myself in my time."

If Newman was rattled, he didn't yet look it. So Cooper pressed a little harder.

"Mr. Walker is a Yale geneticist. Quite a rockstar as far as I can see. Also, funnily enough, a member of the tribe. The tribe that adopted your lake."

Another swig of beer and a glance at Newman. Cooper placed his glass carefully back on the bar. He continued.

"Curiouser and curiouser, you might say. Then there are promotions and reorganizations, talk of an entirely new division at Ziegler and a big new role for Mr. Walker and his boss. Amazing what you can pick up for the cost of a few beers in the Fin and Feathers. So anyway — is all that coincidence or consequence, I wonder?"

Still no reaction. Newman was looking intently at his beer as if he may have spotted a misshapen bubble.

"Now why would a mighty multinational like Ziegler need to secretly investigate your fish? And how come you stumbled on those fish in the first place? Unless you really are a conjurer and you produced them from thin air."

Newman displayed his empty hands and pulled up

his sleeves in a dramatic gesture.

"OK look I also know Ziegler is financing improvements here on some sort of under the table quid pro quo deal, and it all started when they got hold of your fish."

"I'm sorry Mr. Cooper. But I'm not sure what the fish have to do with the Ziegler corporation's tax strategies. And 'my' Mr. Walker has nothing to do with me, whatever he's up to. Maybe safer to cut back on the creativity here and return to reporting?"

"Not important but it's Mr. Black, actually. Let's just call me Cooper. OK so we have an unsuccessful resort taken on by a senior manager from a genetics firm, the immediate discovery that the lake contains a unique strain of fish, and shortly after the Parks service hands it all over to the local tribe. Oh and I haven't even mentioned how your own tribal heritage was suddenly spirited into being — yes, I heard about that too. Then — another miracle — that very same genetics firm starts handing over cash to the tribe to turn the whole place around. Am I following this correctly then?"

Newman ordered another glass of beer, waited until it was delivered, and exchanged a few pleasantries with the bartender before he responded.

"That's one way of reporting it. And by the way — I find your questioning my heritage very offensive, Mr. Cooper. How about this as an alternative interpretation: 'the new operator's successful promotion of a previously underutilized beauty spot led to the discovery of a unique strain of fish that attracted the attention of a multinational genetics company, who funded its continued development through the resort's owners, the tribes of the Coldwater Nation.' Not such a pernicious narrative now, is it? But I can see why you prefer your version. Hungry for a blockbuster story, perhaps?"

Cooper was already considerably invested in his version of events, and considered them compelling to the point of incontrovertible. He was inclined to see Newman's reaction as defensive. There was already some sort of cover-up going on here, by the sound of it well-rehearsed, because they surely imagined that sooner or later someone might start digging.

"Ah yes, the tribes. I've been looking into all that too — their long journey toward taking over this place came to an abrupt and unexpectedly successful end with some very recent discoveries. And now, I gather, a senior former Parks employee works for the tribes, yes? I plan to visit the president tomorrow down at Coldwater Bay." Cooper took another swig of his beer. "The more I think about it, the harder it is for me to remember any story with as many promisingly loose threads as yours. And in my experience, Mr. Newman, it only takes one of those threads to begin to unravel for the whole thing to start to come apart."

"It sounds like you already have a story of your own in mind, and I really can't blame you. This is a wonderful place, and if I were you and I could persuade the *National Observer* to give me an assignment here I'd do it in a heartbeat. Beats poking around town looking for the next scandal to whip your readers into a frenzy about. Well done, it'll be a while til you run out of reasons to hang around here and they call you back. And by then you may have figured out how to write a story about us that's a little closer to reality. Anyway, to show there's no hard feelings on my part, I'll tell you that Fred Jesperson's the boss at the Bay that you need to talk to. I can invite her up here to meet with us if you like."

171

"No, that's fine thanks — I prefer to just show up, you know, see what's going on, see what her take is. And by the way, this is no cushy assignment. It's entirely my own project, and I assume none of us wants the spotlight of the mighty Observer brought down on our doings, not just yet at least. They'd likely send a small army down here to sort this one out. So I'd appreciate your discretion in exchange for mine, Mr. Newman, for all our sakes."

"Right. Solo project, eh Mr. Cooper? I've been involved with PR long enough to know a scoop-seeker when I see one, but I think you're barking up the wrong tree here. Or fishing in the wrong pond. But anyway, do go ahead. I certainly don't need the Observer down here getting in the way and I know Ziegler is always sensitive to any sort of publicity. Discretion is my middle name."

"I may be a little out of my depth, I'll grant you that. But I'm in the right pond, and I'm a strong swimmer, Mr. Newman."

"Just as well."

Cooper finished his beer, then swigged the last of his whisky. He was increasingly satisfied that he was most definitely on to something. Newman was far too casual about the whole thing. After all, he'd just been accused of some sort of chicanery and what did he do? Laugh it off, act as though it didn't matter. "If it were me, I'd be more surprised, more baffled, more angry," Cooper thought. "I'd probably take a swing at me."

"I should have hit him," Newman said, "should've decked him there and then, little shit." As casually as he could, Newman had finished his drink and left Cooper in the bar with an on-the-house whisky chaser. Once he was out of sight he'd sprinted up to his office and called Fred at the Bay.

"He was taking potshots right left and center, and after he'd voiced his suspicions about fish and Ziegler he turned to the whole Parks thing. He'll be showing up at your place tomorrow, so he says."

"What does he want, do you think?"

"Oh he has some vision of himself as a hotshot reporter breaking a national story I'm sure. He's going it alone — afraid it's too big of an opportunity to share with his colleagues. And I bet part of it is he's thinking bigger than his newspaper — that'll be why he's kept it all so quiet. He'll have an eye to *60 minutes*; our man at the lake, our man on the reservation, our man interviewing the National Parks. Oh god, I'll have to clue in poor old Trefor, I'm not sure he's up to it."

"Steady on, Newman, you're getting ahead of yourself. I'm sure you have it all worked out far better than he does. Let's slow down for a moment. Where's his evidence? All circumstantial. Best possible result for him would be to create some unresolved scandal. And you never know, that might just end up in more people showing up at the lake."

"But Ziegler. They're key to your plans, right? They can't get a whiff of this. I'll tell you, when I was there I'd have run a mile from any project with this sort of publicity risk. And it's not just the PR — what happens if he publishes his poking around and the original transfer from Parks goes sideways?"

There was a moment's silence from Fred. Then in low, measured tones she said:

"Newman. Slow down. When he shows up I'll sound him out. I want to get a handle on how much he suspects and how much evidence he thinks he can get to back it up. Sounds to me like he has a great story all worked out, and he's looking for just enough material from us to ground it in reality. We don't need to hand it to him. Tell you what — you should be more worried right now about the fishing. There are just a few reports of impressive catches, but many more about the overall numbers dropping right off. If there's something going on with the fish and they're dying off there may be no story for him to chase before long, and you'll have to think of a new attraction to bring in the tourists in the meantime. Check it out with Dave, will you? I'll let you know what happens with Cooper Black."

As soon as she got off the call, Fred stepped out of her office onto the balcony and called down to Fargo on the museum floor below. He was helping drag into place what looked like a large, unwieldy piece of sodden driftwood.

"Fargo — be here in the office first thing, will you? And what the hell is that?"

"Partially carved canoe. Tribe as yet unidentified. Saturated. Found it deep below the cliffs, North side of the lake."

"Really? Looks like a piece of wet driftwood."

Fargo looked at Fred, then the driftwood. "Well, then opinion is divided."

"OK. Just be here in the morning, will you?"

In everything she did, Fred seldom used only a single strategy. She liked to combine approaches, to hedge bets, to attack from more than one angle. This technique had been her pitch to the Council when she ran for President; no more "stay the course" for the Coldwater Nation. No more "keeping on track" or "making the most of it". It was time to take what was theirs while consolidating what they had. Give and take; they shouldn't hesitate to take when outsiders' gifts fell short. They needed to become who they would be, even while they held true to their roots. No-one else had their interests at heart; the future was in their hands, the past in their favor. And her approach had worked well; the council recognized that the long overdue success in extending their territory upriver to include the Lake, and in funding enhancements to the Bay, were almost entirely due to Fred's contribution to their evolving history. So it wasn't with anxiety that she anticipated Cooper's visit. She felt excited. Energized even. She naturally rose to meet a challenge ("like a boat turning into the wave", was Fargo's observation) and in this case, despite Newman's concerns, she could hardly wait.

But she did choose to have Fargo with her for the meeting. His could be a usefully intimidating presence. He wasn't beyond thirty years or so, but he somehow exuded authority, cultural awareness, weight, and integrity. "You have a bit of a shamanic thing going on, Fargo — without the regalia of course. And do keep covered up," was Fred's observation.

Fargo was sitting in her office when she arrived, the expansive bay view behind him, silhouetted by the bright blue and yellow morning sunlight streaming through the seamless windows. "Perfect day," he said, "though my pastry was disappointing. You want coffee?" Fred nodded and told Fargo that a reporter was due to arrive, probably sooner rather than later, and that he seemed to be trying to build a story about the history of the lake. In particular, the most recent history. That last phrase was accompanied by a nod to the museum below.

"He sounds like a disappointed man," said Fargo. "He hasn't yet learned the impossibility of building anything worthwhile by ruining something worthwhile that already exists."

"He may well be. I certainly feel he may be looking to ruin something here for his own advantage. I'm told this is his personal project, that it's the extent of his current ambition to make a story of us, and that he's confident he's already nailed the plot."

"Then why does he need to speak to us?" Fargo asked. "It sounds like he may already know more than I do. Perhaps despite his ambition, he's not used to working alone and he needs people along with him, especially powerless people who only exist in his story."

"My goodness Fargo, you're on form," said Fred with only the hint of a smile. "Well maybe he doesn't fully understand the forces with which he's about to engage. Do you think?"

The phone rang, Fred picked it up. "Send him up," she said.

Cooper intended from the outset to be abrupt and businesslike, and avoid falling for any of the intimidating tribal nonsense he was expecting to face. But he couldn't help looking slightly wide-eyed around the room as he walked in, clearly impressed by everything he saw, including the expansive, sunlit space, and the incredible bay view. Not least, Fred was pleased to see a slight double-take when he saw her standing in front of the conference table.

Before anyone else could say anything, Fargo said,

"You are a historian? You know about history?"

Cooper was taken by surprise.

"No I'm a writer. Journalist. Cooper Black. Cooper. How are you, sir."

"How are any of us, you know? We just are, I think. How we come to be is a question that could occupy us for some considerable time. But if that is your interest, I'm happy to discuss it with you."

Fred decided to help Cooper out.

"My colleague Fargo is a student of Wittgenstein, among many others, Cooper. Can you tell? You'll find that sometimes he'll pull you onto his philosophical ferris wheel and your only option is to jump off and hope for a happy landing. Pleased to meet you; I'm Fred Jesperson, I head the tribal council."

Fred offered Cooper a seat at the table, and then she and Fargo sat down on the same side, so they all three ended up sitting facing the windows. That way, she thought, they would need to deliberately choose to look at one another during their conversation.

"I don't know if Mr. Newman up at the lake has spoken with you about my visit," said Cooper. "I'm here because I'm interested in the story of where this all came from." Fred was sitting between him and Fargo. He leaned forward and looked toward Fargo: "To that extent, I'm interested in your discussion about how things came to be, Mr. Fargo."

Fred's opinion of him immediately changed. He wasn't the desperate hack she initially suspected. He was ready to get to grips on their terms; maybe not so easily thrown off his game, this Cooper Black. Now she wondered if it had been wise to include Fargo in today's meeting; he might just fly off the handle and give this man unsought grist for his journalistic mill.

"Impressive museum you have here, Fred. I only got a glimpse as I came upstairs, but all sorts of interesting artifacts by the look. I noticed a huge piece of driftwood being put in place down there — what's that all about?"

"Relic of a totem pole from the hilltop above the lake, brought down by a mudslide six hundred years or so ago," Fargo said.

"Really?"

"No, not really. It's a half finished canoe, probably from an abandoned fishing village on the lake shore, that got swept into the water in the early eighteenth century."

Fargo stared at Cooper.

"I think it may be a piece of driftwood," Fred said, leaning in between them. "But I'll leave it to the experts to determine once they've looked at all the evidence. Wouldn't want to jump the gun and miss an opportunity to preserve something of value."

"Ah I see," said Cooper, "well I agree it's a good idea to make sure things are what they seem before making any important decisions about them. For example, those rainbow trout up at the lake. Do you think they're what they seem? A unique strain developed from generations of a landlocked species? I think that's how Mr. Newman described it in an interview for *Angler's World*."

"There's never been anything like them found anywhere else," Fred said.

"My point exactly. And Mr. Fargo — your discovery of relics, many of them unearthed I think when the soil moved just recently. Remarkable, by any account. Certainly made an impression on the Parks service."

"They are only relics for so long as they remain undiscovered," said Fargo, "once found, they return to the present to take their place in shaping our current affairs."

Cooper feared another rathole, but Fred intervened.

"Alright, cut to the chase Cooper. Life's too short. What do you want?"

"Just a story. I'm just following a story, that's all."

"Following or fabricating?"

"Really, Fred. While we're being direct with one another, I just may be the only one around here who isn't making stuff up."

Fargo had been staring out of the window. Now he stood, walked toward the window, and said:

"I saw the papers that we signed when we took back the lake from the government. Those papers were made up, Mr. Cooper. There were very many references in them to earlier papers that were made up. There was a time when outsiders first arrived here, and all they had were papers, all made up, all declaring their ownership. It's what they call precedent."

Both Fred and Cooper moved as if to interrupt but Fargo was having none of it.

"Precedent is what makes papers more important the earlier they were made up, and the more subsequent papers you can find that refer to them. We had no notion of papers or of ownership — they made ownership up, they used it to occupy the land, and they compensated us with papers. Those papers turned things round, so that our land became our claims to the land. They created ownership, they gave us claims, they took away our rights, they justify everything with papers."

Neither knew quite how to respond, until Fred brought the conversation back on track: "Do you see, Mr. Black? I think Fargo is suggesting that if you're not making anything up, then we're all on the same side. Do you understand?"

Cooper had thought he understood very well, but now wondered whether there was anything about this whole business that these people couldn't spin into some impenetrable nonsensical mish-mash. This was becoming even more frustrating than dealing with Newman.

"I'm not talking a couple of hundred years ago. I'm not talking Lewis and damned Clark here for god's sake. I'm talking since just before you started negotiating with Parks. I'm wondering whether the strategies used around here to boost tourism and to gain ownership of the lake were entirely above board. You can rehearse your paranoia about outsiders arriving here and all that as much as you like — that's not where the story lies. I want to know how nature seems to have conspired with everyone to bring about a series of unpredicted and very profitable turns of events. Now maybe it's magical," he glanced at Fargo, "or maybe it's political" he turned back toward Fred. "Either way is fine by me — it's a great story, and I intend to figure it out."

Fargo said, "Paranoia?"

Fred stood up.

"Would you like to tour the museum before you leave, Mr. Cooper?"

"I see. No, thank you. I'll return to the lake and make arrangements to be here a little longer. Perhaps I'll come up and see it in a few days, and we can speak some more about conspiracies, natural and man-made. I may ask if we can take a closer look at those artifacts, maybe bring in an expert or two? At the very least we can clear up some of Mr. Fargo's confusion over the totem pole canoe driftwood thing."

"Expertise, that's your answer then," Fargo said. "Bring in expertise, tell us what's what, clear up our confusion for us, tell our story for us, will you? Explain things to us. Make it clear to us how things will be. That's a very familiar story to me, Mr. Cooper."

"Take it however you will," said Cooper as he walked to the door, "but I'm here, I'm an accomplished reporter on a national newspaper, I see a story and I won't leave until I have everything I need to write it. Thank you both for your time."

"Thank you too, Mr. Cooper. I hope your trip proves to have been worthwhile."

Fred, a good few inches taller than Cooper, placed a hand briefly on his shoulder and was pleased to feel him flinch slightly. She closed the door quietly behind him, and turned to Fargo.

"Well!"

"I can't stand it, Newman, I'm fit to bust here. I have news."

Steve sat at one end of the boat; Newman the other. In the face of Steve's complete mechanical inadequacy, Newman had taken charge of the motor and was navigating them across the water toward the Discovery Store and Cafe for breakfast. Recently opened, the Discovery catered to campers, boaters, those leaving the highway for a break from their journey to the Bay — as Newman put it, anyone finding themselves on the wrong side of the water.

Steve had been thinking the news was juicy enough to save for the second or third beer later that evening, but he just couldn't wait.

"I can't damn' well wait, and anyway it wouldn't be fair. There's a plot afoot Newman; I got it all from Geoff. Surprisingly frank after a bottle of light beer, that fellow. Ziegler, yes — that Ziegler with which we're both so familiar — Ziegler wants to get together some sort of lease arrangement to build some sort of research, HQ, executive visitor place on the lake. Bit vague on the details I'm afraid, but what do you say to that?"

"Well I must say, I am surprised."

Steve seemed to completely miss the fact that Newman didn't sound at all surprised.

"Exactly. Geoff is here to discuss it with Fred, but that Walker hire wasn't all about the fish so much as the lake itself. I thought Geoff was about to spill the beans last night to be honest, but he's sworn to secrecy of course, by Ziegler and Fred both. So I asked him why, and he said they were still looking for a great field place, and your lake fits the bill on just about every count. I mean, you said yourself years ago Parks was the only thing that disqualified it as a prospect."

"Yes."

"So now they're out of the picture, Coldwaters are in and it appears Fred is more open to the proposition. What do you think?"

"Initial thought is it's good to see where all that cash is coming from. Closely followed by 'What the hell does a person need to do to shake those Ziegler bastards off for good?' Then I'm wondering just how much of the detail in plans I put forward for a field facility they'll take on."

"Yes you had all sorts of stuff in there, didn't you? You made it sound more like a PR stunt than a testing facility, I remember. I liked it."

"Well the value for Ziegler was as much in the PR as it was in the product — at least, I saw that as the best way to sell it to the higher-ups. I suppose I was also looking for a nice place to work. I had accommodation for students and execs, I had tie-ins to local business, infrastructure improvements where necessary, lots of educational tax advantages — the works. Now they've got the tribal angle to play off too as they try their best to come across as biological and cultural philanthropists. I wonder how much of all that plan Ziegler will actually build out?"

Steve laughed. "Well so far it looks like they've already upgraded the toilets."

"Yes they're already spending so I assume they've already reached some sort of a deal. That rascal Fred is playing her cards close, eh. I thought we had an accord."

"Well you're as good as family after all, aren't you Newman?"

"At least on paper I am. Fargo will vouch for it I'm sure."

"Well you can always throw in the towel and take the tribal pension or whatever. Ha."

Steve was enjoying himself, though relieved to approach dry land as Newman tied the boat to the dock. They unsteadily disembarked before heading into the Discovery.

"Hello hello," said Steve as they walked in, "Ham and eggs twice, a big pot of your strongest coffee, and a pitcher of juice please."

"Anything for you?" the assistant asked Newman.

"Oh, half of that is for me, I think."

"You want an extra plate?"

"No, I mean I'll be having the same."

Steve stepped in. "No no — we'll each have ham and eggs, and we'll each have coffee and juice — sorry to confuse the issue."

"Oh alright, I thought that was a lot of food. That would be easier for us, no extra plates or double helpings and the like, thank you."

"Geez Newman, good job you're not doing any negotiating today. A bit rattled are you?"

"Let's just have breakfast and take stock, shall we?"

They sat by the window. Steve picked up a crayon from a box next to the salt and pepper and idly filled in the outlines of a fish on the disposable table cloth. After a moment, Newman said:

"Damn it. And now I have some hotshot gumshoe reporter type from the Observer sniffing round for a story."

"*National Observer*?"

"Yes, the damn *National Observer*."

"Ho ho shit, Newman. Or rather, fan, eh. Inevitable I suppose? I was hoping it would be a favorable piece though — sounds like he's a non-friendly?"

"Decidedly. We had a friendly piece done shortly after I arrived as part of our big fish push. Now we've got the backlash I suppose — this one's a lone hunter with a chip on his shoulder, and of course he's starting with the fish."

Steve laughed.

"Oh, I see" said Newman. "Chip, fish. I'm glad you feel you have the distance from all this to take time for a laugh. Well how about this: next he's coming after the whole transfer thing by the look — off to rattle Fred's cage today I believe."

Steve took a moment to follow the logic. "Oh crap, that would take Ziegler out of the picture then. Geoff says Ziegler will be paying them a shitload. In fact, they may already have started; goodwill and all that. I gather the Coldwaters intended to cross-fund the Bay with revenue from the lake."

"Well I know Parks only signed up for a share of straight visitor revenue, so Fred probably has the Ziegler cash untouchable, in a separate stash. She'll have to get her hotshot accountants to sew that up somehow. But she'll be looking to use that loot for her college funding project as well as general improvements at the Bay."

Newman downed a glass of orange juice in three purposeful gulps.

"Did Geoff give any detail on the terms?"

"He claimed he didn't know, that was up to facilities and the negotiator folks. But it's probably along the lines we talked about when we were scouting locations."

Newman thought aloud. "Well let's see how that might go. How about Fred agrees to a leaseback. All infrastructure development financed by Ziegler on behalf of the tribes. No upfront investment for Fred, and a guaranteed term at the lake for Ziegler. Amortization blah blah Fred ends up with lake plus developments and enhancements at the end of their lease. Sounds pretty good all round."

Steve resumed his coloring. "Goody for them if they can pull it off then. But what if they can't — what if this reporter sticks a terminal wrench in the works? Aren't you worried about what'll happen to the resort? To you and your job? I know I am. Have to take up golf or something to pass the time after all."

"I'm just taking it day by day. So far all the changes have been for the better. Toilets are better already, aren't they?"

Steve was surprised by how quickly Newman seemed to come to terms with all this news. He'd never known him to be phased by the unexpected, of course, that was one of the reasons he'd found him indispensable all those years. But here was another kink in Newman's plans, just as the place was starting to settle down again, and he seemed almost pathologically calm. First Ziegler of all people, coming back to call the shots. Now this investigation — who knows how much that reporter would be able to dig up. Maybe Newman was surrendering to some sort of fit of conscience to resolve all that stuff with the tribes, Parks, and the fish. After all he'd been out of corporate long enough for at least the semblance of a conscience to resurface. Oh yes, the fish.

"The fish, Newman. So what about the fish?"

"Right now, Fred owns the fish. Assuming things go ahead and Ziegler takes a lease, then I'd insist that they own them. And whatever happens to them. How's that for a game of pass the karma?"

"Hadn't thought of that. Spent so many years taking credit, didn't consider the merits of avoiding it. Have to feel sorry for the mighty corporation though, coming up against your mystery fish."

"I don't know. Lot of smart people at Ziegler. If anyone could play the fish, surely they could. I think it'd be a fair match."

Steve finished up the last purple stripe on the tablecloth trout.

"Well there's my fish. Look at that. Apparently I can invite our server to judge whether my effort's worth a free soda."

It didn't look like Newman was listening. Steve leaned forward. "Well. What about you and Fred? I thought you had an understanding?"

Newman was staring out of the window. "It's her place, Steve. She can do deals if she wants — I'm just running it for her. I can make suggestions of course. Provide a guiding hand behind the scenes even. But we don't necessarily rush to share everything with one another. Mind you, she's never been anything other than straight with me I can tell you that. As far as I know."

"You're both a little economical with information, eh. That seems par for the course round here."

"Well you know how sensitive these sorts of things can be. Need to know and all that. I'm sure Fred has her reasons. I know I do." Newman turned back from the window and called over to the server. "Excuse me — do you think his fish deserves a free coke?"

"Let's see — did it manage to keep all its coloring between the lines?"

Doris's breakfast was an impromptu affair taken with Robert, who enjoyed exercising the control he had over his own time these days by engaging in just such spontaneous behavior. "Why, I think I will have a spot of toast and tea. Property will still be there when I'm done." They had shared what they'd overheard; the rumors, the idle gossip and the blind guesswork. Now Robert sat proprietorially in the big chair by the fireplace reading the Observer, and from behind the reception desk Doris kept an eye out for Newman. She wanted to get up to date on the goings-on with Cooper.

Before long she saw a lone motorboat arrive at the dock and she could just about make out Steve and Newman standing up inside it, each waving at the other to sit down. After a couple of attempts to breach the gap between boat and dock, they had managed to get out and walk up toward the lodge in apparent good humor.

Newman flung open the door.

"Hello Doris, here we are. Survived another voyage despite Steve's lubberly behavior. The relief makes what promises to be a perfect day even more welcome!"

"Really? Well it all sounds better than I expected then. I was wondering whether you might have gone into hiding from Mr. Black."

"Me too," said Steve, "thought you would be happier beneath the wire, Newman, now you're out and in the full glare of the national spotlight, eh?"

"Is that the respect I get after spending an otherwise pleasant morning giving sailor Steve here a tour of the lake? We went in a fruitless search — I think even the fish are shy of Mr. Black, to be honest. Or maybe it's Steve's thrashing around panicking about falling in that puts them off. I'm beginning to think there may be nothing here for Cooper to write about. Ooops — speaking of panic."

Cooper walked in, and seemed surprised for a moment to see Newman in reception.

"Mr. Cooper," Newman said, "Not leaving us I hope?"

"Cooper. It's Cooper. Pull the other one Mr. Newman.

Sorry to say I need to extend my stay for a couple of days. Can we do that, Doris?"

"Let me take a look at the book."

Doris thumbed through a few pages and glanced toward Newman for any indication that they should be fully booked. Newman appeared to be smiling; that alone was unusual enough to suggest he wasn't entirely comfortable, but she didn't see any indication that she should deny Cooper's request so she told him she'd put him down til Friday.

Steve, as usual, was more direct. "Have more business to conduct then Mr. Black? A few promising leads? I hear you're on the trail of a blockbuster of a story."

"Don't tell me Fred was anything other than forthcoming," said Newman. "Surely she helped fill in a few gaps for you? Did you meet Fargo? He's a great resource for local history, you know."

"As a matter of fact I do have to follow up on a few points with Fred. I'd also like a word with your man from the National Parks service — Mr. Evans, isn't it? And I would like to speak with a few of the staff round here. Get some opinion, some local color. Unless of course you have any objections?"

"No not at all, knock yourself out," said Newman.

"Great. Now — where do you think I'll find the ranger this afternoon?"

"Dave'll be down at his station if his truck's outside; otherwise he could be anywhere I'm afraid."

Once Cooper had left, there was silence until Steve said "You do know he'll get his story one way or another. What do you think he's looking for — everybody gives up and spills the beans? He must think he's entitled to know.

Common enough, isn't it — journalists who think people are obliged to provide them with any and all the information they want. Pushy lot."

"I imagine he's smarting after visiting Fred. Can't think he got too far there," said Newman. "Couldn't have been there long at any rate. I assume he wants to stir up the whole thing with Parks, put the deal into the papers and have the negotiations spelled out for his readers to play judge and jury while he gets to preside."

"Just for grins," said Steve, "what would happen if he had his way? What if your powers of misdirection failed you, and Fargo cracked and gave the game away. How d'you think it'd play out?"

Newman turned and leaned back against the reception desk.

"End of story, basically. Worse case is the whole place unwinds, Ziegler withdraws, reverts to Parks, litigation, bankruptcy, the works — turns back into a third rate campground and we all live in tents dreaming of the good old days."

Doris said, "And the best case?"

"That would be some sort of divine intervention by which Mr. Black foresees that tragedy play out and decides to leave us alone and look for a story elsewhere. He's seen how creative we can be down here; you never know, maybe we can help him with that and come up with an even better story. Or — here's a thought — we send him out on a tour of the lake with sailor Steve and he's never heard of again."

"Impugning my seamanship, Newman?"

Doris diverted an incoming call to hold. "Well Trefor's rattled. He told me Cooper had asked him if he could see the paperwork that was sent to Parks for the transfer negotiations. He also asked for contacts for all the people involved. Trefor didn't give him anything; referred him to PR at Parks, and to Newman for the paperwork."

"Well well I'm beginning to think we only have to say the name," Newman said as Trefor walked through the door.

"Morning Mr. T, and what's going on with this Cooper fellow?"

Trefor got straight to the point. "He ferreted me out for some reason and was asking all sorts of questions about fish and so on, what the hell do I know about it, relics and the like. Then he started on about Parks and the transfer. Even asked me which tribe you were a member of, Mr. Newman. I told him, in all honesty, look you here I haven't a clue. Tribe? What's going on?"

As Newman gave him the short version, Trefor became increasingly alarmed.

"Good grief, are you suggesting there's a shred of truth among all that for him to base his story on? Is that what you're saying?"

"I'll just say this," said Newman, "Fargo once pointed out to me, in so many words, that the truth in these kinds of situation is the jetsam that gets washed up on the shore of a lakeful of fact flotsam. Plausible truth jetsam."

"That's brilliant, Newman. Now do Fred," said Steve.

"I mean it's pointless worrying the details, what's more of a concern is that he's already got a story to tell and he's just looking to anchor it here and there in little bits and pieces, true or false. You know how these stories are. Could lead to a bunch more reporters following up on details of his story. Could go on and on."

Trefor sought clarification. "So you're saying that we should behave as though the truth were irrelevant?"

"Pretty much," said Newman, "we should press on, be as unhelpful as possible, only tell him stuff he might want to hear that's impossible to verify, and rely on the fact that he's going it alone. We can encourage his fantasies and give him all sorts of blind alleys to get stuck up. I mean he can't bring in the heavy guns because he doesn't have any — doesn't want any chance of being scooped. So he needs to get all his ducks in a row to make his story compelling; our job is to keep 'em scattered."

"Wait — Newman. He questioned whether you are in fact descended from the tribe. Are you saying there's even a hint of an issue there? Because if you're not, then we've already broken the contract with Parks. And if that's broken, your job may be in question. Have you thought about that?"

"Would that that were the extent and the end of it, Trefor. Tell you what I'll deal with that if and when it becomes an issue."

Steve said, "Burn that bridge when you come to it, eh Newman?"

Doris was less inclined to find anything amusing in the situation. "Thing is, Trefor, all our jobs are on the line. At this point we are all in with the Ziegler money. That is dependent on the agreement with Parks. And that is dependent on Newman's truth jetsam, right Newman?"

"In a nutshell, yes."

"So I'm thinking we should perhaps do something more than just try to confuse the issue. That's Fargo's specialty, anyway. No. We should be more decisive. How do we turn the tables on Cooper and go after him and his story?

Get the jump on the whole thing and make his scoop a nonstarter?"

They fell silent for a moment. Newman was looking at the floor and shaking his head. Steve glanced eagerly from one to another like a quizmaster looking for the first to come up with the right answer. Trefor was the first to speak.

"Look here, I'm going to proceed along the lines of ignorance being bliss, just for the moment. Nevertheless I agree with Doris; rather than stonewall him, we should look for ways his story could fail before he gets it started. So, there's the sensitivity around the Coldwaters. I mean the story so far has a whole lot invested in the cultural stuff, the history, the relationship with the government and so on. Mr. Newman made a great deal of that — very successfully, I may say."

"Why thank you Trefor. I see what you mean — characterize his investigations as an attempt to undermine the sovereignty of the nation? I'm sure we could get Fred behind that."

"Then there's the ecological angle." Trefor was on a roll. "We start building up the benefits brought to the resort since the Coldwaters took over, and since the latest investments started kicking in."

"You mean the new toilets?" said Steve.

"The toilets are a definite improvement, I grant you, but I was thinking more of how we might leverage Ziegler's ecological spin — they've put a lot of effort into that as part of their pitch, and we can suggest Mr. Black has his own anti-ecological, earth-killing agenda in trying to destroy all that they plan to achieve on behalf of the planet." Trefor paused and looked at Newman. "Too much?"

"No," said Newman, "sounds great, couldn't have done better myself. The man is clearly a menace. I should add, there's also the disgruntled partner angle. Not on the same scale as Trefor's eco-political strategy, but nonetheless a significant thorn in Cooper's side, perhaps. I looked him up and it turns out he has a former partner at the newspaper who he thinks cheated him out of a major story they'd worked on together."

"Where d'you get that?" said Steve.

"Well that former partner also did the feature story on the fish for us years ago — remember that? Sitka Small, at the Observer. Gave her a call to see if she knew anything about this guy, and she said she used to work with him. Apparently he tried to muscle in on a big story of hers, she couldn't shake him off. She says he went so far as to have a root canal just to get in on the deal — not sure what that was all about. Anyway he went crazy when he couldn't get any credit for it. She says, confidentially of course, he was in therapy for a while over that and since then he either can't work with anyone, or more likely can't find anyone prepared to work with him."

Steve was still puzzled. "OK so we already knew he was ambitious. How does this help?"

"Oh just a little leverage maybe to get him to play nicely. We can at least threaten to work directly with Sitka to scoop him. Can you imagine — scooped for the second time by his ex partner. My pitch to Cooper is that I have all the material she would need, ready at hand, just in case we decide he's not working with us well enough to come up with something that benefits us all."

It took a while for this last strategy to sink in with

the others.

"Last resort of course. But maybe, with everything else, enough to get him to back off. Or jump in the lake."

In the lull that followed, Robert finished reading his paper, shook it, folded it, and got up to leave.

"Doris. Gentlemen," he said as he strode out of the lodge.

"There's Robert," Trefor said. "Wouldn't be fun for him to lose his property department and go back to being the handyman. And what would Dave have to talk about? He'd probably be reassigned to trails or facilities. Cooper could end up snagging all sorts if his net's broad enough, and I can't see him throwing any of us back."

Robert would say he wasn't one for gossip, you understand, but it's always important to stay informed. A man shouldn't make his way through life not knowing the ins and outs of what's going on around him. And it was according to this general principle that he had taken careful note of what was said in reception regarding that reporter's visit. Who knows what the man was really up to or what was to be done about it; he was clearly up to nothing good for the lake.

And Robert had come to regard the lake as more than just a workplace. He'd lived and worked there for longer than he had anywhere else, so it was also more than just home to him. In fact years ago he had been chatting to one of the many visitors he met who claimed Scottish heritage. This one was also a genealogy enthusiast. It hadn't taken them long on their computer to find Robert's probable ancestral home in the Scottish Highlands, and subsequent detective work by Robert (with considerable help from a "cannie wean" from among the contingent staff) had led him to pictures of the highlands above Inverness. It was a strikingly familiar place to him; a glacial landscape with a huge lake extending hundreds and hundreds of feet below sea level, rivers carved into ancient fault lines leading down the rugged coast a few miles below. That was his old country, where the McAlisters strode through the hills, raised their sheep, fished their lake, and tended their crofts; the parallels with his current home he found unavoidable. And that was why he increasingly of late felt like he belonged here. Working and maintaining this little settlement by the lake, he felt a particular affinity for the place. A sense not only of belonging, but also something like ownership. He saw visitors come and go each year, busy people taking a break from their routine to enjoy for a moment the very fact that this place wasn't where they belonged, and for that very reason was a source of temporary respite. Robert thought of them not so much with condescension, but with a benign resignation; he would sometimes scan the throngs on and around the lake and sigh. They work hard and make plans, they struggle among themselves so that one day they might enjoy the more complete, more rewarding life he was able to live every single day.

Robert bore all this in mind as he approached Cooper, who was seated at a picnic table by the dock, computer, phone, and related paraphernalia spread out before him.

"Mr. Black, isn't it?" Robert said. "Robert McAlister, Property."

"Property, eh?" said Cooper. "Property. What belongs where and to whom. Maybe you're the man to help me figure out what's what around here."

"How might that be, Mr. Black?" Robert opened up the boathouse and prepared to haul a boat toward the water.

"Oh come on, Mr. McAlister. I'm sure you're a straightforward man. You must get tired of the lack of straight talk around here. I know I'm already sick of the runaround."

"Robert, please. Mr. Mcalister would be my father. Or maybe his father. It sounds like you're having a bad day, Mr. Black."

"Well I am, but I'm sure Newman and Fred will do their best to make tomorrow even worse. How do you put up with all this, Robert? Do you just ignore all the goings on and hope for the best?"

"I'm not sure of your meaning, but I do have a generally optimistic frame of mind, I can tell you that. Maybe it's the fresh air, the place, or maybe it's the people, but I don't so much hope for the best as plan on it you know."

Cooper slapped his forehead in a demonstration of his exasperation. "Well I'm planning on more frustration tomorrow when I meet again with that woman from the tribe."

"That woman being Fred Jesperson, the president? Now she's brought many good things to the lake, that's for certain. I can certainly speak to that. Oh yes."

Robert pulled the boat to the water's edge.

"That's my point, Robert. Where do you think it all comes from? The fish. The new museum. The never-ending upgrades to what I've seen described online as 'a health-hazard run by graceless misfits that's an embarrassment to the lake.' And why the Ziegler interest?"

"The brand new toilets?" Robert took a pair of oars

that were lying in the boat and returned them to the boathouse.

"Yes the damn' toilets too. Where oh where does it all come from Robert? Does Fargo spirit it out of thin air? Newman evolve it all, along with those extra special fish? What shall I say about it?"

"Well that's a bit rich if I may say, you being a writer Mr. Cooper. Asking me, a former maintenance man and now property manager, what you should write. But since you ask, here's my advice to you. I would say, spend some time here before you rush to write anything. Fish, hike, boat — whatever you like, but get to know the place a bit before you rush to judgment. Always best I'd say to get first-hand experience rather than depending on what others have to say, don't you think?"

Robert saw Cooper scan the lake and take a deep breath. He could see from Cooper's frustration that he probably didn't have a story he could publish without getting something definitive from someone in the know. Otherwise, it would just be a more or less interesting work of fiction with a nice location. Well good luck with that, Mr. Black, as far as Fred or Fargo were concerned. And from what he'd overheard, Cooper was swimming against the current trying to get anything from anyone here at the lake. Sounded to Robert like he'd be branded a desperate earth-killing business-hater, bent on libeling the indigenous people and destroying a popular vacation spot. On the other hand, there was a lot at stake to risk any sort of deeper investigations. Those insurance policies described by Trefor and Newman were no guarantee that something wouldn't get started that might one day end in disaster. And living under that shadow would not be fun for anyone.

Robert picked up the fuel tank in the boat and sloshed it around a little before replacing it. He locked the boathouse door, and returned to sit on the other side of the picnic table, facing away from Cooper and looking toward the lake. "Mr. Black — I hate to see you struggling. If you don't mind my saying, you may be looking in the wrong place for your story. Or at least, on the wrong side of the lake if you need to get some inside information, that is."

And with that Robert smiled, turned, and strode back up the path toward the lodge with a backhand wave as he went.

"Fred. It's Newman. Seen Cooper?"

"No. Fargo and I managed to upset him, he said he'd be back, I guessed he'd be back here yesterday but he never showed up. Assumed he was up there harassing you about the fish at the very least."

"Right. Let me know then."

Newman hung up and asked Doris to have housekeeping check Cooper's cabin. "Maybe he's done a runner. Dare we hope?"

"Doubt it. He seemed frustrated but confident last time I saw him."

Newman headed over to Trefor's office.

"Trefor — Cooper been giving you any grief lately?"

"Not seen him thank god. Not sure I'd be any match for a professional interviewer, mind. Who knows what beans I might spill."

Of course, the bar. Cooper liked his whisky chasers. Newman called in at the Rainbow Bar but everyone was pretty sure they hadn't seen any shady looking character with a laptop bag skulking around lately.

He called the Discovery across the lake — that was something he hadn't considered before. Maybe Cooper had decided to cast his net a little wider; but no. No sign.

Newman rolled up at the Bay for a one on one with Fred.

"I can't think what he's up to, Fred. He seemed in such a hurry and now he's gone quiet. Still around though as far as I can tell — his stuff's still up there even though he was due to check out yesterday."

"Spontaneous combustion?" said Fred. "Look for a smoking pair of boots. That or the rapture maybe. I'm sure Fargo may have some suggestions, too."

"You of all of us I thought would take this seriously, Fred."

"Little bastard I'm just glad he didn't show up back here as he said he would. I was about ready to call out the ancestors."

"I dunno, Fred. I'm thinking more along the lines of that scene in Jurassic Park where the toothy lizard disappears then whips in sideways from nowhere and causes havoc."

"Oh that's good Newman — let's hope he's extinct, too. Look, I can see you're rattled by this but how likely is it he would come up with anything in a week's time? By then, we'll have settled everything with Ziegler and it'll be more likely he'll drop it."

"Right."

"What do we have. On the one hand, a half-baked conspiracy theory concocted by a demonstrably paranoid loner with no hard evidence to back it up. And on the other, very shortly at least, a global corporation to share our vested interest in closing him down. Plus, for the moment, it looks like he's disappeared. Maybe he's holed up somewhere with his little laptop, desperately making stuff up."

"OK. That's helping," said Newman, "I can work with that. And when he does show up, maybe we can string him along a little until the legal stuff with Ziegler is all done. Besides, Dave got on my case yesterday, confirming your concerns, complaining about declining numbers of fish and what could possibly be the reason. Fish out, Ziegler in, would suit me."

A partially reassured Newman returned to the lodge, sat by the window, and ordered coffee and pastry. He deserved it, he thought, after a tough morning's detective work. He sipped, nibbled, and people-watched. It was a combination he always found helpful when trying to wind down a little. People came into the lodge, browsed the information on the 'Things to Do' rack, stared out of the windows, considered the dinner menus, interrupted Doris, and generally took in the relaxing atmosphere. As he swept up the remaining crumbs of his blueberry scone, he recognized Robert's hushed yet distinct highland burr at the reception desk. "Enough rope, so to speak, Doris, enough rrrrope."

Newman got up and walked across to join them.

"Robert — how are things?"

"Ah, Mr. Newman. Doris here was asking me if I'd seen that Mr. Black fellow. Last time I saw him he seemed to be feeling me out, so to speak. Well I'm a generally cautious man, and I dare say a little suspicious of newspaper people, especially the ones who are up from the city."

"Oh — when was this? Was he looking for a story?"

"Couple of days ago, down by the boat shed. Always looking for a story I'm sure, and he seemed particularly bent on coming up with something or other about the lake, or the Coldwaters, or whatever. I really didn't take to his tone, you know, and I thought it better not to leave him entirely to his own devices. Idle hands and so on. So I gave him something to chew on, some nonsense about a man he might find over the other side by the Discovery Cafe. Just across the lake there, I said, little place just up in the hills, lived here forever and knows everything. Generations, I said, generations on the lake — there's nothing he doesn't know. I must say, I began to believe it all myself before I was done." Robert clapped his hands together and grinned. "So! Let him chase up a story about that."

"I see. Enough rope not so much to hang himself, as get himself a little tied up, then."

"Indeed, that's my thinking. Told him he could drive round the east end of the lake, but a boat would be very much quicker — motorboat like the one I keep dragged up on the shore there would be my choice."

"Maybe that's it then — didn't look like much of a sailor, probably drove over there and got waylaid somehow. Maybe got lost. I checked and they haven't seen him."

"Aye, I expect so. Of course, I don't like to jump to any conclusions, but my boat went missing sometime after I left him. Could be some young whippersnappers larking about — wouldn't be the first time."

"The boat's missing?"

"Yes, but not for long I'd say. Wouldn't get far without fueling up. I checked and the tank was almost empty.

Plus I don't like the boats filling up with rainwater, so I leave out the plug. They'd have to remember to put that back in."

Newman was trying not to jump to conclusions himself, but from the look on Doris's face she was thinking along the same lines. Robert was apparently — no, on second thoughts determinedly oblivious to the implications of his story. They all stood contemplating for just a moment, then Doris broke the silence.

"What plug?"

"Oh it's basically a wee stopper that fits a hole in the bottom of the boat, you see, tucked away under the seat. A self-bailer, they call it. You pull it out, and as long as you're moving forward any water in the boat gets sucked out of the hole; when the boat's dry, why you stick the plug back in."

"And if you don't?"

"Oh you'd be just fine as long as you kept moving. Then again, if for any reason you stopped, well then the laws of hydraulics stop working in your favor and so, you know, the boat will fill up. Wet arse is often the first sign of your mistake."

Dave had asked Doris to set up a meeting with Newman. That in itself was an unusually formal event, Newman thought, as he headed up to his office for the rendezvous. Dave's habit was to head off Newman as he took his morning walk around the grounds, engage in predictably idle banter, then manufacture a supposedly spontaneous comment, request, or complaint. This time, thought Newman, he must have something in particular he wanted to say.

"Something I've noticed that we need to talk about, Newman," he said as he walked in through the open door.

"You know fish are few and far between lately. Now people are even starting to complain. Been getting worse for some time — started a while back when we decided the water was too warm in the shallows. Then I put it down to those louts in their ski boats with the blaring so-called music forcing the fish out and away from the shore. I even read it might be acid rain. Now I always like to keep tabs on who's pulled what out of there, and I haven't seen or heard of a catch for a good few weeks. My evening 'Ranger's explainers' are more like history lessons these days — nothing recent to talk about, and come dusk when I do the dramatic pause for everyone to watch for fish: nothing."

"I know Dave, if we can just push through til the end of the season maybe things will buck up next year. If all goes well we'll have Ziegler folks do a survey and find out what they have to work with, possibly farm a little, restock so we can rejuvenate your lectures. Something like that. In the meantime if there's a drop-off on visiting anglers the Ziegler money should more than make it up and we can just quietly drop the fish from our advertising until things change. You have the whole glacial landscape thing you do — visitors love that. I dunno Dave — I really don't have time to think about it. Right now I don't see there's a lot I can do."

Rather than take his cue to leave, Dave sat down. "It's not what you can do, Newman. It's what the heck is going on? There's nothing to explain it. Temperature's good, no toxic algae or anything, oxygen levels fine, and I see plenty of insect activity. The lake was suddenly teeming, again for no apparent reason, and it lasted for a good few years. Every square foot was alive. No problems catching 'em either. Then this last season they've been on an accelerating, downward spiral — getting bigger mind you — considerably bigger — but fewer and farther between. 'Course, the bigger they get the more they'll stay out in the deeps. Good for 'the one that got away' stories, but that's about all."

Newman was happy for the resort to move on from the fish. Diversification is always good, he thought. And though any liability associated with the fish would soon, and appropriately enough, be assumed by Ziegler, it would be ideal if Ziegler's investments in the place brought new reasons to sing its praises and a whole raft of new visitors with the potential for more disposable income than the anglers ever seemed to have.

With diversification in mind Newman had once instigated end of season waterside concerts in the hope of bringing in a smooth jazz crowd that would buy expensive wine, eat expensive menu items, and stay in otherwise empty premium accommodation. As it turned out, what few tickets he did sell brought as many watch-and-run busloads of picnic-hampered freeloaders as would pay at most half of his expenses. Complete disaster, and Fargo, who saw the event as competition for his casino ballroom, didn't take kindly to the decision made by the highschooler assigned the task of promoting it to call it *Smooth Indian Summer*. Poor kid had to endure a lecture from Fargo on xenonyms and a mercifully summarized version of his *Historical Error and the Casting of First American Nations* piece originally worked up for the transfer negotiations with Parks. (Fred said at the time that it may have been the threat of having Fargo present it that had swung the entire deal.)

But nevertheless, Dave had a point. It would be nice to know where the fish were, and get a more precise handle on where they were going. They may as Dave said be confined to the deep, darker, cooler waters of the central trench, but even if so it still wasn't clear when, where, and what they were eating. From what Geoff had said, it could be the wild west down there. Still it'd be Ziegler's issue soon enough, and until then no news was definitely the best option.

Meanwhile Dave was still talking.

". . . kayaker in the bar pretty shaken up, probably been drinking, pretty sure he saw something. Overgrown eels? Didn't know there were any, but the lake is big enough to hide 'em. Trolls, one Norwegian guy claimed. Mind you he'd definitely been drinking."

"Well well, do these trolls look anything like reporters from the Observer? Maybe the first of them's already arrived."

Dave said he just wanted to voice his concerns, give Newman the opportunity to offer his opinion in private, and then he took off down to his post to rehearse his excuses for why the fantastical fish he described would probably not make an appearance that evening.

Newman walked down to reception to find Doris.

"Seen Fred? No calls?"

"No. Nor Cooper. He must be spending his time down there working on her."

After having become sick of the sight of him, Newman was now a little unnerved by not knowing where Cooper might be. Nobody but Robert and Trefor here at the lake had spoken with him yet, to Newman's knowledge at least. Anyway, Doris would know for sure. He couldn't have got what he wanted and gone back to his paper. Could he? Worth checking in with Fred though. Good luck getting a quote from Fargo that the Observer readers could make sense of.

"It's been a couple of days since I saw Cooper — when's he due to check out?"

"Today."

"Alright."

Robert returned to his cabin that evening having spent the main part of the day "pushing a pen". As property manager, he had to conduct reviews with his team every three months, report on progress made, and put together a plan for the following three months. As of today Robert didn't technically have a team, just a single student helper during the busy season. That meant his other obligation, to conduct 360 degree team performance assessments, became more like 180 degree affairs. Nevertheless he took his obligations seriously and would spend an hour or so documenting in painstaking detail his achievements this period before turning to his intentions for the next.

He called in on the way to pick up his mail from reception.

Since becoming head of the property management division he'd signed up for all sorts of related promotions, catalogs, associations, and opportunities for professional advancement. As a result his mailbox would very often be packed with ultimately useless but nonetheless reassuringly instructive packets of all sorts. Who knew when an improved system for the installation of interlocking paving blocks might prove essential? How many times had he wished he had detailed information on the elimination of moisture incursion during the installation of replacement vinyl windows? And even if he would never join the Institute of Water Feature Architects, it was nice to be offered a pre-qualified invitation.

On this occasion he rifled through the bundle of envelopes and one item stood out, mainly because it was an air packet with a return address in Scotland. "MacDonald, Douglas and McIver, LLP. Edinburgh. Hmm. Lawyers. I hope they're not expecting any money from me. They can whistle for that," thought Robert as he carefully opened the envelope. Inside was a single, impressively embossed, headed page that opened with, "Regarding McAlister House and grounds on the shore of Loch Lomond." He read the page twice, and gathered that great grandfather's house, or the remains of it, with outbuildings and its impressive stretch of lakefront, had been gifted, with covenant, to the National Trust in Scotland many years ago. The gift was in return for the McAlisters being able to live there and work the place on behalf of the Trust, for as long as they were alive and able. Once the last resident McAlister had died, the covenant defined a period after which, if no further members of the clan came forward, the grounds and buildings would pass entirely to the Trust to do with as they wished. The firm had tracked down Robert as the last surviving family member, and were notifying him of the impending expiration of that covenant and the actions he must take if he wished to exercise his right to extend it.

Robert was by nature suspicious of officialese, and even more so of legalese. And he considered this to be both official and legal, in which case his best option would be to consult with Newman who, after all, had a proven track record in dealing with this kind of nonsense.

Robert went straight down to the Rainbow Bar where, as he expected, Newman was propping up the bar before dinner. Next to Newman was Steve, who seemed to be engaged in wild gesticulations, mimicking someone falling out of a boat it turned out, as Robert walked over to join them. "Easily done, Newman, easily done — in my own experience those boats of yours are not exactly stable, are they — only have to fart and you may be overboard. Oh, Robert! What you having?"

"Very kind. I think I'll have a dram, if I may. With a splash. And I have another favor to ask of you gentlemen. I've received a letter from Scotland. A first ever, would you believe, so I'd like help figuring out what it's all about."

Newman laughed as he took the envelope from Robert. "So it turns out they can take the Scot out of the man as well as the man out of Scotland, eh? You wouldn't be the first to fail to understand a Scot, Robert."

"Ah, very good Mr. Newman I'm sure. But I find lawyers are a challenge in any language. Since you and Steve here have some experience, I thought a second and third opinion would be wise."

Newman scanned the letter, then after a nod from Robert handed it to Steve. Steve looked at it with a deliberately serious frown.

"Geez Robert, you're doing a Fred here," said Steve. "You do realize you have an opportunity to declare rightful ownership of — what would it be — a bogful of shit and a hovel in the highlands?"

"Rightful ownership, you say?"

"I'd say the covenant is designed to give the McAlister clan the right to live there without paying upkeep, and pretty much do as they like with it. Though it looks like things have been let go a little. Let's see. When the last McAlister kicks the bucket, the National Trust is ready to take over. You should stake your claim!"

Robert sipped his single malt, and stood a little taller at the bar.

"I see, I see. Well I have to say, I spent some time a while ago tracing my ancestry back to the Trossachs, you know. The McAlisters lived and worked the lake; beautiful spot, beautiful spot by all accounts. This would hardly be a hovel and a bogful of shit, gentlemen."

"Really?" said Newman. "How hardly then? Don't tell me you're descended from Scottish aristocrats that had to sell the farm to pay the bills?"

Now Robert leaned back a little, held his glass close to his chest, bounced slightly on his toes and assumed the expression of one slightly amused by something said by a child.

"Close, Mr. Newman, close. The McAlisters were gifted the house, the outbuildings, and a good number of lakeside acres by the Montgomery-Scott-Dalrymples, in thanks for generations of service. Of course, they couldn't really afford the upkeep, so in that regard you have a point. I had no idea they'd done some deal or other with the National Trust, you see. And I wouldn't know what state the lodge is in by now. Big place mind you. You can see it on the Google earth — Doris's intern showed me a bird's eye view of the whole spread when we were tracking down the family tree. Amazing what you can see with that Google thing." Robert cast his eyes upward. "Probably watching us right now."

"How about another round?" said Steve. "On you,

Newman."

Newman bought more drinks, and they talked about technology that let you peer into your own backyard, aristocrats, castles, lakes and lodges, the costs of keeping any roof over your head let alone a crumbling early eighteenth century one in the Scottish highlands, and how unlikely it was for any government department here or over there to subsidize the maintenance. By the time they'd finished they'd had another round or two of drinks and almost forgotten where they'd started, until Robert said "So what do you think I should do?"

"About what now?" Steve said.

"Well I feel the weight of responsibility for being the last of the McAlisters. And since someone's gone to the trouble of tracking me down all the way from the Trossachs, I should at least do him the courtesy of a response don't you think?"

"Oh yes, the National Trust, family seat and all that. What do you think, Newman? I'll have another, by the way."

"Sit tight Robert. Let's take a closer look at your options. It may not be quite so cut and dried, you know? Might not need to just hand it over to the Trust, and you might not need to jump across the pond in order to hang on to it. Maybe Steve and I still have a contact or two in Ziegler's international law department who can look into it for us, eh?"

"Thank you both, it's a weight off I must say. Hold on to the letter will you. I don't like being in any way beholden to a lawyer, and I don't want to sign up for anything that might bankrupt me, you understand. And I don't know how I could manage the property here all the way from Scotland. A miserable commute, eh. Haha — well, good night and thanks again gentlemen — I regard you all here as family, I must say, and I appreciate your helping me out with this. And now I should take my leave, I must retire to my stately cabin while I'm still capable of finding it."

When Robert had left, Steve and Newman spoke about potential candidates in Ziegler legal who might be able to help. Neither Donoghue nor Stevenson, despite their names, would likely know anything useful about Scottish property law. They reminisced about the number of times they'd been told either "that's not within my field, of course", or "well it all depends, you know."

"But there was an international property lawyer who helped with the location scouting," said Newman. "Name of MacLeod, as it happens. That certainly sounds well qualified, and I do recall him rattling on about the implications of Scottish independence that time at the July fourth picnic. Liked his single malt too, I remember — his favorite from the lunch menu he called it."

Newman and Steve spent a little longer exercising their joint ignorance of European geography, debating the differences between lakes in Scotland, England, Italy, Switzerland and — were there even any in Wales? Trefor would know. They proposed differences between tribes and clans, and they even made some less than polite proposals as to how Robert might keep his clan alive with future progeny, given the resources available to him in the wilds of Loch Lomond. It was at that point that Newman called it a night.

"Right, night Newman," said Steve. "I'll get Geoff to have a word with MacLeod if he's still around. Buy him his lunch, pick his brains while he's drinking it."

*＊＊

MacLeod was indeed still around and was happy to give Geoff his off-the-record opinion on "the McAlister case". He went so far as to express more than passing interest in a trip over to the highlands for any hands-on work that may be required. He and Geoff were ensconced in the Pig and Whistle, Geoff enjoying a sandwich and a pint, MacLeod choosing a double whisky washed down with a double whisky (because during a busy lunchtime you never knew when you'd be able to get the bartender's attention.)

MacLeod had been a Queens Counselor back in Scotland, wig and all, representing corporate property interests in all sorts of international wranglings, and had joined Ziegler in later years in exchange for less stress, a massive salary, and the promise of a handsome golden parachute. By now he'd worked at U.S. corporate for some four or five years, having originally come over for just a quick trip to sort out some arcane European legal issue. The landscape, the weather, and the thriving micro distillery industry of the North West he said suited him.

Geoff wasn't too invested in the whole process, he was just doing it as a favor for Steve, really. It may have been that, the subject matter, possibly the beer, and maybe even MacLeod's accent which Geoff struggled, for a while, to decode, but he couldn't avoid tuning out as MacLeod spoke. The relaxed nature of his current position as Legal's head of globalization was reflected in the languid rhythms of his speech, which were almost the precise opposite of the technical fire-hosing Geoff generally underwent from engineers. MacLeod had a tendency to offer few opportunities for interlocutors to contribute to the conversation. In fact he didn't converse. He constructed a legal opinion in real time, verbalizing slowly enough to allow him to formulate quite eloquent phrases, with enough complexity in those phrases that the natural features of the language signaling conclusion, pause, or hesitation were almost entirely obscured. Even as he took a sip of his lunch, where you'd expect someone else might be able to get a word or two in, MacLeod would murmur a preceding "hmmmm", a "notwithstanding", or a "don't forget" that would preclude any interruption.

As a result of that and the second half of a third IPA, Geoff felt his attention span shorten and was caught staring, almost mesmerized, at the carpet when he suddenly noticed MacLeod had stopped. Geoff wiped a tiny amount of drool from the corner of his mouth with a napkin.

"Mmm well that is very interesting, and thank you for your thoughts," he said. "Now I'm going to need to relay the gist to Mr. McAlister who confesses to never having been involved in anything of a legal nature. He'll need a very boiled-down version and I'm uncertain about doing that myself in case I misinterpret something of what you've said. Wouldn't want to unintentionally mislead the man. Could you, perhaps, in a few words, summarize the gist for me?"

"You weren't listening, Geoffrey."

"Well I got a little distracted, Mr. Macleod. I think it's the heat in here maybe."

"Aah well that's alright, I get that all the time these days. Good job I was listening. I always need to listen to myself anyway, see if I'm making any sense. Tell you what: he needs to file some paperwork that'll give him more time to decide what he plans to do. Entirely reasonable. After all this time the National Trust will hold off and he could have another year or more to decide if he wants it. He'll have no taxes or other expenses in the meantime. 'Course, from what you've said, the place will continue to dilapidate and decay and in these cases there's no obligation on the Trust to do anything about that. No legal recourse for decrepitude — otherwise I'd have taken it myself years ago. What?"

"Very good, very good. And what about liability, and any potential revenue from the place?"

"The Trust assumes all that. If he does eventually decide to hang on to it, then he has the option to organize it in several ways — he can simply manage the place on their behalf, or they keep the land, he owns the buildings, revenue sharing, or he could potentially rescind the entire deal and take everything back — for a lump sum payment of some sort to cover their existing liabilities and so on and so forth. Which expense could also be mortgaged on the property. Maybe I should help him with all that — pop over there, take room in his lodge, sample the local distilleries — what do you think? Pro bono plus travel expenses?"

"I'll certainly mention that to Mr. McAlister — very generous of you, I'm sure Mr. MacLeod. And thanks for your help so far."

"Pleasure."

Geoff wasn't off the hook quite so easily, MacLeod taking full advantage of the opportunity for a substantial lunch in the style of what he called "the good old days", meaning days before it was frowned upon to return to court "three sheets to the wind." As a result it didn't end up being a late lunch so much as an early night for Geoff by the time he had cajoled MacLeod into a taxi and returned home.

It was the following evening when Geoff got back to the Lake and was able to report MacLeod's opinion to Robert, Newman, and Steve over dinner.

Robert confessed to a newfound fondness for the old country, now these new roots had been discovered for his largely overlooked family tree. He had assumed that all ties and certainly any property would have been long gone; he thought his only remaining connection was his expired British passport, in which his place of birth was proudly proclaimed as Argyll, Scotland.

"You'll have to renew that thing for starters, Robert," Steve said, "you can't be a damn' Laird on a visitors' visa."

Robert wondered what he might find in the buildings where his family had lived for generations. There might be photographs; diaries, maybe. Keepsakes abandoned, around which he could start to construct something about how his folks had lived.

Newman, too, seemed to take it all a little more seriously than was usual when Steve was around. "What do you think you'll do Robert? Surely worth a visit, if nothing else? It's an inheritance, after all, and from what Geoff says it comes with no liability, no strings; if you like it, you have plenty of options. If don't like it, you can hand it to the Trust. In any case, you'll surely learn something. Be a great experience."

"I don't know, I have a pretty good life here at the Lake, you know. And I'd be away for a couple of weeks maybe; what would they do? I'll have even more responsibilities any time now what with all the new development work. And as property manager, it's my professional opinion that the buildings over there are in an even worse state than this place was before you took it on."

After some research and close inspection of all the information that the internet could provide, it had become clear to Robert that there was quite a spread up there on the lake shore. A twenty or so bedroom house, a huge stone barn, boathouse, stone outbuildings and storage all slowly decaying but with plenty of historical interest and national as well as local heritage.

"Could be a goldmine though," was Steve's assessment. "Once you've fixed it up a bit of course. I could see it as an easy sell for the likes of Newman here. How would you deal with it, Newman? How would you turn a collection of lakeside bog-hovels — no offense, Robert — into a high-flying, highland flinging destination?"

"Oh I'd look at every angle. Hunting, shooting, and fishing of course. Build a banquet hall, plenty of accommodation. Luxury rooms, finest dining — pull in a Michelin chef. Historical tours, lake stuff, hiking. Weddings. Off-sites. Retreats. Hype up the Scottish stuff in general — no offense again, Robert — clans and things. Heritage. History. Hmm. Maybe get a consult from Fred on that. Work up some stories about the place, dig up a few characters who used to live there."

"Dig stuff up, eh?" said Steve. "Maybe get a consult from Fargo, too, d'you think?"

Robert was warming to the idea. "You know the Loch is famous for its trout, there would be plenty of visitors for the fishing. And there's talk of the Lomond monster, though that would be nothing compared to its Loch Ness cousin. But maybe Mr. Newman could make something of it? Oh and we do have a connection with King Arthur that may be worth something; he's claimed to be a Scot you know. And anything to piss off the Sassenachs."

"Good god you're off and running," said Steve, "somebody hold him back."

"Aye but don't forget, one way or another granddad McAlister might've left me the place, but that's why he put it in trust — he didn't have the cash required for the upkeep. It would take a fortune to fix it up for what we're talking about, Mr. Newman."

"A fortune but perhaps at most a small fortune, Robert."

Geoff relayed MacLeod's advice to file paperwork to register his interest and gain time to decide what's best. He also told him MacLeod was very keen to visit and provide on-site advice for dealing with the Trust. Robert said he was getting no younger, and would have to make a decision soon enough.

Newman and Steve would revisit what Steve called "the Scottish play" over dinner, Steve making great sport of a property manager inheriting property for which he might have to hire a manager. He even, shamefully enough, attempted a Scottish accent at one point but on Newman's advice swore he wouldn't ever try that again. He wondered if there might be oil; that part of Scotland was famous for it. Or was that under the sea. Maybe there was a bog — what was the current market price for peat? Anyway, he suggested, if Newman could turn out to be a member of the tribe, maybe Robert could be a member of the damn' royal family. As his suggestions became increasingly far-fetched, Newman only stopped him when Steve thought the Lomond monster might be developed as a viable competitor to Nessie — they might even propose that Nessie had moved home and was under new ownership at the McAlister resort. "Any connections among the lakes over there? Could we claim she had migrated, do you think? I mean, how the hell would the people at Loch Ness prove Robert's invisible monster was originally their invisible monster anyway?"

"Let me stop you there," Newman said, "I don't think I would advise him to mess with the contents of the lake, that never gets anyone anywhere. There'll be no Ziegler to join in, and the only tribe who could help him out would be the clan McAlister, of which it looks like Robert's the last remaining McOne."

"Agreed. But you know, he just needs something to jumpstart the place and it could be a nice little earner. From the sound of it a lovely place to live. Remember the conference we went to — that was North of Glasgow, wasn't it? Round there somewhere — lovely. And I do remember you delivering your paper with one hell of a thick head after a night sampling the local distillates."

They reminisced some more, tossed around a mix of viable and ludicrous ideas, and each reached broad conclusions on what he would do, were he Robert.

Newman did his best to look attentive as the Ziegler contingent were making their final presentations before signing the lease, while he stared over their heads, through the window of his office, and across the sparkling blue lake. After all the planning and preparations, the actual signing was a tedious affair during which everyone was expected to say a few words to congratulate everyone else and confirm the great job everyone had done. Right now Geoff was talking about something or other to do with mutual endeavor for the betterment of all, and Newman could only think about how confident he seemed, compared to not so long ago when he was Steve's lab geek poking around with dead fish.

So the implication of that clear, calm, silent scene outside in which Dave cut an almost filmic figure standing at the wheel of his craft, towing a partially submerged boat across the lake and towards the dock didn't immediately register. By the time it did, Newman had become sufficiently numbed by Geoff's presentation that his exclamation of "Oooohhh...crap" unintentionally came out aloud.

"Mr. Newman?" said Geoff.

"Oh, sorry, sorry. Excuse me — I just remembered an engagement I forgot to cancel. If you'll excuse me for a moment, please do carry on."

Newman left the meeting and tried to walk, not run, down to the dock where Robert was already standing watching Dave's approach.

"Robert!"

"Mr. Newman."

Dave tied up his boat, then walked his waterlogged catch up the dock before he and Robert lugged it up onto the beach.

"Found it among the weeds in the shallows down at the South end. One of yours, I assume? You really need to keep better tabs on your boats, Robert, I don't want to have to speak with you about pollution. Bad enough you have these old two-strokes buzzing around the place as it is. Lucky there seems to have been no fuel spill from this one, but still — hell to pay from Fargo if he finds out."

Robert smiled and thanked Dave for his efforts.

Newman took Robert aside.

"This is it then, is it? This is the boat — the one you lost last week? The one that was last seen sitting there while you spun Cooper the yarn about the Oracle across the lake at the Discovery?"

Robert made a point of looking the boat up and down carefully. "I believe it is, yes."

"Crap. The one whose drainage bung thing you had in your pocket?"

"Oh yes, that's right now I think of it. These things happen, you know. Bit of wash from a ski boat might come ashore and sweep one of these out into the wind and it's gone. And if it's taking on water, once it's down low like that it'd be hard to spot from the shore."

Robert looked at Newman and shrugged. "Well he's right, I should keep better tabs on them. Maybe leave the plugs in."

Newman returned to his office where Fred had by now cracked the champagne and everyone was standing around chatting convivially. Copies of freshly autographed documents, neatly stacked on the table, indicated that agreement had been robust enough to withstand even Fargo's *Historical Error* presentation (which, for the sake of brevity, Fred had distributed in hardcopy while Fargo gave a ten minute overview.) The Ziegler people were ready to take a trip around the lake, hosted by Geoff and piloted by Dave, for the management and legal crew to review in person what they'd just signed up for.

Newman asked Fred for a word.

"Fred — about Cooper. There are a few circumstances you should be aware of."

"Didn't see him after he said something about never leaving til he got his story. So he's still here? Or did he get his story? Not too fussed either way at this point, Newman."

"I'm thinking maybe the former. His car's still here, stuff's in his cabin, we've heard hide nor hair, and now we think he may have taken a boat out to cross the lake and not come back."

"He rented a boat? Didn't look like a sailor to me, I must say."

"Strictly speaking it looks like he stole a boat, which is good. Turns out the boat wasn't exactly seaworthy — Dave just found it half sunk in the shallows, far side."

"Oh dear. Have you called anyone?"

Newman thought for a moment. "I think I'll tell Dave the guy may be missing, and we think he may have taken that boat. Dave doesn't know anything about anything, so he's the best person to deal with it."

"Well it looks like our Mr. Black may have come up with a way to both stick around and come up with a great story. Let's hope he's still capable of writing it. But they'll need to find him, one way or another. You never know, he may even be hanging out somewhere watching us to see what we do. This whole thing may be a story in progress, Newman."

Newman hadn't thought of that — maybe when he accused Cooper of making up his story he wasn't too far off. What was it he'd said? He was a creator as much as anything else. Yes, maybe Cooper was one step ahead, testing the waters to see how they would all react, then he could plan his next move accordingly. Newman decided to react as anyone might given the circumstances.

"I'll call Dave."

Dave, in turn, had done what he might have been expected to do and called the police. He pointed out that there hadn't been any sort of incident like this since 1941 when a young couple had robbed a bank and crashed off the highway, drowned while attempting to outrun the police. And now, as then, there were police all over the place scooting around the lake, asking questions and combing the shoreline. But this time they were looking for a missing guest who stole a boat and, either before or after it began to sink, parted ways with it.

"That's about the thick and the thin of it," said Inspector Pilchard, after introducing himself to Geoff. "Pilchard, George. Inspector, Coldwater Bay police. Here to find your missing boater."

Pilchard had a habit of introducing himself backwards, as though from the index of a book. In his view this had two main advantages; it sounded suitably professional, and the Inspector part served to help wipe the smile engendered by the Pilchard part from any nearby faces. Other way round, he'd explained more than once before, and the Pilchard part hangs in the air — or flaps on the deck — with nothing to temper its comic potential.

It was particularly challenging for Geoff to overlook his name, because he'd just been thinking about fish. And he was in a particularly lighthearted mood when the Inspector called.

Regarding the fish, Geoff had found no evidence that the transgenic mutations among the fish at Glacial Lake had extended beyond their color. Granted, there had been some trophy sizes caught a while back, but they might well be anomalies and now things had quietened down. If anything, the fish appeared to have been sterile, and they were dying out as they should. He looked forward to the lake presenting a blank slate for the next round of experiments, which he would oversee from his offices in the planned executive briefing center. So now, as the Inspector announced himself, Geoff couldn't avoid thinking that a Pilchard was the most unlikely thing yet to show up at the lake.

"People think Pilchards are fish, don't they. I wonder if they would find it so amusing if I were to inform them that there is no such fish? Pilchard's the way they're packaged, you see, not the fish." Pilchard raised a forefinger by way of punctuation, before adding "Sardine similar."

Pilchard waited for that to sink in. Geoff thought better of seeking clarification. The Inspector continued.

"So Pilchard is a police inspector, and there's an end to it." Pilchard maintained a broad, fixed smile. "And here we are, dealing with your absent boating journalist. It's not so much that he went missing, as it is where he went missing." Pilchard was in the habit of asking questions in the form of statements, such that it sounded like he was disclosing an observation or reaching a conclusion when he was in fact looking for an answer.

"He may never have been on the boat. He may have gone down with the boat. He may have jumped off the boat and back onto the shore, leaving the boat to drift off, you see. He may have swam for it. Swam for it. Let's think about that for a moment. Officer!" he called to his assistant, "Officer, is it swam? Doesn't sound right."

"Think so sir. Or swum."

"Oh no, not swum. I don't think our man swum, whatever else he did. Anyway, he may have left the boat in a determined manner under his own steam, and ended up who knows where. From what our ranger said, the where in question may be largely unrelated to the final location of the boat, which would be subject to wind, currents and so on. Do you see?"

"Yes, sounds awful," said Geoff.

"Well possibly, possibly, but of course we don't know that yet, that's one thing we can be sure of. The officer here will tell you — one thing we can be sure of is that we never know absolutely everything, so knowing the importance of what we don't know can be very important information. Something like that — long time since officer training for me. Anyway, all that aside for now, you just moved in here to, ah, to what, to oversee things?"

"My company, Ziegler Genetics, has just leased the lake to develop and farm fish here, and to build a sort of center with various educational and business facilities. All in concert with the local tribes. This resort is a part of their reservation."

"Fish, eh? In the lake? Makes sense of course, even to a humble policeman. Mind you, we have another potential occupant of the lake to worry about now, don't we? I say — officer — may be something other than fish out there, eh?"

"Yes sir. I suppose it would depend on how well he might have swum, sir."

"Uh-oh — going for a promotion, that one!" said Inspector Pilchard, with a sideways wink to Geoff. "You watch your grammar a little more closely and you might be destined for great things, son. But yes, of course, he may only have been a temporary occupant and may even as we speak be stumbling around somewhere in some uncertain condition. All the more reason to make haste in finding him. Now. Geoff. We've established that you've only just moved in, but you may be able to help me. The task at hand is to identify the one round here who would best know the ins and outs of the lake, who could tell me more about our lost boater perhaps, who can help me cut through the nonsense and get this thing sorted. Someone clued in, involved."

The fish were never far from his mind, and Geoff was still thinking about the ambivalence of "potential occupants" of the lake when he realized Pilchard had asked a question. "Oh that would be Mr. Newman, I'd say. He's operated the resort for a number of years, and was instrumental in the divestiture from the Parks Service, working with the tribal council. So he's pretty much at the center of things here."

"Thank you sir," said Pilchard, "I'm sorry this has come up in — what, your first week here? Well don't worry — we'll sort it out and be on our way soon enough. We'll sort it with Mr. Newman and be on our way, won't we officer?"

This time he didn't wait for an answer, he marched out of the door with the officer in tow. After a moment he ducked back in and looked at Geoff with a furrowed brow.

"Try the bar. This time of night, sitting at the end with a beer most likely," said Geoff.

"Thank you," said Pilchard.

Newman nursed a beer, deep in thought. His somewhat emotional, empathetic side may have cost him a good few rungs up the cutthroat corporate ladder in the past, and coming to terms with the current situation had required him to undergo a fair amount of self-analysis. In the end, he had decided that yes, of course he was disturbed by the potential loss of life on his lake. But he was comforted by the fact that no-one could reasonably hold him or any member of his staff responsible for it. He felt he'd played a relatively neutral role in Cooper's misadventure, and looking back on it he didn't see any way he could have prevented it other than giving Cooper everything he wanted on day one. Cooper had arrived unbidden, and he'd initiated a chain of events, almost a game of strategy in which it looked like he'd then made a poor move. As a result, things at the lake were more or less as they were before Cooper had shown up. No harm, no gain, no foul.

And anyway, with a bit of luck he'd shared his fate with his damn laptop along with any notes he'd been keeping on his story.

"Mr. Newman?"

Newman was jerked out of his comforting reverie.

"Oh Yes."

"Pilchard."

"I'm sorry?" Newman wasn't sure if he'd been misidentified, or insulted. He smiled momentarily, then looked like he might have taken mild offense.

"I see my reputation has in this case failed to precede me. George. Inspector. Coldwater Bay police. You, on the other hand, are already known to me."

Newman's offended look turned to one of surprise. Pilchard was suddenly amused, as he often was by a person's reaction when he announced himself, or more likely, his rank and profession.

"No no not in that sense of course! Ha ha — no no. No Mr. Newman, Geoff told me you were the hub around which all things revolve."

Pilchard often surprised himself with his own eloquence. From time to time, he would say something that, even to him, sounded particularly apropos. Apropos was another word that might just slip out, who knows where from, maybe from this morning's crossword. But out it might pop, surprising Pilchard as much as anyone with its — with its — what was the word. Apropriety? No that probably wasn't a word. Anyway, he'd end up smack bang to rights with a particularly apropos turn of phrase, bringing, he ventured to think, a heightened elegance and clarity to the conversation.

"It's true there's not much goes on around here that I'm not aware of. But I have to say, this thing with our Mr. Black has me looking for answers too. I hope we can sort it out, for his family's sake and for the good of the resort. Not helpful to have people going missing here like that, Mr ... "

"Indeed, indeed. Pilchard, by the way. George Pilchard. Inspector, and so on. Well anyway not much in the way of family that I can find. Seemed to be a bit of a one-off. He hadn't been here that long, I understand. Know anything more about him, Mr. Newman?"

"Well he did say he was a reporter from the *National Observer*, so when he seemed to have disappeared I did call his office and spoke to his colleague, who couldn't really help. Said nobody knew he was down here, actually."

"Sitka Small? Followed up with her. Some sort of rift by the sound of it, this Cooper Black a bit of a loner. Actually, bit of a loony more like. Now don't tell anyone I said that, specially not if he shows up. But I was beginning to wonder whether he might have, you know, committed suicide by unseaworthy boat, given his state of mind and so on."

This was one explanation even Newman hadn't considered. "Oh that's perfect. I mean, that would explain it, too. He did seem to take off a bit suddenly, if that was him with the boat."

"Spur of the moment thing. Happens, you know. We've searched his cabin of course, and his car. No sign of any note but we did find a Post-it on the floor, might've fallen off the wall or something. Officer — what exactly was it on that Post-it note you dug up?"

Pilchard's assistant had been silently standing more or less to attention alongside his Inspector. Now he pulled out a notebook and flipped a few pages. "'Starts and ends with the fish', sir."

"Starts and ends with the fish. There's a conundrum for us. Unless it's just a comment on your dinner menu, eh Mr. Newman!"

"Well we have had quite a few reporters up here to do stories on our fish, that's for sure. Been a feature here for a few years now."

"Hardly warrants a Post-it then. Maybe he had a memory issue. Certainly forgot his boat needed a bung from what I gather from your property manager. I'm told by the bartender he spent an evening in the bar with you the other night. Bartender mentioned he was no stranger to the demon drink. Notice that, Mr. Newman?"

"I'll admit he was drinking whisky chasers all night but I put that down to his profession rather than to an addiction."

Pilchard slapped his assistant on the shoulder by way of punctuating the close of their meeting. "Onward and upward — let's be off then officer. Mr. Newman here seems unable to make our jobs any easier for us. No rest for the wicked, so never a break for us, eh? We're off to speak with Fred Jesperson at the Bay, Mr. Newman. Due diligence and so on you know."

Geoff called to set up a meeting with the new "steering committee" at Ziegler who would be running the operation now the lease was in place. They asked that all invested parties be available, which meant Newman and Fred.

"Here we go then," Newman said as he and Fred prepared to leave for the meeting, which was taking place in the current Ziegler executive briefing center at corporate HQ. The center was planned to be relocated to a completely new, all glass, highest of tech affair at the lake, for which architectural renderings had already been prepared. It would occupy an elevated platform carved into a bluff, it would provide a watery blue reflection of its surroundings, and to Fargo it would be like a noxious smell, practically invisible but almost completely overwhelming.

"Here we go; it's begun," said Newman.

"What's begun?" Fred asked.

"Oh I know these corporate chicaneries. They want us up there to put us on the back foot. And there's likely a good reason they want us on the back foot. They have new information, a significant decision, something they need to tell us to our faces — so must be important I'd say. Probably the first of many, actually — corporate moves and changes, new brooms, about faces pretty much the norm. What do you think Fred — you're no stranger to the back-footing tactic yourself!"

"Thank you for that Newman, I'll take it as a

compliment. But I really can't say why this is all so important, so soon after I thought we'd wrapped everything up during the lease signing."

They announced their arrival at building 101 front desk, and the receptionist seemed to be expecting them. As they waited for their visitor badges to be printed, Newman noticed someone through the inner glass wall tap a colleague on the shoulder and gesture toward them. The other nodded, and they turned away in huddled conversation. Very soon Geoff burst through the door with outstretched hand, offered a brief but, from Newman's point of view, overly cheerful welcome, and ushered them upstairs to a huge meeting room containing a dozen or more people, Walker being the only one they recognized.

Walker lifted the fingers of one hand slightly toward Fred, who nodded back in his direction. They sat down, and were introduced to attendees with variously impenetrable titles from legal, facilities, development, public relations, and so on.

One of them, apparently the most senior, disclosed his fairly recent "onboarding" to the "lake project" by insisting on delivering an extemporary and to Newman, familiarly tedious monologue. First he bored his own people by reviewing established facts about Ziegler, then he turned to boring Newman and Fred by making facile and familiar observations about lakes and resorts. After twenty minutes that seemed like an hour or more, almost everyone round the table was in a state of near torpor.

Geoff thanked him with an unjustified enthusiasm that Newman thought was probably due to him being Geoff's boss, and not, more reasonably, due to his having stopped talking. Then Geoff, and all eyes around the table, turned to Newman and Fred.

"OK, now I think we can all see why Glacial Lake is such a good fit for Ziegler's future direction. On the technical side we are investing heavily in food research, and on the political side we are making a big push to swing GMO toward the positive. The lake serves both of these ends, and during the term of our lease we expect to make it a showcase for Ziegler as a technical, economic, and cultural powerhouse. If you don't mind, Mr. Newman, I borrowed a phrase from one of your presentations, I think it was to the government genetic science watchdog a good few years back: 'the development of health and wealth go hand in hand at Ziegler.'"

Newman recognized the tactic; draw your opponent in by using his own words to flesh out your own position. He glanced at Fred, who was looking down at the table.

"But of course, as you know, and as has been said, advantage in this industry relies upon discretion," Geoff nods toward his boss, who smiles knowingly, "and there will be a need to maintain vigilance with regards to the security surrounding our work at the lake. We are all familiar with the need to protect patentability by preventing our intellectual property from escaping into the, err, into the wild." Now a slight nod toward Newman.

Newman couldn't wait any longer, and was surprised that Fred didn't seem more eager to move things along. "Excuse me, Geoff — can I just ask — where is this going? I'm not sure at this point why we're here, or what your pitch has to do with the resort."

"Ah. Sorry. I guess I was just trying to outline the

path that led us to our decision, specifically regarding the resort option at Glacial Lake."

"The 'resort option'?" Newman looked at Fred, who was looking at Geoff.

"Yes, meaning that side of the lake operation as described in the lease that involves largely seasonal visitors. Management has reviewed the situation, and feels that it is in the best interest of satisfying the requirements of the lease, vis-a-vis supporting Ziegler's corporate development and providing a stable revenue stream for the Coldwater Nation, to de-emphasize the resort side of the operation."

Newman was already ahead of him as Geoff's boss seized the opportunity to make his presence felt at a point where he was capable of making a contribution.

"If I may, Geoff. You see, Mr. Newman, Ms. Jesperson, we have done a 360 evaluation and have decided to shut down the resort in favor of a closed campus for the duration. I mean, to put it bluntly, we can't have campers wandering around our research facility snapping pictures and asking visiting dignitaries and the like for directions to the cafe, can we? You can see it just doesn't work. Also we feel that the resort was a particularly inefficient use of the location. If you consider resources dedicated to operating a resort, compared to that effort redirected toward operating the briefing center, the economics are compelling."

Newman saw Walker staring intently at his tablet. He saw Fred writing something on a notepad. It was dawning on him that he was the only one in the room with any skin in the resort as a resort. Everyone else, for one reason or another, would be quite happy with it as a Ziegler outpost. Just then, he realized the room had gone silent and all eyes were on him. He spoke after a fruitless moment spent trying to gather his thoughts.

"Well. That is, as you can imagine, a surprise. I guess it provides some sort of closure, doesn't it? An inefficient use of the location, you say. I mean, I left Ziegler for the resort, now Ziegler's followed me up here to take the resort. Briefing center versus resort. Huh. For the duration you said? By the time you're all done with it, what happens then?"

Geoff and his boss looked at the one earlier identified as being from legal.

"I can help with that, Mr. Newman. Without prejudice of course. At the end of the lease we do have the option to renew, pending negotiations with the Nation. Substantial changes to the lease terms would at that time be subject to arbitration in the court of our choosing. If we opt not to renew, then the buildings and associated improvements will become the property of the Nation, since they are built to lease by Ziegler. So to answer your question, in my personal opinion and without prejudice I imagine the location could be reverted to previous use if that was deemed appropriate at that time."

"What do you think, Fred?" said Newman. Fred showed no inclination to respond. Geoff's boss stepped in again.

"We wouldn't want to eavesdrop on employer-employee conversations, I'm sure. Why not take a day or so to discuss it among yourselves, and get back to us with any questions? I'm sure Geoff will be pleased to help out, and he has the support of the internal teams represented here."

The meeting was over.

* * *

Newman and Fred had agreed not to talk about the Ziegler meeting until they had returned to the lake. And during their journey they managed to do that, apart from a couple of "You knew"s and "no"s from Newman, and intervening "Want to talk about it then?"s from Fred.

Newman certainly did want to discuss it, but he wasn't in the right frame of mind during the trip back. What he wanted was for someone else to share his disbelief in what he felt Fred had done, before he heard what she had to say about it. Someone to validate his outrage. There had been no-one in the room at the time that he could even bounce a "can you believe it?" kind of glance off; no-one to at least implicitly share an "I know, it's unbelievable". Walker had avoided all visual contact with anyone during the entire meeting, and Geoff clearly enjoyed the isolation from any unpleasantness that came from toadying up to his ignorant boss. And Fred — Fred looked like she was hearing unpleasant but nonetheless welcome news, as you might if you heard that your intentionally leaving a window open had resulted in a cat you never liked in the first place going missing.

So he arranged to visit Fred the following day, ostensibly to hash out the logistics of the new situation with Ziegler, and to discuss the situation once he'd had time to take it all in. But this evening he went straight to the bar, where Steve was already in conversation with Doris.

"Oh crap, give me a beer will you?" Newman asked of the bartender, before any greetings had been exchanged. "Doris. Steve. Just back from a trip to Ziegler with Fred. You won't believe it. I know I didn't."

Newman gave them the overview before he'd taken the first sip of his beer. He was succinct, and not at his most eloquent.

"Ziegler. Closing us down — Fred knew it I know it. Closing us down — bloody believe it? I don't. You better believe it. Geoff even had the bloody nerve to use my soft landing approach against me. They were all in on it I know. 'Research center, executives, security, can't have visitors' and his boss is a complete turd I can tell you that much. Classic corporate crap. Walker — geez." He paused to suck down a good quarter of his glass of beer.

"Wait — 'closing us down?' How? What do you mean?" Steve said.

While Newman was still swallowing his beer, Doris said "Well I have to say Newman I warned you about Fred and her plans. So this time we're out of a job then?"

"Not yet, not yet," said Newman, "I'm meeting Fred tomorrow to figure things out. I still can't believe things are as cut and dried as Ziegler had it. And I'm not confident I can figure all the angles Fred may be playing — wasn't obvious to me why this was such a good deal for her."

"Bit late for self awareness in dealing with Fred," said Doris. "She never wanted the resort, she wanted the place. Actually, the income from the place. All that nonsense about tribal history. And I don't know about corporate visitors, but I can tell you that vacationers are more often than not a pain in the ass so she probably feels it's a good thing to be shot of them."

"I hope that wasn't directed toward me," Steve said, in a half-hearted and, judging by Newman's glare, horribly inappropriate attempt to lighten the situation. Newman banged down his glass on the far edge of the bar, leaving the bartender no need to ask if he wanted another one.

"Looks like they planned all along to close the resort once they had the lease in place — some legalese lets them do it, and as long as they see all parties right financially for the loss of tourist revenue, I assume they can get away with it. They had the room packed with legal, PR, corporate VP goons mind you, as if they had expected some sort of resistance that needed countering."

"Christ," from Steve.

"I was blindsided. Maybe with all those experts there they were expecting me to say something that might give them a reasonable argument; maybe there was something I could have said that would have at least stalled it. I don't know. I expected them to talk about investment in the place, not closure. All along I thought the resort piece was an essential part of their PR story. Thought Fred was there to hear about all the improvements. I was dumbfounded, I don't mind telling you."

"You mean all those years of experience in corporate bullshit failed you? Must've been a real shocker," said Steve, risking being doused in Newman's freshly poured beer.

"Well I suppose I'm about ready to retire," Doris said, "but I never would have, of course. I would've hung on way past due and only gone if I was shoved or carried out. Maybe this is the push I needed. But poor old Trefor, not been here long and likely out on his ear then, unless Parks'll take him back. And Dave. He'll miss giving his lectures. Doubt whether there'll be much he can tell Ziegler about anything in the lake."

Steve, for just a moment, was uncharacteristically serious. "Saw it coming or not I still have faith in you Newman, above anyone else, to spot a silver lining. No-one

I'd trust more to make something out of this, I have to say. What's your next move — had a chance to think about it?"

"Meet Fred. She agreed to come up here to enlighten me, poor sap that I am. So best case is I'll see exactly what she's been up to and what she may be planning next, and there may be a side to it I hadn't considered I suppose. Worse case I'll fall for more of her bullshit. Well, I suppose that was unfair. But I'll let everyone know what's going on once I have a clearer picture. I didn't want to get into it with her today, still too shocked, angry, surprised — embarrassed to be honest with you. Should have asked Ziegler about a timeline I guess — how long do we have. At least she should know that."

Newman motioned to the bartender.

"Just keep 'em coming, please."

The following morning saw Fred arrive at the lake and occupy her favorite chair at the water's edge. Newman had a sense of déjà vu as he dragged a second Adirondack across the grass toward hers and sat awkwardly down.

"Something I will not miss is this damn' chair," he said. "The one thing around here that never suited me." He sat precariously forward, as if the chair-back were freshly painted and he was wearing a brand new jacket.

"I'm sorry, Newman" Fred said. "But you know, you put this whole thing in process as soon as you decided to use the lake for your retirement project."

"Oh yes? It's down to me that the place is closing down? I thought I was the guy that saved it."

"I'll tell you, Newman, when you showed up along with your fish it was something of a revelation to me. I'd been struggling for so long trying to figure out how to bring the Nation into the twenty-first century, and here you come straight from that very place, and offered us the chance for us to join you. It's ironic, really. All of the historical, cultural, and political stuff we'd been trying for ages never worked, and then you come along and a plan is hatched that works in an instant. You must understand, Newman, it was far, far too good of an opportunity to pass up."

"I thought we were more or less on the same side, Fred. Things were going well, even before Ziegler. You'd got your lake, and all the financial advantages that came with it. Not enough for you?"

"Not enough, Newman. You know the resort really isn't of any interest to us. In fact, the lake itself isn't important; Fargo will tell you, confidentially mind you, none of us ever lived or worked this far up the valley. It's the revenue from the lake that we need. And compared to a little tourism kickback, the option of exclusive use of this place was very, very valuable to Ziegler and the lease terms we were able to extract from them reflected that. But you know — it wasn't exactly my idea to ensure that the closure option was buried into the lease agreement."

"Geoff?"

"Walker."

"Of course."

"Yes, he was my unexpected fish in the Ziegler lake, you might say."

Newman's smile was one of resignation. "I get it. Parks was an immovable roadblock, so for all this to pan out you needed to get them to give you control. And I actually helped you do it."

"Don't understate your role, Newman — you were

absolutely essential to the entire plan. Don't think I don't know it. And I also know at some point you planted the seed with Walker about them leasing the lake. He was all fish then suddenly, all lake. And I remember him being surprised by the enthusiastic reference you gave him for Ziegler. So maybe you're another odd fish I have to thank."

Newman made another attempt to get just a little less uncomfortable in his chair, which creaked a little before refusing to give way.

"Oh dear. I may have encouraged him to talk lake with Geoff. Just using my initiative, Fred, to open up a much richer potential revenue stream. Didn't expect him to turn all entrepreneur on me and come up with the closure — never considered it. Anyway, result is that in some nefarious symbiosis, you get the lake, Ziegler gets the lease, then Ziegler cuts loose the resort and you get hooked into Ziegler cash. Of which there is a lot, I do know that. Maybe you should have had me involved in that — I hope you got a hellofa good deal out of them."

"Yes, Geoff was very helpful there. Very generous. Helped by the fact that his boss is so clueless, he has to rely on Geoff almost entirely. But I understand Geoff will be elevated considerably within his organization as a result, so it was very important for him to grease the wheels and make it work."

"And we, meaning the people you referred to once as your friends up at the lake, we get kicked out — is that about it?"

Fred got up, stretched her arms above her head as she surveyed the lake, and said, "Let's walk, Newman."

Newman thrust himself forward and out of the chair,

determined not to allow an accompanying grunt to betray discomfort or decrepitude as he did so. "Ah. OK. I'm walking here."

"I've been thinking about it, Newman. Putting myself in your place, seeing things from your point of view."

"You'll have been pretty pissed off then, I'm sure" said Newman.

"I don't just mean with regard to the most recent events. You're a smart man. You will have had your own plans all along — you didn't cook things up overnight either, did you? So I ask myself, were I in your position, leaving Ziegler and arriving here as you did, what sort of insurance policy would I have against things somehow going south."

They walked past the dock, and Newman waved toward Robert. "Go on," he said, "while you were in my position you might have thought of something I didn't."

"Well, I would have held onto something by way of a safety-net. Have to. Something that would serve to protect me against future misfortune, in particular at the hands of my former employer. Get my drift?"

"Yes. So far, you're doing a good job as Newman."

"Walker says there are no records of any sort regarding the work you were doing there. Yet we have clear evidence in the lake that the work was done, don't we? And if that evidence were discovered, it could only mean one of two things."

"Go on."

Fred smiled and looked directly at Newman.

"First possibility: Ziegler wasn't aware of what its own division was up to — the experimentation, the potentially illegal transgenics, even the release into the wild

241

by one of their employees. So not just ignorant, but incompetent, and clearly not to be trusted with any sort of related work by any regulatory body worth its salt. In an industry that I'm told runs on image and trust, they would be pariahs."

"And the second?"

"Worse. If they knew all along what the evidence reveals then they must have done, well frankly, they must have done an egregious cover-up job. Absolutely shocking, and another blow to an industry that normally treads so carefully around legal, technical, and public relations issues. Heads would roll, all the way up to the top I'm sure. Oh no; a cover-up would be the worst of it."

"I see your point, Fred. But supposing such evidence existed, and Ziegler already had an inkling of it."

"Well then they would already have factored just such a potential outcome into their plans. They're also too smart not to have some sort of contingency. They would already have a prepared response, even if they'll withhold it til the last minute."

Newman stopped Fred as they were about to enter the lodge. "Look, Fred, let's get back to me being me for a moment. If I were me, and I had such evidence, and I was as pissed off as I clearly am, I might be tempted to tell Ziegler I'll blow the lid off your whole enterprise here, be damned with what happens to me or anyone else involved, including you and your plans, Fred. Sorry."

"Oh that's OK Newman. You should go ahead. I would say that's about your best — your only — move right now. And while we're at it, if I were me I would have anticipated that, too. I would have imagined you threatening Geoff with spilling the beans and not giving a whole lot of a hoot about the Coldwaters given how you would feel about them. Wouldn't blame you or expect anything less."

Just as he was feeling as if they were at last on the up and up with one another, Newman felt the return of that familiar feeling that Fred was most likely at least one step ahead of him. He felt she had done a far better job at being him than had he at being her. She was like one of those characters in a spy story that it was impossible to anticipate or outsmart. Just when you thought you were done and you had everything settled, she would have that one additional piece of information, she would always have that last word that made you doubt yourself all over again.

"Know what? Think I will."

Newman held the lodge door open.

"After you, Fred."

Newman needed a little time to decide exactly how he might best pitch the additional information, and his compensation for withholding it, to Geoff. Not only did he have the raw data describing the fish that Geoff had already seen, he had a huge amount of project documentation too; e-mail, design and planning documentation, presentations, texts, voice-mail — pretty much everything that Donoghue and Stevenson had advised them to destroy. He thought Geoff was definitely the right person to go to with it if he wanted the quickest reaction. If he took the legal route it might get mired in the machinery, but Newman could imagine Geoff and that stupid boss of his falling over themselves to come to terms with what he had to say. A kink in their otherwise perfect scheme, they would struggle with whether or not they could somehow deal with it themselves, or whether they would need to involve more and more outsiders, all the time risking the disclosure of their incompetence to increasing numbers of people in their organization.

Newman could imagine the highest level meetings, the hushed audience while senior managers' managers wondered who could have possibly screwed up either the fish project that should never have existed, or the location deal with the Coldwaters that they'd been assured was a done deal. He considered the inevitability of the spotlight narrowing on Geoff and his team, requiring them to explain when and where it was, exactly, that they let things get out of hand. He was really starting to enjoy this scenario. There would be one or more ambitious juniors, already snapping at heels, associating themselves with the good bits of the lake deal and isolating themselves from the bad, expressing surprise and disbelief at the concealments and proposing that with their new guidance the project might yet be saved. For them, the situation presented only opportunity for advancement, it was all upside. And for any disasters, however unlikely, the fall guys were already in place. Eventually, the dreaded term 'reorganization' would be heard, and the fate of Geoff, his boss, and his organization would be sealed.

They wouldn't be fired. Much worse. They would be sidelined.

Before he could spend too much time rolling that prospect around in his imagination, Newman felt something he hadn't felt for quite some time; a pang of conscience. He was no blackmailer, and this felt a lot like blackmail. He'd twisted a few arms in his time, maneuvered people into situations where they had few options, and so on. But he didn't remember doing anything that would cause harm, only advantage. The only casualty might be a competitor organization — such as Drugs — but that sort of large scale corporate chicanery was essential to the success of the overall organization. At least, that's how he chose to see it. This case was a little what you might call grayer, and that grayness intervened to temper the satisfaction he was taking in weighing potential outcomes. Until now he really had no axe to grind with Geoff, and despite his concern about losing a little control over his retirement when Geoff, Walker, and Fred took over the driving seat, he had to admit things had turned out pretty well.

And he really couldn't blame Geoff for looking out for himself at Ziegler; his was a classic corporate story of geek made good. Geoff had figured out what he needed to do to get ahead, and gone out and done it. He could even have taken a leaf out of Newman's book, come to think of it. So it would be tough to threaten him with disclosures that could bring down his entire house of cards like that. On the other hand, what did Geoff expect him to do? He'd seen the data, he must've been as surprised as Newman at the extent of what was likely going on with those fish. But he clearly didn't think any of that could come back to haunt him now that everything seemed so neatly sewn up with Fred.

Alright then, Newman thought, he would have to call to arrange a tête-à-tête with Geoff. If nothing else, it would make him feel better about things. Take back a little control.

Just then the phone rang.

"Mr. Newman? Geoff. We need to talk, urgently I think. Can we set up a meeting for tomorrow afternoon? At the lake. Party of three my end. We're on the way."

Geoff, his boss, and Stevenson from legal arrived and introduced themselves to Doris in reception. Steve had spotted Geoff's arrival and was already looking pleased with himself. He'd been joshing Geoff about his weight, pointing out how weight always increases the higher up the corporate ladder you climb. Probably why so many end up toppling off, he said. All a question of balance. Geoff did say something about nostalgia for his days in the lab, doing the real engineering work without all the politics. "Ah," said Steve, "the real work. The bigger the organization, the harder it is to identify exactly where the real work is getting done, isn't it?"

Newman had spent the previous evening and most of the morning stealing himself to deliver an ultimatum. Whatever Geoff had planned, he was confident his news would trump it. He had no intention of losing the resort and the livelihood of all whose occupations depended on it to what amounted to a corporate land-grab. And for himself, he would gladly go down with the Ziegler ship if it meant the resort could survive. That's just the way it was; hard for them to negotiate with a guy who, at the end of the day, didn't really give a crap. And regrettably but unavoidably, Fred's source of revenue, for all her planning, might just end up among the collateral damage.

"Here he is," Steve said as Newman walked in. "Now we can get the band back together, eh!"

"That one's getting very old," said Newman. "Mr Stevenson — hello again! Geoff." Newman didn't get the name of Geoff's boss, whom no-one bothered to introduce, and who made no attempt to conceal his ill humor.

"Face like a bulldog sipping vinegar that one," Steve said, in an aside to Newman as he left.

"Gentlemen — I have the meeting room ready. Shall we?"

Newman led the procession upstairs to his lake view conference room, where a coffee machine choked and burbled and a selection of oversized cookies was available to help break ice.

"We should probably get straight to business," Geoff said.

"Just a moment," said Stevenson as he opened up his laptop and took a file out of his briefcase, "need to get some things in order here before we start." Stevenson caught Newman's eye, in what Newman swore was as close to a wink as was possible without actually winking.

"Quite the team you've brought with you, Geoff. If everyone who visited brought along two friends we'd be in no need of Ziegler cash in the first place. And you'd definitely not be planning to shut us down."

Geoff seemed more awkward than usual, and avoided looking at Newman let alone speaking with him. Instead he turned and addressed the room in general.

"OK well if you're ready, Mr. Stevenson, perhaps we can get this over with. I'd prefer we speak off-the-record unless and until we all decide on officially documenting our discussion. Mr. Newman — Stevenson is here just to ensure nothing is said that might imply unforeseen prejudice on either side. Is that what you said, Mr. Stevenson?"

"Close enough."

Geoff wasn't looking at all as confident as he did in their last meeting, and Newman began to wonder if he might have a conscience after all. His boss, on the other hand, was looking downright dyspeptic.

"Mr. Newman, I heard from Fred Jesperson regarding your position regarding closure of the resort. In particular, she reminded me of the possibility that there was a complete body of evidence regarding a prior Ziegler project, a small part of which you had earlier made me aware."

Geoff's boss looked at Geoff and raised both hands slightly from the conference table before letting them fall back again.

"Of course, at that time we could only assemble a very incomplete picture and we had no idea of the chain of events that would come about as a result of that work, allegedly conducted in our Food division. Seemed to me at the time that it was largely a midnight oil affair conducted by one or two rogue engineers. Anyway, Ms. Jesperson went on to point out that much had depended on, and continues to depend upon the tenting surrounding that project; it remains important to all concerned that no reckless disclosures take place that might threaten to undermine Ziegler's credibility in that regard. This is the gist of her call to me. Though I have to say, she was a little more direct in her description of the situation, the options, and the potential outcomes."

Since the point at which he heard "Fred Jesperson", Newman hadn't been able to pay close enough attention to what Geoff was saying to feel he completely understood what he meant. "Perhaps you could take a leaf out of her book, Geoff, and leave a little less to the imagination? I'm not sure I know what the hell you're talking about."

"Get on with it," Geoff's boss said, seizing his first opportunity to make a confident contribution. Geoff looked increasingly harassed.

"Right yes, sorry, old engineering habit gets the better of me sometimes. Talk a bit too much. Right. Newman: she told us you have the means to ruin the entire enterprise here. And if the fish fall, then everything unravels. She even said the legitimacy of the property transfer from Parks could be threatened. She ended by saying Ziegler could end up looking like a bunch of incompetent buffoons."

"Perish the thought," muttered Stevenson as he typed.

Geoff's boss shot challenging glances around the room.

Newman felt an uneasy mix of empowerment and emasculation, a sensation that had become increasingly familiar to him the more he worked with Fred. But from what he'd just heard, it sounded like somehow or another he was back in the driving seat. He decided to see how far Fred's intervention had gone.

"I was hoping things would never come to that. Are you still hell-bent on closing us down then Geoff?"

"Our position is that there are two separate issues here, Mr. Newman. One is the direction that Ziegler intends to take the current lease. The other, and one which Mr. Stevenson here might best handle, would be your actions were Ziegler to take that direction. And, of course, whether there might yet be any opportunity for us to seek some sort of synergy between the two. Mr. Stevenson?"

"Yes, hello Newman. How are you doing? Been a while since we worked together! Lovely place you have here. Might take a few days myself — make some recreational hay while the sun still shines, eh? I mean before it all goes . . .

Well then."

Stevenson's familiar tone with Newman engendered surprise, if not alarm, in Geoff's boss. He stepped in once again.

"Mr. Stevenson, please, you're here representing Ziegler, not vacationing with Mr. Newman. Can we get this done with? I'm sure we all have other important matters to attend to."

"Doing great, thanks, Mr. Stevenson," said Newman, "nice to see you again. Let's see — last time was another closure, wasn't it, working on winding things up over there! Given the success then, I can't think of anyone more qualified than yourself to handle things this time round!"

"Well thank you for the kind words. Now I would just like to add that Ms. Jesperson — I'm reading a transcript of what she said to us here — Ms. Jesperson did mention that the extent of the potential to, let's say, revise the basis of Ziegler's contractual agreement regarding the resort extends beyond events surrounding the retirement of the fish project. She mentioned in fact that — let's see — there may be challengeable historical evidence on which tribal rights were established."

"Indeed", said Newman, who was starting to get a clue but was looking forward to Stevenson spelling more of everything out for all present. He was also, as usual, keen to hear everything Fred had said in an attempt to figure out what she might have meant.

"Now it would be one thing if Ziegler's work — the fruit of a rogue project or otherwise — were to be shown to have found its way into what was, at the time, national parks' property. But it would be quite another if the legitimacy of the other party's claim to ownership in our contract for the resort were to be legitimately called into question."

Stevenson turned to Geoff's boss, as if assuming he above all would require the situation to be spelled out for him.

"The first, you see, is at best an internal mishap and at worst a legal disaster pitting Ziegler against the government. But the second, the second you see, whichever way you look at it, voids the contract and reverts the entire area to the parks service. This sort of historical evidence, you see, is always subject to revision and such revision may trigger the voidable terms in the contract with Parks. D'you follow? No winners there, we feel."

Stevenson closed his laptop as if to indicate that his contribution was over.

Newman felt the air inside the room suddenly infused with fresh oxygen. Time for him to pick up Fred's proffered baton and run with it.

"Speaking for myself, I'm not looking to win. Or void, for that matter. I'm simply looking to preserve something we have built here, in the face of an unexpected and, frankly, unreasonable turn of events. Of course these developments are relatively recent, and I'm still considering my options. But the President of the Coldwater Nation has it pretty much right I think, in that if it became unavoidable that the ship sank then we'd all by necessity I feel go down with it."

For a moment, Newman imagined himself a runner at the end of a long race, with a downhill stretch all the way to the finish line. He sat back and addressed no-one in particular. He appeared to be thinking aloud, rather than threatening some sort of suicidal retribution.

"So the question becomes, who has the most to lose? Fred Jesperson — a source of additional revenue, so she'd be set back to where she started a few years ago. Parks. Who knows what Parks would do? I, and all my staff, might end up working for the government once again. But Ziegler; Ziegler I suppose could end up amid all sorts of accusations of harmful ignorance, incompetence, illegality, espionagery, buffoonery we've already mentioned I think, skulldugg..."

"Yes yes alright Mr. Newman we all know that," Geoff's boss said, getting up out of his seat and then standing at the table awkwardly for a moment, before sitting down again. "So what are you saying Newman? What's your intention?"

"No choice I'm afraid, have to go public with the lot. I have a contact at the *National Observer*, so I think that'll be the way to begin. I mean, as I say, I have little to lose and my staff have only their continued employment to gain. And speaking for the overall credibility of the GMO industry, not to mention the safety of the general population, it may be my scientific and civic duty to blow the whistle on a bunch of corporate cowboys. Don't you think? I'm interested to hear — I wonder what you would do if you were put in my position."

The table went silent for a moment. Newman noticed that Stevenson had stopped typing and was looking at Geoff's boss with a slight smile. Of course; he saw this coming, and had already told them all as much. They had arrived at the point where negotiations would start, and everything before had been to simply rule out the unlikely scenario in which Newman capitulated and walked meekly off into the sunset.

"Well I might count my blessings and head off into the sunset," said Geoff's boss. "I mean, you've had a good run here and it couldn't be to any advantage to yourself or to Ms. Jesperson to rake up all that past stuff, could it? If I were you I might consider myself fortunate to have got away with it. From what I've learned, you've sailed a little close to the wind on more than one occasion."

Now Newman was upset. He had never liked being patronized by idiots, and this man seemed to typify every patronizing idiot he'd ever met during his time at Ziegler. If his intention had been to cajole Newman into a sense of gratitude for past gifts, and for being let off the hook in the present, then he needed to be corrected. Now Stevenson had turned his smile toward Newman; he was poised to resume taking notes on his laptop, eyebrows raised in anticipation.

Newman addressed Geoff's boss directly.

"Well now I do wonder what could have distracted you for the past half hour to the point where you completely failed to grasp what's going on here. Fred called you, presumably to give you the bottom line, the context for our discussion. Mr. Stevenson has summarized potential outcomes from a legal perspective. I have attempted to further impress upon you how precarious is the entire enterprise that you've inherited. Geoff knows me and has at least some history with Ziegler; I can't believe he hasn't provided you with at least an inkling as to how unlikely it would be that I would lay down and let your organization roll over me, as you forge advancements in your own careers out of the ruin of good people here at the resort. You must surely think you're dealing with some other person, a former colleague whose name you've half forgotten, some smart, well-intentioned, hard-working unfortunate you used as grist to the mill of your own unearned, unjustified, overpaid, sadly short and ultimately unrewarding spasm in the backwaters of know-nothing faceless corporate middle-management."

Newman paused for a moment to let that last bit sink in, to catch his breath, and to let Stevenson catch up with his typing. He was sure the only bit that would have hit home with Geoff's boss was "sadly short", but he continued.

"Anyway, and to put it into terms you understand, I and my staff will need compensation. Compensation and plenty of it. And just to be even more clear, that means cash, not sinecures such as yours, stock options, corner offices, or company cars."

Geoff's boss by this time was doing a very poor job of concealing his outrage. He leaned back in his chair, fingering a non-existent beard on the tip of his chin, determinedly avoiding Newman's gaze. He had only recently laid to rest initial qualms about why he had been given his current position; his wife had been instrumental in persuading him that it was clearly and entirely justified by his obvious talent and hard work. Now he felt that old self-doubt return, and wondered whether he might just have been set up.

Newman continued. "I'll speak with Fred and for now I won't involve the *National Observer*. Why don't you take a moment, pop back to HQ and consider your position? I'll expect an offer soon. Let's say in two days. How's that? You send me those blessings you spoke of, and I'll count 'em, see how they measure up."

"You son of a—" Geoff's boss's containment failed him for a moment, but Newman was ready for it.

"Now now — if you were a real geneticist I'd consider that an insult. We done here? Mr. Stevenson — can you share your notes with your colleague? I think he may need them."

10: The Scottish play

THAT NIGHT, NEWMAN had met Steve in the bar after his meeting with Ziegler, and would have downed far too much beer even without Steve's enthusiastic encouragement.

"Oh my god Newman I wish I was there. Don't suppose you can get me the transcript? And that Stevenson, I always liked him. I'm sure he had a hand in setting you off. Oh god, I wish I'd been there."

As a result, the following morning Newman was feeling on less than top form when he spoke with Fred.

"Before you say anything, Newman, I would like you to consider whether there was any better option available to any of us. I believe I took the only possible course of action."

"Well I've been thinking about it. And I have to say, apart from feeling a bit left out of the whole process — a feeling I'm getting used to, by the way — I think it's a stroke of genius. There was a time when I'd have been proud of that sort of thing myself, you know. Now I'm left to admire it from the wings."

"You know I could never have involved you in the resort closure thing? I mean as soon as I saw it was written into their plans, I had to figure it into mine first. Couldn't have them refuse the lease, and before they'd signed that, we had nothing."

"You were right. I still have a few Ziegler chips on my shoulder — although I shifted a good many of them yesterday

I can tell you — I would have scuppered it somehow before seeing any possible advantages. Worried about the job losses for one thing. But now I'm seeing plenty of golden parachutes to be handed out, a bit of déjà vu I might say. Of course if it doesn't work out for the folks here it's still very much scupperable. But the most remarkable thing is that where I would never have had the inclination or the nerve to offer to throw your takeover under the bus at this stage, you had the brass balls to do it yourself. Have to say, it was a first for me to be in a negotiating position with absolutely nothing to lose and every potential outcome being a win. I mean, you actually told them your claim to the lake was on questionable ground, right? You used Fargo's hidden skills as a threat?"

"Yes. You would have appreciated the affect that had on that boss of Geoff's. He said he'd been tricked into buying stolen goods. I told him no, the issue was just goods of questionable provenance. Mind you, I'm not sure we should ever divulge that side of the deal to Fargo."

"Really? But surely provenance is right up Fargo's street, isn't it? I mean, a relic is just old junk without its provenance, right? Fargo is right there at the center of things. Oh god what I'd pay to see Fargo arguing that point with Geoff's boss."

"You're probably right, but Fargo's been in the provenance business for so long he takes his creations very seriously. I think he even forgets sometimes he had any sort of hand in their genesis, you know. Might take things personally."

"If it wasn't for you teeing them up, I'd have had nothing but bluster and threats when that Ziegler contingent walked in. Fantastic. You know, I told them I'd give Cooper a story — better than the one he came here for. And I might well have, too."

"What's up with Cooper? I'm hoping this will all be done and dusted before he's caused any damage."

"Robert spun him some tale that should keep him occupied for a while at least, he's off somewhere or other chasing that. I gave Ziegler a couple of days to make an offer to buy us out, more or less, so let's hope."

"I always wondered about your exit from Ziegler in the first place. That's your déjà vu there is it, Newman?"

"Let's just say that if anyone has the experience required to put this deal together, it's Stevenson — possibly with Donoghue's help. What a team they were."

Newman agreed to let Fred know as soon as he heard anything from Ziegler, and headed back to the cafe for more coffee. He was feeling a little better, an unusual sensation after a meeting with Fred. She seemed to know what she was doing, even if it wasn't always immediately obvious whether or not it was in line with Newman's interests. And increasingly of late he'd felt subject almost entirely to the whim of fate as he struggled with fish, reporters, and corporate shenanigans. Fred always had a plan but on this occasion he felt like her plan was something he could work with.

Besides, from what he could remember of it he'd really enjoyed putting Geoff's boss in his place.

"Yes Ms. Jesperson, myself and the officer here need to speak briefly with you. By way of due diligence more than anything else, really. Ms. Jesperson?"

Pilchard had called Fred from reception at the

Coldwater Tribal Museum, and it took him a moment to realize that Fred wasn't there, and he was instead speaking with her answering machine.

"Oh I see, apologies. Pilchard, George. Inspector, Coldwater Bay police. Calling about the missing reporter. I'll call again, Sir. Ma'am."

Pilchard turned to leave and was confronted by Fargo, who had overheard his message.

"Fred is up at the lake, speaking with Newman."

"Oh I see, thank you. Pilchard."

"No, Fargo. I work for Fred. I run this museum."

"Sorry — Pilchard, George. Inspector, Coldwater Bay police."

"I see. No need for apologies."

"Yes, glad we got that cleared up. Now then, perhaps you can help, Mr. Fargo. The officer here and myself are making some general inquiries about a missing person, a Mr. Cooper Black. Reporter. I believe he visited you looking for information for a story he was working on."

"I understand."

There was an awkward pause until finally it was the officer who realized that Pilchard's question in the form of a statement hadn't worked with Fargo.

"The inspector wondered whether you might be able to shed light on Mr. Black's whereabouts, Sir."

More silence, while Fargo stared intently out of the window toward the Bay.

"I know what'll work," Pilchard said to the officer. "Mr. Fargo — have you seen the man?"

"Not since he was here a couple of days ago. Perhaps three."

"Now," said Pilchard, "Now we are getting somewhere."

"He was not a happy man," said Fargo, turning toward the officer, "he seemed to be looking for a way out of his unhappiness I think. He was creating a story, he said."

Pilchard said "Yes yes, well that's likely, you know, he worked for the Observer."

"The Observer, yes. Observer. I wonder about an Observer who asks so many questions."

"Oh — and what sort of questions was he asking?"

"He asked about this beam, from a longhouse," said Fargo, having led them toward his latest installation. "He seemed interested in the past, but he questioned evidence of it in the present. I think evidence of the past is all we have, isn't it? How else does the past exist?"

"This is a beam from a longhouse?" asked Pilchard. "Looks like a piece of driftwood, doesn't it. Officer — what do you make of it?"

"Just a guess sir, could be an old boat or something."

Fargo raised his eyebrows slightly. Pilchard said, "Old boat? Old boat?" He made a show of inspecting the exhibit very closely. "Oh dear, officer, I think your imagination may have run away with you a little there. Old boat, eh? Anyway, did this Cooper Black give you any idea of what his plans might be, Mr. Fargo? Any hint of where he might be going, what he planned to do next?"

"A boat is a possibility. So much of what we know about the past hangs upon our interpretation of the present, doesn't it? As a policeman, you must have observed this."

Pilchard had a look of slight exasperation about him. Fargo continued:

"Actually, he did say he was going to come back here. But I haven't seen him since. I assume we were not useful to his story."

The officer had stepped away and was exchanging words on his radio. He ended with "I'll tell the Inspector straight away." Now he whispered something to Pilchard, who said aloud "Oh — progress then. No need for cloak and dagger, officer, after all it's on Mr. Fargo's patch isn't it." He turned to Fargo.

"All a bit of a telephone game I'm afraid but it looks at first blush like we have a development from the search team up at the lake. Body washed up on the North shore. Officer: lights and sirens, I think."

And with that the officers swept out of the museum into their vehicle, and off toward the highway and the lake shore beyond in a flurry of wailing and flashing.

Fargo immediately called Fred. "Pilchard says there's a body on the beach. North shore. He's on his way."

Fred said, "Pilchard?" but it was too late; Fargo had hung up. She called Newman.

"Fargo just said something about a pilchard and a body at the North shore beach."

"Pilchard? Body? That's the police. I have to go."

Newman didn't know what to do first. Of all people, he called Steve. "Body on the beach. Pilchard said. Keep in touch. Gotta go."

He almost jogged through reception on his way to his car. Doris and Robert were at the desk. "Body on the beach on the North side. Don't tell anyone. Pilchard is over there. Who knows. Back later."

Newman got into his car and drove round to the North shore. On the way he thought how this wasn't the story Cooper had imagined — it wasn't the story any of them had imagined, actually — but it was, thankfully, in line with Pilchard's troubled mind scenario. Poor paranoid ink-slinger frustrated in his ambitions once again, scuppers his boat in a final defiant raising of the middle finger to the entire establishment. Very tragic and all that, but wraps up this entire sorry episode nicely without too many loose ends. Fred can use the period between now and the next time any scandal-hungry news-hound appears on the scene to shore up all the angles, tighten up the history a little.

As he drove round the North end, Newman could see a collection of police and emergency vehicles in a lay-by, lights flashing, and a couple of boats, including Dave's inflatable, pulled up onto the beach.

"Newman, I'm the guy that runs the resort," he said to the police officer barring entry to the shoreline.

"He's alright, let him through," shouted Pilchard, looking up from a dayglo-clad huddle. "Newman — not a great day to visit the beach. You heard then? Well I was about to call you anyway. But it looks like our body is a red herring, if you don't mind!"

At the water's edge Newman saw not so much a body, or even a herring, as he did a carcass. A massive carcass. It was enormous. He'd seen something on this kind of scale at the Bay once, but then it was a beached whale which, despite its size, still looked somehow benign toward us humans. Not so this thing. It had the trappings of a Glacial Lake trout; it had speckles the size of trash-can lids, and huge swaths of that neon color that was a key characteristic. But it was horrifically, almost cartoonishly magnified. Like a hideous carnival caricature, or a bloated, malevolent inflatable from some satanic parade. Gaping serrated jaws looked as though they could easily accommodate a clydesdale, and even in death they were terrifying enough to cause the assembled photographers and forensics experts to give them a wide berth. It was lying on its side, a huge, gluey eyeball staring up as Newman walked from the back of the fish toward the front where Pilchard stood. There he saw the gaping hole in the midsection, where once the entire abdomen would have been. Ragged edges and torn trailing flaps of flesh suggested either a very poor attempt at fishmongery, or a bite from something at least as big as this thing and maybe bigger.

It looked, and smelled, horrific.

"Not too many of those to the pound, eh Newman."

"Good godness," Newman said. "I mean god gracious. What the hell."

"Pretty clear where it came from, question is what do we think it is," Pilchard sort of asked. He looked at Newman. Newman looked horrified and disgusted in equal measure.

"God it stinks too. I suppose we can assume it's dead? I mean it looks like some sort of gross throwback or something. But I was expecting Mr. Black from what you said; thank heavens it's a fish at least, however hellish it looks."

"Ah well there's the rub — no culinary reference intended, you understand. Particularly not given the unsavory stench around here. There's the rub Mr. Newman. Officer, if you please."

Pilchard's assistant handed him a reasonably intact shoulder bag from a polythene sack marked 'EVIDENCE'.

"This was half way down that thing's throat. Strap

here stuck in its teeth would you believe. Computer and remains of a notebook inside, few other bits and bobs."

"Good lord," said Newman. "No good trying to recover anything from that computer then, judging by the look of it?"

"No, completely ruined I'm afraid. But we did manage to find out that it belonged to our Mr. Cooper Black."

"How do you know?"

"He stuck his temporary pass on the outside when he visited the Coldwater Bay Museum. There it is look: 'Cooper Black, *National Observer*'. Didn't take too much detective work, that, did it Officer? I say, didn't take too much detective work!"

"No sir; spotted it straight away, sir."

"Good lad."

There was a pause while Pilchard smiled at how easily he could bait his assistant, cameras flashed and clattered, and Newman let the implication of the orphaned laptop bag sink in. Eventually Newman said:

"No sign of Cooper, then."

"No sign I'm afraid. Let's keep this under wraps for now, shall we? No need to get everyone excited til we sort out the facts from the alternatives. We have a couple of alternatives to consider as far as Mr. Black is concerned, I think. Officer: what are the alternatives we have to consider?"

"Well sir, I would say based on our observations so far, either Mr. Cooper's boat sank and he swum away leaving his bag to be swept up by this fish. Or, Mr. Cooper could have been swept up and swallowed by the fish leaving his bag here, him having no means by which to get similarly stuck in its teeth as such."

"Very good, very good. And observation being, as per police training, the intense and cultivated use of all of the faculties, I would venture to further observe the possibility that owing to a good hundred and fifty pounds or so of missing fish, Mr. Cooper could be the first person I've come across to have been eaten by not one, but two fish in one sitting as it were. What do you think of that, Mr. Newman? A sort of doubly unlucky Jonah, you might say."

But Pilchard received no response. Shortly after hearing him offer his further observation, Newman had dashed away beyond the immediate vicinity to deposit his own lunch among the assorted debris washed up along the shore.

This was not how he had imagined things might turn out.

Meantime the Ziegler offer had arrived in the form of an online document that required both Fred and Newman's digital signatures. Newman recognized the work of Donoghue and Stevenson in the lengthy preamble, designed to indemnify Ziegler against any charge that they were buying their way out of anything or paying anyone off.

The entire affair was structured as compensation for future earnings Newman may have received as licensee of the resort. There was quite a laundry list of additional items for which Ziegler offered cash in exchange, each of them at least as surprisingly generous as the last. There were provisions for Newman to compensate his staff, remuneration for lost value in advertising commitments, retraining and benefits allowances, housing and accommodation, travel — the list seemed endless, but eventually did end with a startling lump sum for vague but apparently invaluable items like outreach, counseling, and reorientation.

"Makes the fish deals look like small fry!" Steve said, when Newman ran the whole thing by him in the bar. "I don't get it. You seem to be followed around by shitloads of cash just waiting to fall in your lap. I mean, there's enough here for mass retirements; Doris, Robert, Trefor, the entire crew. Mind you, looks like once you sign it you're done with Ziegler for good. 'Right to sue; domestic or foreign; irrevocable'; let's see, 'cede, forfeit, relinquish and renounce'. What the hell, Stevenson earned his pay on this one by the look."

"Fine by me," Newman said, "assume it's fine by Fred. Need to run it by the folks though. And sooner rather than later."

Running it by the folks involved getting everyone together in one place. This, in itself, was an unprecedented event and took a surprising amount of organization on Doris's part, who was given the task of pulling it off hastily without bringing the resort to a standstill. It was early evening when Doris, Trefor, Robert, and Dave gathered around the conference table to hear what it was that Newman had to tell them.

He reminded them that the past few years had been pretty tumultuous, that there had been ups and downs, but mostly ups. They'd been fortunate to get out from under Parks, and the Coldwater Nation had proved to be great neighbors and even better owners. And Ziegler. Ziegler's bounty was welcome (the new toilets, Robert murmured with a nod of the head toward Newman), but it turns out it had come with one significant drawback, and that was the reason he'd called the meeting.

"I hadn't realized that the lease Fred entered into with Ziegler gave them full control over the operation of the resort, as well as any business facilities they chose to develop here. They do have a duty to pay Parks a modest tithe, but as it turns out that doesn't need to come from the operation of the resort. And the rent provided to the Coldwaters isn't dependent on the resort either. So they met with us, and they explained that they wanted to concentrate on their core business requirement for the lake and, unfortunately, that means closing the resort at the end of the season."

Newman thought it best to pause there and allow the others to react. Doris was the first.

"I'm surprised, Newman. Very surprised. You mean to say you really didn't see that coming? You thought, first, that Fred was interested in a pond up in the hills and then that Ziegler would welcome a bunch of tourists with fishing poles wandering around their campus? OK. Show of hands. Anyone here surprised by Newman's news?"

Dave was surprised that he and Newman were the only ones raising their hands.

"Actually, Dave," Newman said, "for you there's an opportunity to continue to be the overall custodian of the lake. They need a Parks affiliate to watch out for the flora and fauna, and I believe they'll have an education program that would showcase your lectures. They have said they will compensate Parks for your service, and they have an offer specifically for you."

"Ah. Oh. But what about ... " Dave looked around the table.

"For everyone else, there is, not to beat about the

bush, cash to make up for the fact that their jobs here are going away."

"Damn' right," said Doris.

"I'll be talking to you all tomorrow individually to make sure your specific requirements are met. Be assured, though, we got a very, very good deal out of Ziegler. And Fred was a big help with that."

There was general discussion and a few questions, more about the process of closure than the implications for specific individuals. Everyone agreed with Doris that, before Newman arrived, closure was regarded as inevitable and even though the resort had met with more success of late, no-one thought that was any guarantee of its future. Robert wondered what would become of the stock of single malts in the bar. Trefor said he'd be glad to get shot of Parks for good, but he'd miss working with everyone. Dave said now might be the opportunity for him to go for a Park Manager position within the service; Newman told him he'd do well to at least consider Ziegler's offer before making any decisions.

When the meeting was over, Newman sat at the table and looked out of the window. Whatever he'd been expecting from everyone, it wasn't exactly that. He surprised himself that he hadn't remembered how information spread regardless, and how hard it was in any organization to keep anything completely under the covers. Nevertheless, everyone seemed to accept it readily enough when it came. Maybe they could each see advantages. Maybe they were just stoic. Turns out it had been Newman himself who was most sideswiped by this particular turn of events and, now he came to think about it, it was maybe he who was the most disappointed. For whatever reason, he'd come to enjoy his work at the lake; he enjoyed the place of course — who wouldn't — and he enjoyed his coworkers. He liked most of the visitors, and those he didn't like, Doris could deal with. Working with Fred had been both a joy and an education, and he had to admit that Fargo, along with a number of questionable artifacts, had brought perspective that otherwise he might never have considered. What would he do next? Whatever he liked, when he considered the fact that he was about to receive his second payoff.

Problem was, he was already doing whatever he liked, but something was inevitably going to change.

Newman sat down to breakfast with Steve, ahead of his individual meetings with the others that he'd set up for later that day. Of course, Steve already knew everything. But he seemed, even for Steve, more than usually excited to speak with Newman. The server waited patiently for their order.

"One thing I always said when I was at Ziegler. I said 'don't worry about it; Newman always has a plan x in his back pocket for when everything else goes to hell.' And I was right, Newman, many a time one of your plan x's saved our bacon. Ooh — that sounds good, actually, I'll have the Anglers' Start, please, ham, eggs, hash-browns — the lot."

Newman ordered a similarly robust breakfast, the server picked up their menus and departed, Steve continued.

"But this time, Newman, this time I think you're a bit nonplussed. Am I right? A bit at a loss, eh? Go on. Tell me your plan x this time round."

"No plan x Steve. In fact, I'll admit to being a bit at a loss. I was annoyed with Fred for a moment there, but I think that wasn't so much to do with her covert plans but because for the first time, I realized that I didn't have any. Out-planned, you see. Pride took a hit. But once I accepted that, all I could do was congratulate her. I didn't expect things to pan out this way, but on the other hand . . ."

"Yes, on the other hand you'll all make out like bandits."

"To be honest, Steve, I'd rather we'd been able to keep things going as they were. Doris, Robert, now Trefor, Dave doing his ranger thing. It was a great life here, I liked it even more than I expected. And you — you'll surely miss coming up here. Geez, you almost live here too."

Steve stirred cream into his coffee for a moment in silence, then he said "I've been thinking of a little project, Newman. Involving all that cash you've got coming. And a similar amount of mine, of course."

"Oh yes? Don't tell me you're doing financial advice in retirement."

"Just a one-off. We use that cash to move and take the resort with us."

"Right. Sounds like pitching the relocation of the entire lake might stretch even my powers of persuasion. You talking magic Steve? Seen something similar on television I think, involving a mountain, or the Washington monument or something."

"Not the lake, Newman, but everything else. People, facilities, marketing, general idea, me, you, success — everything but the lake. Robert can supply the lake."

"Of course, of course. Yes we'll descend on Robert's ancestral seat and turn it into a Scottish Glacial Lake. Alright, Steve, I'll come clean. I already spoke with him about something similar. That was before all this happened of course, and I was just talking about cutting and running myself at some point. Not that I took myself entirely seriously. I think I was just comforting myself that at least there was the potential for a plan x of my own, however unrealistic."

"I know you spoke with him, Newman. He mentioned that when I spoke with him a few days ago."

"Wait a minute. You've already spoken to him about it too?"

"Oh yes. I already had plans for a partnership for the three of us. Don't want to sound disloyal, Newman, but I thought it was only a question of time before all this came to shit even with a man of your accomplishments at the helm. So what did he say to you?"

"Actually he said something like 'well Mr. Newman that's certainly something to bear in mind when all this business here comes to shit, as I'm told it will.' And you?"

Steve laughed, leaned forward and slapped his hand down on the table. "Now I understand what he meant when he said the highlands were getting so popular these days he was in danger of being trampled in the rush."

"Who'd have thought," said Newman, "the old boy can play his cards as close to his chest as any of us."

"Well now we have a new situation. We have something better than cash — we have even more cash, and we have a bunch of additional folks who may be interested. What's not to like about that? Go on, Newman, just when I thought things were petering out. There's your plan x."

Newman and Steve discussed, proposed, and debated possibilities over their breakfast. Newman was surprised at how much thought Steve had already put into the idea. Steve specialized in what he called "broad brush strokes", and those allowed him to create quite complex pictures that looked immediately impressive, but nevertheless needed Newman's input before they could bear any sort of close inspection. He spoke about rehabbing buildings and grounds, about involving the Scottish tourist board, all those film and television opportunities, offering spas and fitness centers, boat trips and seaplane rides. Look, he said, pretty much all Americans consider themselves at least a little Scottish — those that aren't Irish, anyway. He said Robert was sitting on a goldmine that just happened for the time being to look like a peat bog. Just imagine what could be done with it by playing up Robert's Scottish ancestry, adding a little good old American creativity, perhaps working showers, and giving it a smidgin of the Barnum treatment.

"Goldmine? P.T. Barnum? You may be getting just a little ahead of yourself here. I'll speak with the others today then we can get back to Robert and see if he's in, given the support he might get. You never know; he may prefer to take his payout and go it alone, reclaim his seat, and live like a highland hermit. Might already be thoroughly sick of all this fish, resort, lake, tourist nonsense."

Newman fully expected the amount and the immediacy of the cash compensation would surely exceed even the most optimistic expectations of everyone involved.

In the event, Doris took it as further evidence of the benefits of her spiritual awakening. To her, something or other — not sure what — must be in alignment. And whatever it was, its alignment had now been given a stunning monetary value. She seemed quite positive about Newman's suggestion regarding what Steve had termed "the Scottish play", and besides, Robert had already spoken with her about it.

"He's already spoken with you about it?" Newman was a little disappointed, given the effort he'd spent preparing to break it to her.

"Oh, yes. He said it looks like he may be moving to Scotland to fix up his family place as a resort on a loch. Sounded quite dramatic, all lake and heather and inherited mansions ripe for development. Wondered if I would be interested in helping to run the place. No firm plans as yet, but he said he had things in the works, possibly with you and with Steve, and wanted to give me time to think about it."

Doris was clearly enjoying having news to deliver to Newman for a change.

"From what I heard, the place would suit my wardrobe at the very least. And I always liked a man in a kilt, so the more the merrier over there, eh."

Newman, for his part, was beginning to wonder if there was anyone who hadn't already spoken with Robert.

Trefor was almost embarrassed by the amount of money he'd be receiving. As a relative newcomer, he questioned whether he was entitled to it; did he deserve it? How can it even be justified? Newman told him he'd just have to accept the fact that he was getting a boatload of cash, and try his best to live with it. Question was, did he want to work in PR as part of the Scottish play? "Oh yes." Trefor stopped Newman as he began to talk about Scotland. "Doris mentioned that to me, you see. Sounds very exciting, doesn't it? I shall have to have a think, once you've spoken with Robert."

Part of Dave's compensation was the offer of a position at Ziegler as natural resources custodian, or some other title to be determined by Dave himself. A dream job, as he put it, with stock options (nothing to do with fish, Newman had to explain, and went on to describe just how stock options worked), guaranteed bonuses, golden parachutes — the works. Dave had never really traveled outside the boundaries of the Park until, as he pointed out, they moved the Park boundary to exclude the lake. Scotland was not for him, in no small part because he would have to fly in order to get there. Boats, for Dave, were exotic enough as far as transportation went, and if he couldn't walk it he'd be happier if he didn't have to go much further than he could drive. Besides, he'd spoken with Robert about it and although it sounded very interesting, he didn't feel he was ready to start again with a new lake, not at this point in his career. He was already heavily invested in this particular lake, and he wasn't sure he had the time or energy to start again with a fresh one, even bearing in mind superficial geological similarities, of course.

Newman had arranged to meet Robert at the boathouse later that afternoon, and as he walked across the lawn toward the dock he thought of what Dave had said about the energy required to start again, to reinvest in an entirely new project. He didn't have to of course; he had no obligation to join the rest of them in this new plan. But he did feel responsible in part for the way things had panned out. If he hadn't shown up, they would probably still be struggling on as they were, not exactly thriving but at least with no immediate threat of losing their jobs. So he did have the option of helping set everything up with the Ziegler compensation and with MacLeod's legal work for Robert, then he could with a clear conscience free himself of any further responsibility and simply enjoy being a visitor, just like Steve.

Just like Steve? No, maybe in spite of everything he wasn't quite ready for that.

Robert emerged from the boathouse and greeted Newman. They sat on a bench on the dock.

"Another beautiful day in the neighborhood," Robert said as they looked out across the lake.

"Certainly is — good to be outside, I've been tied up talking to everyone about the whole Ziegler deal this morning."

"Ah yes — I hope that worked out well for everyone."

"Yes, it did. I sounded them out about the Scottish play of course, and would you believe, someone had already talked to each of them about it."

"Yes I did that, Mr. Newman, yes I did. Get in front of people, speak with them, give them the story from the horse's mouth, you understand — always best I think. And I can get a better measure of folks' thoughts when I'm speaking with them face to face. I mean I have every confidence in you and Steve. In your abilities to get things done and make progress and so on. But I wanted to see for myself what the others really felt about such an outlandish proposition as moving to Scotland."

"Do you think it's that big a deal? Similar latitude. Same language."

"Same language you say? You'd be surprised, Mr. Newman. Until you examined the local food, perhaps. Then you'd certainly be surprised."

Newman got down to business. The compensation meant that Robert could pretty much do as he liked for the foreseeable future.

"So. What are you thinking then, Robert? You going to retire here, make the move, or what? Lot of options."

"Unexpected options, yes. I was undecided, you know. But although the old place just arrived out of the blue, it seemed somehow irresponsible to just let it slip through my fingers. That's maybe not enough reason to make such a life change though, is it? And drag others into it to help make it happen?"

"Maybe I'm the wrong person to ask, Robert. I dragged enough people into my life change and look where it's ended up."

"Oh I think most people are happy enough to have been involved, Mr. Newman. But I will say, it was talking to young Fargo that helped me see things a little more clearly."

"Fargo? Helped clear things up? Well there's another surprise."

"He was very helpful, you know. He came to see me, actually, when he got wind of the loch."

Fargo had more or less told Robert that fate had intervened in a way that he, Fargo, could only have wished for. Here Robert had been given the sort of legal documents the tribe would have regarded as ancestral intervention; asserting Robert's right to land that his forebears had lived and worked on for generations. No need to lend fate a guiding hand and risk upsetting the balance of forces, said Fargo with a nod toward his archaeological dig across the lake; everything was coming together, unbidden, around Robert resuming the life of his predecessors. Fargo asked

Robert to consider his life to-date as being part of the inescapable arc of the McAlister clan, the indirect but absolutely necessary path of an arrow before it reaches its target.

"Fargo saw things very clearly. My choice wasn't whether to return to the loch; it was whether I felt I had the nerve to refuse to return to the loch. I can see his point."

"And what about the rest of the folks? What sense did you get about whether they were keen?"

"I can't imagine pulling it off without a team, however done and dusted the whole thing may seem to Fargo. Doris is a natural, isn't she? She tells me she's up for a change, and she credits you for that, Mr. Newman. A few years ago, she says, it would have been a very different matter. And Trefor's her first choice for PR and advertising, eh? And no way he'd let her go without him. So he's up for it, he says, barring having to wear a kilt. Not to say he wouldn't do a great job, even without a kilt — he has the Welsh way with words, I'm sure of that. Now Steve says he's on board, and I believe him. I'm not sure how committed he is to the details of the project, you understand; he always seemed to me like he wouldn't risk details spoiling the bigger picture. I do think he feels it's the most fun he can imagine for the time being, but I get the idea he may find something more entertaining in future, so who knows. But he's the sort of man you want in the bar, isn't he? I could imagine him a fixture there, as he is here. And besides that he does have plenty of cash he's prepared to invest in the development. So."

"What about me, Robert?"

"Well of course, Mr. Newman, I don't know how any of this could happen without you. I admit I was relying on you being on board the highland express, you know. And when I think about it, the main thing is I'd always welcome a fellow Scot to return to the old country with me."

"Fellow Scot? I can hardly claim to be that."

"Really?" said Robert. "Well now it's you surprising me, Mr. Newman."

11: The headline

NEWMAN SETTLES BACK into his business class seat for the remaining nine hours or so of a long-haul trip to London. MacLeod, next to him by the window, has already consumed enough whisky to nod off, finding himself able to overlook it being "a damned blend" and the plastic bottles being "a bloody insult". It's good to have a break from conversation. And a relief to just give himself up to the experience, hand over all control for a change to those in charge, and wallow in pleasantly cushioned quiet.

Sunlight streams unimpeded through the cabin windows; outside the sky is clear blue and the wispy clouds they pierced just minutes ago must now be way below them.

He's enjoying the enforced idleness offered by air travel. He's indulging in what he considers earned nostalgia; reminiscing, recalling selected events from his recent past that led to him being on a plane with an American, two Scots, an Englishman and a Welshman.

The steady whine of the engines and the roar of air over wings combine to lull Newman into that semiconscious daydream state that comes as a blessing to all long-distance travelers. He's numbed to the present and enlivened by a meditation that surrounds him with images more immediate than the tube in which he sits, hurtling East, faster than time.

Geoff's boss settles into the executive chair in what was once

Newman's office, breathes deeply, and takes in the expansive view of the lake. Well strictly speaking it's no longer Newman's office, not since the closure of the resort was made official and Newman and his crew of no-hopers took off with their undeserved gains for wherever it was they planned to go. Happy trails and good riddance, he thinks, bunch of losers. A man could spend the better part of his life manipulating his career or messing with the stock market before he could hope to join the ranks of the truly wealthy and amass as much spare cash as Ziegler dropped into the laps of those talentless wasters.

Where'd they gone? On a plane to England or somewhere. Good.

Well then. What a beautiful morning. The lake looks absolutely splendid, and all the better for not having tourists and kids and things running all around it. Geoff's boss imagines the lake as his own backyard, there for his sole enjoyment on this bright, wonderful day.

He pushes the one button he's figured out on his oversized, colorfully screened desk phone and shouts to his assistant, who sits downstairs in what was once the reception area.

"Send up coffee and Danish, will you?"

He'd come up with an unrealistically aggressive plan for remodeling the existing buildings and grounds into more corporate-friendly facilities. He'd made sure there were people committed, on paper, signed up and subject to performance review, to making it happen per his impossible schedule. There would be high-profile reorganizations and a many careers sidelined when, inevitably, it didn't. There aren't too many above him in the current Ziegler hierarchy,

Richard writes for a living in the Pacific Northwest. Twenty-odd years ago he flew over from Reading, U.K. for just a couple of years.

He's still here.

Thanks to Nicki Primrose for supporting this effort from reviews through related trips, food, and even fish-related office decorations. Tom Jenkins for coffee and encouragement and for so thoroughly enjoying the whole teeth thing. Cliff Didcock for meticulous debugging, and Lily Didcock for providing such thoughtful feedback in the midst of her busy YA schedule.

Chris Norris for being so smart, lucid, encouraging, and enthusiastic throughout my postgrad years.

And thanks to my sons Jack and Tom for giving me a reason to enjoy and remember everything the Olympic Peninsula has to offer, all those vacations ago.

but he'll see to it that those who are will take notice of his no-holds-barred, no quarter given moving and shaking round here. This place was his to use as the latest and probably the greatest springboard yet for his recently stagnating career, and in his experience it was always good to throw a few others under the bus in the process just as a way of asserting your influence, showing who really must be boss. Nothing like putting people on notice, he thinks.

Coffee, Danish, and the morning paper arrive.

Let's see; what's on the agenda today? Maybe he'll revisit the site of the new briefing center, see how that's coming along. Maybe another look at the boathouse. He had an idea to convert the boathouse into a world-class rowing facility, and could imagine presiding over a Henley-style royal regatta on the lake. Never been a rower, of course, but he'd once attended the regatta during a business trip. Or was it the Cambridge Oxford boat race? Anyway, those affairs definitely attracted his sort of people, the elite crowd to which he was confident he belonged, and could realistically aspire to join now he had his lakeside foothold. Maybe add some ethnic flare with canoeists from among those people down at the Bay.

The coffee is good, but a little too bold perhaps? Make a note of that. Need a larger selection of Danishes.

Geoff's boss picks up the *National Observer* and shakes it open. One day soon, he thinks, it'll be him hogging the headlines. He'll be able to give them a real blockbuster story, they'll be falling over themselves to get a piece of the success he's made of Glacial Lake. Or should he say, the Stammbaum Campus, a name he chose in order to favor the chairman of Ziegler, Fabrizio Stammbaum who, eventually, he planned to report to directly as Corporate Vice-President.

He turns straight to his favorite section, Features.

"Ziegler Corporation Commits Fraud to Cheat Government" is the headline.

"Widespread Organizational Malpractice, Incompetence Threatens Public Health Crisis" is the sub headline.

"By Cooper Black and Sitka Small" is the byline.